SUCH A KILLING CRIME

ROBERT LOPRESTI

The author gratefully acknowledges permission to include excerpted lyrics from the song *Mr. Tambourine Man* by Bob Dylan. Copyright © 1964 by Special Rider Music. All rights reserved. International copyright secured. Reprinted by permission.

The quotations from *archy and mehitabel* are taken from: Don Marquis, *the lives and times of archy and mehitabel*, New York, Random House. 1935.

Cover design: Karen Parker © 2005.

ISBN: 0-9723706-3-3
Library of Congress Control Number: Pending

Robert Lopresti
Such a Killing Crime
First KSB printing (July, 2005).

Printed in the United States of America

Kearney Street Books
Po Box 2021
Bellingham, WA 98227
360-738-1355
www.kearneystreetbooks.com

Preface

This book is fiction, but it is as accurate as I could make it. Most of the main characters are fictional, and all the major actions are made up (except for the last death in the book, which really happened when and how I described it). One of my goals was to recreate the world of Greenwich Village in 1963 as best as I could.

In this regard I received help from the librarians at William Paterson University, Fairleigh Dickinson University (Rutherford), Western Washington University, and the Lincoln Center Branch of the New York Public Library. I also had invaluable help from the legendary songwriter Tom Paxton and my friend Richard Tucker, both of whom were there when it happened. Tom gallantly offered to be the villain in my novel, and I apologize to him for giving that role to someone else.

Which brings up a point I have already alluded to: some real people appear in this novel. Each of them is used in a fictional manner, which is to say their words and actions are a reflection on my imagination, not on their personalities or histories.

One last acknowledgment: the Riding Beggar used to be the name of a newspaper column by Dr. Robert Bruce Mullin. Bruce kindly permitted me to borrow the title for the name of a coffeehouse, and I would like to make it clear that he is not responsible for the nefarious, not to say liberal, things that occur within.

I want to offer my heartfelt thanks to everyone mentioned above. If the book gives you a feel for the time and place, I owe them a great debt. The errors are strictly my own, or those of my characters.

This is for Terri.

There is a ship and she sails the sea
She's loaded deep as deep can be
But not so deep as the love I'm in
I know not if I sink or swim.

The Water Is Wide, Traditional

Chapter 1

Until the mugging, the night was damned near perfect.

The March air was clear and crisp and I was walking through Greenwich Village with a beautiful girl. She wasn't my girl, true, but she was beautiful and she seemed to be enjoying my company.

"Good God," I said. "They're opening another one." I pointed across Third Street to an old storefront, now showing off a proud new sign: Café Santo.

"Unbelievable," said Carol Meisel. "Where do they all come from?"

It was three in the morning and we were headed home from the Riding Beggar, the coffee house where we both worked. The other waitresses usually walked home together, but Carol often stuck around until we locked up. She lived on Waverly Place, on my way home more or less, and I wouldn't have felt right asking a girl employee to walk home alone that time of night.

"Where does *who* come from?" I asked. "The cafés?"

She shook her long blond hair. "I mean all the people. The owners, the performers…. Two years ago, back in 1961, how many clubs were there in this city where you could hear folksingers?"

"Not many. And now there are must be twenty just on MacDougal Street alone. Anybody who can hit two chords and remember most of the words to *Freight Train* is heading to the Village. Ever since *Time* did that story on Joan Baez."

Carol laughed. "The cover girl. That's what Katy Poe calls her."

In November *Time* had published an article on Joanie, written by a guy named John McPhee. They put her picture on the cover, all right, a drawing that made that beautiful woman look like a cross between a cocker spaniel and a stick insect.

"Well," I said, "naturally Katy gets mad when a traditional singer makes it big. It takes away her excuses."

"You mean she'd rather think that she's not a star because people prefer the Beach Boys to ballads? You're probably right about that."

"She's a good opening act, but...." I shrugged. "She's got no stage presence."

"Well, you'd know, Joe," said Carol. "I've never seen anyone who could pick out talent like you."

I laughed off the flattery. "The Ed Sullivan of Greenwich Village."

"Well, not with the budget Max gives you." Max Karzoff owned the Riding Beggar. "And all this competition—"

"That reminds me. Have you heard the Max Karzoff theory on the folk revival? He traces it all back to one main factor."

"No, what's that?"

"The New York City Cabaret Law."

We were under a street light and Carol stopped and gave me her serious frown, the thing I remember best about her. She was trying to tell if I was kidding. "The *what* law?"

"Cabaret. A bar or a club in this city needs an extra license to have certain kinds of live music. A very expensive license, too. The law was passed a long time ago to keep jazz out of *nice* neighborhoods."

"So how does that effect folk music?"

"The law forbids wind instruments, or bands of a certain size. That created a seller's market for anyone with a guitar."

"Huh," she said. "And that's the cause of a national rise in folk music? What a cynical point of view."

We started walking again. "Max has been running restaurants and clubs in this town for thirty years. That would make a cynic out of Dr. Schweitzer."

"I'll bet no one ever mentioned them in the same sentence before." We had reached Waverly Place and were standing in front of the brownstone apartment house where Carol lived. An old sink lay at the curb, in front of the front steps. Pipes dangled underneath and blocked the sidewalk.

"Would you look at this," Carol said. "Don't tell me the landlord is finally fixing up this dump."

"Your rent will go up."

"It's not *my* sink."

"Doesn't matter. Somebody in the building got an improvement. Think of the prestige."

"I'll think of it constantly. Well, thanks for walking me home, Joe." She smiled at me. "And thanks for stepping up tonight. I mean, with Seamus."

I had almost forgotten about that, the one nasty moment of the evening. Seamus O'Hanlon was a big gray bear of an Irish poet. I had started using him as an opening act at the Riding Beggar when Robert Frost died and people suddenly got sentimental for verse.

The crowd seemed to like his romantic ramblings. Unfortunately his hands rambled, too, and that night I had had to chase him away from Carol.

"My pleasure. I'm sorry he bothered you."

"You're officially my hero."

I shrugged. It hadn't been heroic, just good business.

Carol was already unbuttoning the long blue coat she wore over her white blouse and black slacks—what passed for a waitress uniform at the Riding Beggar. She was very pretty when she smiled. "Want to come in for a beer, Joe? Or a coffee?"

"Don't think so. I'm pretty beat and I still want to make a phone call before I hit the sack."

"Now, who would you be calling at—Oh, I forgot. It's already morning in London."

"Birmingham this week."

"How's Sovay doing?"

"Oh, you know. Galvanizing the working classes. Singing for union meetings. Trying to raise train-fare at skiffle clubs."

"Same old Sovay," said Carol. "She's been gone, what, almost a year, now, hasn't she?"

"Yup. The State Department has it in their tiny brains that she's a dangerous alien, a lousy commie rabble rouser. They won't let her back in."

Carol shook her head. "I thought JFK was going to get rid of that kind of nonsense. Protecting us from freedom of speech."

"The Massachusetts cold warrior? Don't hold your breath."

"I guess not. But if—My God, what was that?"

It was a scream. Someone was screaming for help in the middle of the Manhattan night.

"Get inside!" I told her. "Call the cops!" And then I ran down Waverly Place, wondering what the hell I was getting myself into.

CHAPTER 2

The screams came from Gay Street, the block-long connector between Waverly and Christopher. Turning the corner, I saw three shadows kicking a fourth that lay in the street between them. That shadow wasn't moving, and no one was screaming anymore.

Lights came on in a few windows, but I saw no faces there. I thought about Kitty Genovese, who had died two years before, screaming her life away while a Brooklyn neighborhood listened and did nothing.

But not Joe Talley, no sir. I couldn't stay back and watch from a distance. Too stupid, probably.

Maybe I should have tried to reason with them. I wish I could say I thought it out but the truth is: conditioning took over.

I ran straight for the nearest figure, a short blond man with his back to me. He stood with hands on his hips, watching as one of the others delivered another kick.

Well, I could kick too. I brought my foot up, hard, between the blond man's legs. He screamed, doubled over, and hit the street.

The other two turned to face me. One wore a motorcycle jacket and a vacant, almost frightened expression. The third was taller, paler, and he was holding a knife.

Son-of-a-bitch. I crouched, facing him, trying to stay aware of his companion, the motorcycle man. The man

I had kicked lay groaning across the man they had been beating.

"The cops will be here in no time," I shouted. "You better get away while you can."

The knife man didn't take his eyes off me. He stayed hunkered over, holding the blade low, almost casually. This guy had finished on the winning end of way too many knife fights.

You can say what you want about the army and I'd probably agree with you, but you can't deny that their training sticks. I could hear my drill sergeant as if he were standing next to me, yelling: *Watch the man, damn it, not the knife. His face will tell you what the knife is going to do. And don't forget his partner, because he sure as hell hasn't forgotten you.*

The motorcycle man was on my right, dancing around, trying to make up his mind. I took two steps toward the knife man, as if I was making a head-on assault. Then I veered right and swung a foot into the motorcycle man's leg. The sole of my shoe caught the side of his knee with a satisfying pop, and it was his turn to go down screaming.

The knife man was moving. I backed up, keeping his fallen companion between us.

"Cops are coming," I repeated. I probably didn't sound any more confident than I felt.

My heel bumped into the curb and I stumbled. When I recovered the knife man had slipped around his partner and was headed toward me. He was smiling now. He had a broad forehead and sunken eyes, and with that grin his face made me think of a skull. Not the image I needed in my head just then.

Clink. Something landed at my feet. We both looked down. It was a piece of pipe, more than a foot long, and I thought I recognized it as part of the plumbing from the old sink I'd seen in front of Carol's apartment house.

There was no time to wonder how it had flown there. If I could bend over and pick it up, all the odds changed.

The knife man knew that too; his grin was gone. The pipe wasn't sharp but it was probably twice as long as his blade. I could break his wrist with it, crack his skull with it—if I could pick it up.

If.

I could see in his dark eyes that he had no intention to let this little scuffle turn into a fair fight. He was going to keep me away from that pipe, no matter what it took.

Which was fine with me. That made him predictable. What you can predict you just might be able to control.

I danced back and forth, crouched over, one hand stretched out toward the pipe. The knife man crouched too, licking his lips and watching me.

I lunged forward, bending down as if I were going for the pipe. He charged, swinging the blade down toward my throat. But I wasn't there anymore. I had straightened up, and now I forced his arm out of my way, ramming the heel of my hand into his nose.

He grunted and stumbled backwards. I stayed with him, grabbing for his right elbow with my left hand, trying to find the pressure point while my right hand fumbled for his throat.

The knife man hit the cold street with me on top of him. He was bleeding badly from the nose. His blade dropped to the pavement and I pushed off him onto my knees. I was trying to catch my breath when someone shouted: "Joe! Watch out!"

I rolled to the side and caught a powerful blow on the right shoulder. It had been aimed at my head. I looked up at the motorcycle man, swinging the steel pipe. He raised the pipe above his head, ready to bring it down on my skull.

I put my hands down on the pavement, trying to gather the strength for one more dodge. I didn't think I could do it.

Sirens. The motorcycle man turned his head. I rolled away from him, feeling the grit of the road beneath me.

The knife man was standing now, shaking the blond guy, the one I had kicked in the crotch. "Let's go," he said.

The blond man stumbled to his feet and started to walk away. I still hadn't gotten a good look at his face.

The knife man picked up his weapon, holding his left hand to his still-bleeding nose. He look at me and smiled again. "Next time, Jack." Then he turned and ran off toward Christopher Street.

I stood up and almost keeled over. The pain and dizziness had turned my legs to spaghetti.

The motorcycle man gazed at his disappearing partners. He waved the pipe at me with a look of regret. Then, with a shrug, he turned and walked off.

"Joe, help me." It was Carol, bent over the gang's victim. "My gosh, it's Seamus! God, he's all cut up."

Seamus O'Hanlon? I looked down at the bloodied man. Sure enough, it was the drunken Irish poet we had just been talking about. His gray hair looked carrot-red in the street light. His eyes were closed and he didn't seem to be breathing.

"What are you doing here?" I asked Carol. "I told you to call the cops."

"I did. Then I came back." She was flushed and her blue eyes were saucer-wide. "I'm sorry it took so long, Joe. I had to look up the phone number. Are you all right?"

"I'm okay." My heart was pounding hard enough to knock me down. "Dumb luck."

"Like fun," she said. "You were brilliant. I couldn't believe what you did to those creeps, Joe. I'm just sorry I got in your way."

"You? How?"

I threw that pipe at your feet, and that jerk almost killed you with it." She clung to my arm, tears filling her eyes. "I'm so sorry, Joe."

"*You* threw that pipe? Carol, you saved my skin."

"Really?"

"Sure. The clown with the knife would have peeled me like an apple except for you. And then you warned me when the other guy swung the pipe. You saved my bacon twice." I hugged her with my left arm. My right shoulder was too sore.

"Oh, that's bloody touching," said a voice. Seamus was looking up at us through his one working eye. "Any chance you two could arrange a trip to hospital for a poor workingman?"

Carol knelt beside him. "Take it easy, Seamus. The ambulance is coming up."

Flashing lights poured up the street but it wasn't anyone useful. Just the cops.

CHAPTER 3

How do you spell Shamus? Like a private eye?"

"S-E-A-M-U-S." I said. "He's Irish."

The cop wrote it down. "A Mick, huh? I'll tell the Hibernian Society. You say he's a poet?"

"That's right. He read tonight at the café I run."

"Oh." The cop looked thoughtful. "I see." In his eyes Seamus O'Hanlon had changed from a latter-day Yeats to just another beatnik.

Quite a fall from grace.

The ambulance had arrived, finally. The medics didn't look optimistic as they took Seamus off.

"Now, these muggers you described. You say they were in their twenties."

"Right."

"Funny. You mostly get juvies robbing people on the street. Were they wearing names?"

"Wearing what?"

"Gang names. Any symbols or names on the motorcycle jacket?"

"I didn't see any." I looked across the street where Carol was talking animatedly to another policeman. I tried to lean against the wall of the building and wound up sitting down heavily on the stone steps.

"This guy Seamus—did he have any enemies?"

I looked at the cop.

He shrugged. "Maybe it was personal. A lot of these Micks have a temper. What about him?"

Seamus had a temper, all right. And he had probably made an enemy that very night, although I couldn't imagine that the mugging had any connection.

Earlier that evening at the Riding Beggar, while the main act was playing, I noticed some customers looking thirsty. I went looking for a waitress.

Just beyond the kitchen door there was an alcove where we kept supplies. I heard voices coming from there and poked my head around.

I could see the Irish poet's broad back and beyond it, almost pinned to the shelves, the struggling shape of one of our waitresses. "Just a wee kiss," Seamus was growling, but it wasn't her face his hands were trying to embrace.

Damn. If I told Seamus off the way he deserved there would be fireworks and the boss had been riding me lately about our performers throwing tantrums in front of the audience.

The smart thing would be to let Seamus do what he wanted. Who cared about one waitress-groping, more or less? Happened every other minute in New York City. That would be the smart thing, all right.

"Seamus!" I called.

The white shirt straightened up. He turned around—not easy for a man of his heft in that alcove. "Joe, me boy. Carol and I were having a bit of a chat."

Carol squeezed past him fast, her arms full of napkins. She shot me a look full of gratitude.

"A word of advice, Seamus."

He scowled under his bushy eyebrows, ready to take offense at the top of his lungs. "Oh? And what word is that?"

I pointed a finger at Carol's retreating back. "Be careful. She's under age."

"Under—oh, sweet mother of God." Seamus's eyes widened. "The mad, mad laws you have here. *Thank* you, Joe. Thank you so much for that timely hint."

"Glad to help."

"Why, the little minx could have got me in all sorts of trouble, teasing me like that. Could have got me deported." He shook his head at the wickedness of women. "I best be going home."

"Good idea," I agreed. "See you next week?"

He was distracted, thinking about his narrow escape, I suppose. "Next week? No, I'll be in Boston, me boy. For St. Paddy's Day. I did tell you that."

"So you did. Well, have a good time up there."

"That I will. And Joe? Thanks again." He shuddered. "The little vixen...."

As Seamus walked off I realized someone was watching me. Al Perkins, our cook, was standing in the doorway of the kitchen. There was a look of puzzlement on his handsome black face. "How can Carol be working here if she's under age?"

I sighed. "It's a little-known state law, Al. The New York legislature declared that every chick who works at the Riding Beggar is too young to be manhandled by jerks."

"Yeah?" Al grinned broadly. "That's a hell of a law."

"Even Albany gets one right occasionally."

•

"Mr. Talley?" The cop was looking at me warily. "You okay?"

"Yeah." I said. "The adrenalin is fading."

He nodded sympathetically. "You got the shakes. I was the same way the time I had to kill a man."

"I didn't *kill* anyone!" It came out louder than I intended. Carol and the other cop turned and stared at me.

My cop raised his eyebrows. "Didn't say you did, buddy. Nobody's accusing you of anything."

I dropped my face in my hands. I was tired. God, I was tired. But mostly what I felt was resentment at how easily the army training had come back. I didn't want to be a soldier anymore, not even in a good cause.

People were looking out of doors and windows now. Where the hell had they been when I was fighting for my life?

The cop closed his notebook. "Okay, that's it. You better go home and get some rest."

"You have to find out who did this to Seamus."

"Oh, we'll find out. That's our job." He patted me on the shoulder, the one that hurt. "Just don't *you* start playing shamus."

CHAPTER 4

I saw Carol back to her place and dragged myself home. Home was a studio in a fourth floor walk-up on Sixth Street. I suppose it looked pretty much the way it had when I first dumped my stuff on the floor a year and a half before. I was fresh out of the army then, ready to conquer New York.

One thing that had changed, or maybe evolved, was the longest wall in the room. I had started pasting newspaper clippings there the week I moved in, beginning with a photo of the brand-new Berlin Wall. In one corner of that picture, a young G.I. stood gawking at the camera. That was me.

The headlines on the wall ranged from the tragic to the dumb. John F. Kennedy was there, being creamed by Congress on a dozen issues. His baby brother Teddy, looking like a bad mimeo copy of the president, stood smiling as he joined the Senate that January, the youngest prince of Camelot. The Freedom Riders were on the wall as well, getting beaten up all over the New South for crimes like organizing voter registration, and trying to integrate lunch counters. There were a bunch of headlines about the Cuban missile crisis that had driven up the price of fallout shelters last fall.

May you live in interesting times, as the saying goes.

There was even a poem about the wall, written directly *onto* the wall. Richard Fariña had composed it and scribbled it there the previous fall, while he was crashing on the couch; one of many musicians to do so.

And there was a napkin on the wall with the scribbled name of the first musician I had ever asked for an autograph: Dean Coffey. As a matter of fact, he had played at the Riding Beggar earlier that evening, before the mugging.

I found myself a cigarette and sat on the couch and thought about how wonderful the night had seemed until three nuts with knives had kicked their way into it. And that made me think of something Dean had said during his show....

•

"Murder has always been popular," he had told the crowd. Then he played a new song, about the recent murder of a social worker named Lou Marsh by a gang. The audience listened in rapt silence.

Thursday was the best night of the week at the Riding Beggar. Sunday was good in its own way, but the Sunday crowd carried end-of-the-weekend melancholy like a virus. Friday and Saturday nights the tourists flooded in, looking for kicks, gawking at beatniks and folksingers, monkeys in the zoo. So Thursday was best and I had booked three of my favorites to perform.

Not just my favorites, though. The crowd loved Dean Coffey, too. Even some of the tourists were won over by the California boy in the faded corduroy jacket. He had intense blue eyes, a dark moustache and sun-bleached hair ladies liked to touch. But best of all was his voice, warm and coaxing as he finished the song.

The crowd went crazy. Dean had grinned and walked offstage. I stepped on, and in the manner of emcees the world over, pretended the show was over.

The applause stretched out until I finally surrendered. "Ladies and gentlemen, Dean Coffey!" He ran back onto the stage, waving his arms like a kid.

Dean finished his encore, *White Wolf*, I think it was, and came down to a round of applause and handshakes. Pretty girls surrounded him and by reflex I shot a glance around for his current, and very jealous, lover, Irene Fox. She wasn't there, so I relaxed.

I strolled to my long table near the back wall and flagged down a coffee. It tasted good. Bob Braubinger stuck his plump face in front of me. "Good show, Joe! Damn fine show."

"Thanks, Bob." His smile always made me want to check my wallet. "But it wasn't me they clapped for."

"Nope, it was Dean. Good old Coffey. They really ate him up."

"Dean and Katy and Seamus," I corrected. He was the star that night, but there had been two other acts.

"And here's the boy himself!" yelled Braubinger. He held out a hand and Dean Coffey shook it.

"Hello Bob, Joe." Dean fell into a seat. "Lord, I'm tired. And thirsty. If I had known singing was such thirsty work I would have taken up the bass drum instead."

Carol arrived with a soda on her waitress tray and set it down in front of Coffey. "Here you go, Dean. You were great."

"Thanks, sugar." He took a big gulp. "Yeah, that's the medicine. Good crowd, huh?"

"Once you got to them," said Braubinger. "You murdered 'em."

A shadow loomed over us. "Joe, it's almost closing time." Max Karzoff tugged at the skinny necktie dangling over his bulging belly. He was in his late fifties, the oldest person in the room, and by the end of the night he usually looked even older. "Let's get out of here on time for a change."

"I'll get on it, Boss."

Turning to go, he added over his shoulder, "Nice show." Dean smiled.

I offered to buy a last round, but Dean shook his head. "Have to get going, Joe."

"Meeting Irene?"

"Nope, she's modeling tomorrow and needs her sleep. But I want to get home and tinker with a song."

"When it's done, I want to hear it," I told him.

"Sure thing, Joe. As soon as I get back from California."

"You flying out there again?"

Dean made a face. "Family obligations." He stood up. "You coming, Bob?"

Braubinger rose halfway, torn between my offer of free coffee and his desire to cling to Dean. Finally he decided to go.

•

"Nice show?" I said to Max, later.

"What?" He was standing at the dais near the front door, checking the night's receipts while I supervised the clean-up.

"Dean had them eating out of his hand and all he gets is *nice show*? You give out compliments like they were hundred dollar bills."

"If they're rare people value them more." He looked at me over his bifocals. "What's eating you?"

"We can't pay these people much. At least we can treat them right. I don't want the performers to be unhappy here."

"Well, of *course* they're unhappy here, Joe. They all think they should be playing Carnegie Hall." He shrugged. "That's okay. You and I both think we should be *running* Carnegie Hall."

Not me. But I suppose I would have jumped if the Gaslight or Gerde's Folk City wanted a new manager. To run the best folk joint in town was all I wanted. The Riding Beggar wasn't that yet, but I was working on it.

CHAPTER 5

The phone cord in my apartment barely stretched from the wall to the couch, but I was too tired to stand up. After the usual wrestling with the overseas operator, Sovay answered on the seventh ring. "Mmph, what?"

"It's your wake-up call, angel."

"Joe, my love. You bloody yank. What time is it?"

"Almost nine your time. Why aren't you up and at 'em, fighting the good fight?"

"I was up late last night, fighting all the bad ones. Alice has this ghastly friend...."

"Alice?"

"The bird I've been traveling with. I keep forgetting you haven't met her."

"How could I? I'm in New York."

"Don't I know it. Why don't you come visit?"

"I'd love to, babe, but I have a café to run, remember?"

"Oh yes. The Riding Beggar. One of the cutest little rubbish tips I've ever played in. But the management...."

"Thanks a heap," I said. "See if I ever hire you again."

"You can't, damn it. Your bloody government won't give me a visa, so I'm trapped in the coldest winter in Britain since we used to burn Papists for heat."

That was true. She'd ridden trains that fought their way through snowstorms, only to find that concerts had been cancelled due to ice. I suppose her countrymen were more used to needing umbrellas than snowshoes.

"I know, babe." I pictured her combing her long wheat-colored hair away from her face. It was a saint's face, some passionate, militant saint from the crusades.

"Sovay? Do you remember Seamus O'Hanlon?"

"Seamus? That daft Irishman? You told me he looked you up when he hit New York. What's he been up to? Besides the pub, I mean."

"He's in the hospital. Muggers beat him on the street tonight."

"Bloody hell. The poor man. Will he be all right, Joe?"

"I don't know, Sovay. It didn't look good." I didn't tell her I'd been there. I was still embarrassed about my desperate battle with the three stooges.

I wasn't a soldier anymore.

"It's just as I've told you, Joe. That town is too bloody · dangerous. I wish you'd get out of there."

"Leave New York?"

"At least for a visit." Her voice got softer. "I miss you."

"And I miss you. But the club—"

"Let Karzoff run it for a while. Make the ruling class do a bit of the work."

I don't remember what we said after that. Can't separate one thread of that argument from the tangled spool we had been tied up in for months. When the quarrel started the Beggar had been standing on shaky legs and I didn't have money or time to cross the Atlantic.

Maybe I could have done it by that spring, but I don't think either of us expected it to happen. The quarrel was just a ritual, part of the phone call, like saying hello.

I don't know if she realized that one reason I didn't visit was that I didn't want to meet the men she was sleeping with over there. No reason to think she was being faithful; she hadn't been when we lived two blocks apart.

She never lied about it. "You are my very favorite man on this Earth, Joe Talley. But that doesn't mean you're the *only* man. You have to live with that, or live without me."

I had lived with it as best I could. And I had lived with her whenever she'd have me.

Her real name was Sophie Beulah Keech; I saw her passport once. The picture on the passport did her no more justice than her birth name. It reduced that lovely hair to shadow, and cooled the angry spark in her eyes.

The first time I saw her had been on the stage of the Riding Beggar, not long after it opened. It was hoot night and she took the place by storm.

At least, she took me.

"I'm Sovay. Pleased to meet you folks. Glad to see a few of you Yanks remember your heritage." And she began to sing *The Preacher and the Slave.*

You will eat bye and bye
In that glorious land in the sky....
Work and pray, live on hay
You'll get pie in the sky when you die.

That sort of glorious end-of-the-week stew was what I loved best about the folk music scene: an old church hymn rewritten with anti-church lyrics by a Swedish-American anarchist, being sung forty years later to a New York audience by an Englishwoman.

Welcome to the folk process.

It was weird hearing that song in an English accent. It almost sounded like a London music hall number, although Sovay's accent was not Cockney, but what she called Midlands.

Then she sang *Factory Girl*, the British version, and something by Ewan MacColl. I couldn't take my eyes off her.

When she came down I introduced the next act and hurried over to her. "You were great. Can I buy you a coffee?"

She raised an eyebrow. "You the boss?"

I grinned. "Nope, just a working stiff. Max Karzoff is the boss."

"Right. The fat bloke who signed me up. In that case I'll take an Earl Grey tea, if you have such a thing."

"If we don't," I promised, "I'll go get some."

CHAPTER 6

By the next evening the aches and pains were starting to fade and I was able to put the mugging mostly out of my mind, mostly by concentrating on what a lucky man I was. I remember thinking about that as I walked to work: Greenwich Village. March 1963. This is a great place to be young and left wing.

I passed NYU's student center where, a month before, I had watched Pete Seeger, Doc Watson, and Ed McCurdy front a Hoot For Peace. You could do that sort of thing these days without expecting Senator Joe McCarthy to condemn you to blacklist hell.

Eisenhower was safely in retirement. Camelot was playing on Broadway and on Pennsylvania Avenue. Elvis was making stupid movies and rock-and-roll was a dying fifties fad, like hula hoops. Folk music was the exciting new trend.

To find out what's happening, try the *Village Voice.* With all the daily papers on strike since December, it was the goddamn paper of record. Better yet, step into any of the coffeehouses that lined the Village and listen to the songs. As Phil Ochs said: you'll hear all the news that's fit to sing.

Phil came by early that evening to sign up for the hoot. Mike Porco's place, Gerde's Folk City, was the first to start calling talent night a hootenanny. Like so much else in the folk world, that word had been borrowed from Pete Seeger and Woody Guthrie.

Now every coffeehouse had a hoot, a chance for the not-yets and the never-wills to sweat blood in front of a crowd. I scheduled ours for Fridays, figuring it was good enough for the tourists.

The Riding Beggar was on West Third Street, between Macdougal and Sixth Avenue. There was a fake English pub sign hanging outside, an ugly decoration Max had had made up with our namesake on it—a shabbily dressed man on a beautiful white stallion.

Step inside and you faced a staircase that led up to a bar, but turn left instead and you faced the mirrored door of our coffee house. Inside there was a dais where someone stood to welcome people at busy times. Beyond that were the entrances to Max's office and the kitchen, and then our main room.

Our hall was long and a little dark, with a ceiling a bit lower than ideal. Max complained sometimes that it was a goddamned cave, but I thought it was intimate.

I had been the one to suggest that we emphasize the shape with long tables, pointed toward the stage at the far end of the room. I suppose I was remembering the family-style restaurants I saw growing up in Pennsylvania. I liked the fact that strangers wound up seated next to each other, and some friendships—or even interesting animosities—were born that way. Max grudgingly admitted that it made it easier to fit groups of different sizes.

Behind the stage was the green room, where musicians waited for their turn on stage. Some of the clubs had legendary green rooms, dark labyrinths of little chambers where, on a good night, you might find practically any vice being indulged. By contrast, our green room was bright, open, and kept almost clean enough for surgery. Max felt it would discourage people from smoking dope in there, among other things. His lungs always gave him trouble, and he thought dealing with tobacco was bad enough.

I didn't have or want an office like Max. Usually sat at a table under a swag light, far away from the stage, where I could watch all directions. Early that Friday evening I sat down there and started receiving applicants for Hoot Night.

The first man through the door that night was not a performer. In fact, he looked more like my idea of a mugger than the jokers who had been taking Seamus apart the night before. Ray Hegg was a tall, perpetually-frowning man with a shaved bald head and a thick brown beard.

He looked like a fanatic, just waiting for an excuse to start a holy war. In reality I had seldom known him to raise his voice, and never his fists. Ray was one of the few people in my crowd with a respectable job; he was a research chemist who did something scientific and incomprehensible at a big laboratory up town. He must have been good at his job since there were few corporations around in those days willing to tolerate a shaved head and a bearded chin, not to mention a preference for black turtleneck sweaters instead of ties.

"You're going ahead with the hoot, then," he said in lieu of a greeting. "I wasn't sure, when I heard about Seamus."

"Yeah, well. The hospital says he's gonna make it, although they won't let us in to see him. So I figured there's not much point in going into mourning."

"The show must go on. Hey, Carol Meisel tells me you're a hero. Any truth to that?"

I shrugged. "As much as in most hero stories. Hercules, Beowulf, PT-109...."

"I dig." He raised his bushy eyebrows at the opening door. "Here come the troops. I better hit the espresso pot and let you start recruiting. Try to find somebody who doesn't do reheated hillbilly crap, okay?"

"Why do you hang around here, Ray?" I asked. "Not that I object to your company. But you don't seem to enjoy traditional music."

"Traditional?" He laughed. "I'm a jazz fan, remember? If a bopper plays a song the same way twice they step on his shades and kick him out."

A music reviewer once told me that Ray always had a bad word for jazz musicians, too. I guess, deep down, he just liked to heckle.

The first performer to show up that night was a skinny young man with a wild shock of brown hair. "Hiya, Joe. How's it goin'?"

"Not bad, Phil. Haven't seen you for a while. You heard about Seamus?"

"Yeah, that's incredible. Right on the goddamn street. Somebody told me you were there when it happened."

"More or less." I was getting bored with that story. "So Mr. Ochs, where have you been keeping yourself?"

"Over at the baskethouses, mostly. But next week I'm gonna open for John Hammond at Folk City."

"Phil, that's great. A paying gig. Damn it, I wish I'd gotten to you first. Let's set you up for April here."

"Terrific." He was beaming, looking too young to be served a drink, much less performing. He made me feel old and I was only twenty-three.

"I'm glad you came to the hoot, even though you're making the big time."

"Can't stay away from the Riding Beggar, Joe. So many of these dives are run by John Birchers, you know? It's nice to support the old left, occasionally."

"The old left?"

"Your boss. I was talking to some of the crowd at *Broadside* and they say he was in the thick of it back in the thirties. With Woody and Josh and that whole gang."

I thought that one over. I knew Karzoff had been in New York that long, but I never thought of him as hanging out with the Almanac Singers and the Café Society types. He knew them, of course, but hell, he knew everybody. I'd never heard him say a kind word about a Marxist, that was for sure.

"Okay, Phil. I'm giving you a prime slot tonight. If you—"

"Hey, it's the Talley-man!" Somebody yelled.

I sighed. Across the room, three guys in matching blue blazers and white turtlenecks had strolled in. From a block away you could tell they were either a folk trio or a gaggle of waiters.

The one who had called out, a brown crewcut above a ridiculously lanky body, began to sing the Harry Belafonte hit: "*Come, Mr. Talley-man, and tally me bananas.*"

I smiled, but I probably didn't convince anyone I meant it. "You never get tired of that joke, do you, Matty Mark?"

Phil had wandered off and the Southern boy folded himself into the seat Phil had just vacated. "What's your problem, Joe boy? Don'tcha like Harry Belafonte?" His Arkansas drawl was pretty thick tonight. You could measure his beer intake by the length of his vowels.

Ben English, another member of the trio, put a hand on his shoulder. "Joe's busy. Let's just sign up."

Matty Mark Oliver waved him away. "It's okay, Ben. Joe Talley always has time for his old friends. 'Specially when his new ones are out of town."

I checked my pages. "You guys go on at eight, okay?"

"Fine, Joe. Thanks," said Ben.

Matty started to stand up, but couldn't quite make it. "Saving the sweet spot for Coffey as usual? Oh, I forgot: the big man's out of town. Went off to do some field research, I bet. Come back with a few new songs."

I put down my pen. "How drunk are you, Matty?"

"He's okay," Larry Zigler said quickly. Larry was the third member of the trio. "Really, he'll be fine."

"All right. Like I said, you—"

"You're not gonna keep every drunk off the stage, are you, Joe?" Matty tried again to stand, and made it this time. "I mean, what about that Indian fella? Shoot, you have him here all the time. What's his name?"

Matty looked around, frowning. "You know, Tonto. He drinks even more than me. *Lots* more. What's his name again?"

"Pete Lafarge," I said, to shut him up. "And quit playing the redneck, Matty. Someone might believe you."

I looked at my list again. "You guys still the Greenwich Boys?"

"No," said Ben. "This week we're trying the Village Three."

"Village Three. Bleecker Trio. I can't keep track of all your names."

Ray Hegg had loomed up behind me, espresso in his hand. "I offered them a good one but they turned it down."

"What was that?" I asked.

"The Village Idiots."

•

Whatever they called themselves, Matty Mark's group were the stars that night. The tourists had invaded from Scarsdale and Hoboken. Carbon copies of the Kingston Trio were exactly what they wanted to see. They recognized songs like *Greenback Dollar* and *Tom Dooley* instantly, and sang along.

Folk music learned from Top Forty radio is a weird idea. Katy Poe said it was worse than the teenage junk the music industry churns out by the ton, because at least that stuff didn't *claim* any cultural significance.

Credit where it's due, the Village Three, or whatever they called themselves, sang their copies pretty well. Ben and Larry played guitars while Matty Mark switched between banjo and upright bass. He didn't show his booze, not that night anyway.

Later, when she brought me an espresso, Carol Meisel asked me about the quarrel. "What was that about old friends out of town?"

"Oh," I shrugged. "He means Dean Coffey is in California."

"That's what I thought. What's Matty got against Dean, anyway?"

"That's an old story. You know *Let Me Take Your Side?*"

"Sure, it's one of Dean's best songs."

It was. For two verses it sounded like a typical love song. I'll take care of you when times are hard, ad nauseum, like a thousand other saccharine ditties. Then in the third verse you see where he's really headed:

Let me take your side when the deck is stacked
When the cops take cash and the jury's packed
When it's freedom's fight, and for human pride
There's no black or white. Let me take your side.

And you realize that he's singing about civil rights and oppression, not hearts and flowers. It was clever, and maybe it even got a few people thinking—if such a thing is possible.

"The problem is," I told Carol, "it's one of Matty Mark's best songs, too."

"I don't get it."

"Matty taught Dean a banjo tune called *Down Devil Creek*. He used it as the tune for *Let Me take Your Side.*"

"And this was a tune Matty wrote?"

"No, it's traditional. Matty learned it growing up in Arkansas."

Carol frowned. "Then what's the problem?"

"Well, for one thing, Dean offered it to *Broadside* magazine and they published it, words and music copyrighted by Dean Coffey."

Sis Cunningham and Gordon Friesen had started *Broadside* in New York the year before as a place to publish topical songs. If you were a folkie you read *Sing Out!* for the news about the music and *Broadside* for music about the news.

"And Matty thinks it should have said public domain?"

"No, he thinks he should have gotten credit for the tune. After all, he was the collector, as the folklorists call it."

She frowned. "What's the usual way to handle it?"

"There isn't one. The man who first sang *Tom Dula* to Alan Lomax didn't make a penny when the Kingston Trio recorded *Tom Dooley*."

"That doesn't sound fair."

"Nobody's figured out a fair way to do it. *Somebody* gets the composer fee on every recording. If you list is as 'traditional,' you're handing the fee to the record company. So you find a lot of albums with people listed as 'arrangers' of traditional songs. On one album Oscar Brand is listed as the composer of *London Bridge is Falling Down*."

"That's ridiculous."

"The Weavers were involved in it, too. I hear the Lomaxes, father and son, used to argue about it with the Seegers, father and son."

Carol shook her head. "You make it sound like a family feud."

I grinned, thinking of John and Alan Lomax of the Library of Congress doing battle with Charles and Pete Seeger of New York. I could picture those distinguished gentlemen in a musicological version of the Hatfields and McCoys—scotch and subpoenas replacing moonshine and squirrel guns.

A few minutes later I introduced the next act, a scared college kid named Sam Furrell who looked too small for his guitar. I was trying to calculate the odds that he'd throw up on stage. I found out later that night that he'd already done so in the green room.

While Sam was struggling through his first song I passed Matty Mark, who was standing near the kitchen complaining to Janet Grolin, another of our waitresses, about what it's like to be a Southerner in New York.

"Last week some clodhopper from the Klan got interviewed on TV. Next day every time I opened my mouth people glared at me like that jackass was my fault. They ask me to explain what's happening in Mississippi. Shoot, I've never *been* to Mississippi."

Al Perkins, our cook, was standing in the kitchen doorway. He was a tall, strongly built Negro with delicate hands that looked like they ought to have been making jewelry instead of making sandwiches.

And now he was grinning. "The hell you say. That's just how people 'round this joint talk to me. Like I'm Dr. King's right hand man and know what every Negro in the world is thinking. Come in back, man. Let's talk."

After doing my emcee duties I sat down with another familiar couple: Ray Hegg had been joined by Agustina Adler.

Agustina, better known as Gus, had been in the Village longer than anyone I knew, except Max. She was in her late forties and had the longtime non-conformist's fine disinterest in fashion. Her salt-and-pepper hair hung long and loose. She usually wore a white blouse with long frilly sleeves and a dirndl skirt.

In her own way, she was as striking as Ray with his shaved head and goatee. Someone told me once that Jack Kerouac had used her as the model for a character in one of his books—the closest thing to beatification for a hipster— but I've never been able to read his stuff.

"Good to see you, Gus. You haven't been around much lately."

She gave me her slow smile. "I always come back, Joe. You know that. But there are a lot of places that expect to see me. I have to spread my business around."

"Sure," said Ray. "How would any of these joints get by without selling you a glass of fruit juice?"

"Don't pay any attention to him, Gus. You're always welcome here."

"Thank you, Joe."

"What are you working on there?"

As usual Gus had an art pad open in front of her and was drawing something with a fine black pen. She made some money that way, mostly selling the pictures to Village clubs that thought it lent an air of hipster authenticity to have an Agustina Adler sketch on the wall. We had two.

"Just a still life." I could see a wine bottle and a spilled glass. "Is Dean around tonight?"

Gus introduced me to Dean the year before at a party somebody held to celebrate the overturning of Pete Seeger's Contempt of Congress conviction. While most of his colleagues had taken the Fifth Amendment before the House Un-American Activities Committee, Pete had insisted instead on a First Amendment right not to answer questions on who he associated with. It had taken the courts six years to overturn his conviction, and then it had been on a technicality.

Meanwhile, he had been blacklisted, meaning that the commercial core of the folk revival was ignoring one of the people most responsible for the revival happening in the first place.

I remember Ray Hegg astonishing people at the party by saying that Congress was a noble institution. "But," he explained, "you have to remember that to a chemist, 'noble' means inert and unchanging."

At the time of the party Gus and Dean had clearly been a couple, which made him the latest in a long line including, according to rumor, both Ray Hegg and the self-same Jack Kerouac.

"Dean's in California again," I told her.

"California? Is that right?"

"He flies out there every few months, visiting relatives."

"Relatives? I guess that explains it."

"Explains what?" asked Ray.

"Why he'd go." She shrugged. "I've always hated the place myself. And why leave New York? New York is the center of everything."

"You know what they say about the center," said Ray.

"What's that?" I asked.

He raised an eyebrow. "It's the part of the target everybody shoots at."

CHAPTER 7

Damn those bongos," said Katy Poe.

"It's a free country," said Ray Hegg. "Or so they tell me." He tugged at the little plaid cap he always wore when he ventured out in daylight. Without it his bald pate would have gone red as a tomato.

It was the first half-decent Sunday of spring and a few of us had met at Washington Square. The park, ten acres surrounded by brownstones, had been the home of impromptu music celebrations for three hundred years, ever since the Dutch tap-danced with the Indians. The city had tried to stop the music in the park two years before, an attempt that ended with what became known as the Washington Square Riot.

The powers that be had forbidden the usual Sunday music in the park and sent in the riot squad to enforce their ruling. Musicians—led by someone carrying a banjo with an American flag attached—had marched into the square. Dozens of folkies had fought with the cops and ten were arrested while tourists enjoyed the show. The mayor soon put the kibosh on the banjo ban and things were back to normal.

As normal as they ever get in the Village, that is.

On this particularly fine Sunday we were gathered around a bench, not far from the great arch. Katy was trying to play her lap dulcimer, bending over it with great concentration. She was a tiny package of compressed energy, like a golf ball: slim, less than five foot tall, with bright green eyes and red hair cut unfashionably short. She was doing a traditional song, naturally, an old Irish piece called *Love Is Pleasing*. In spite of the cheerful name, its subject was the theme of all folksongs the world over: she loved and he left.

> *If I'd a-knowed before I courted,*
> *That love had been such a killing crime*
> *I'd a-locked my heart in a box of gold*
> *And tied it up with a silver twine.*

She was playing beautifully, but some jazz guys at the other end of the park were drowning her out.

"What can you do?" Carol Meisel asked. "The dulcimer is one of the quiet instruments."

"I don't suppose the Scotch-Irish were much troubled by bongos in Appalachia," said Katy. She shrugged and put the thing carefully back in the strangely-shaped padded bag she had for it. Since a fretted dulcimer looks like a fiddle that has been stretched on a rack—and sounds like the bastard offspring of a zither and a bagpipe—there is no standard size or shape, so you can't get a ready-made case, like you can for a guitar.

Katy didn't learn her music through what folklorists would consider legitimate folk transmittal—orally, and preferably from people in your neighborhood—but she could still claim she came by it honestly. Her father taught in the English Department at Columbia University and studied the *Child Ballads in America*. In his early days he had gone through the southern mountains with a car loaded down with so-called portable wire recorders and tracked down every ballad variant he could find. Katy had grown up hearing those recordings, just like I grew up on Crosby and Sinatra.

Maybe that's why she had a problem with Dean Coffey. He never talked much about how he had fallen into folk music, but if it came from his family he never said so.

The two had quarreled the week before Seamus was attacked. Dean mostly played songs he wrote himself, but he liked to throw in a traditional song occasionally, and that night he had played *Lady Isabel and the Elf Knight*, which tells the story of a wicked young man who talks the inn-keeper's daughter into stealing her father's money and fleeing with him. Then he informed her that it had all been a trick and he was going to kill her. But the heroine outsmarts her wicked lover, pushing him into the river where he had killed his earlier sweethearts:

Then as he sank and as he rose
And as he sank cried he
Pull me out, pull me out,
My own dear love
And you my wedded bride shall be
Lie there, lie there
You false young man.
Lie there instead of me
It's six foolish maids
That you've drownded here
Go keep them company!

The crowd had howled approval. After the show was over Dean had sat down at my long table and beamed while everyone told him how terrific his set had been.

"The audience loved it," said Braubinger. "You killed 'em!"

"It was a shame," said Katy. She had a strong voice for that tiny body, and all of our heads turned toward her. "A shame you forgot the lyrics like that."

"Forgot?" Braubinger was outraged. "When? What?"

She ignored him, still looking at Dean alone. "The last song, I mean. You stopped in the middle of it."

"Oh, that." Dean raised an eyebrow. "She's right, Bob. I left out a whole lot of verses at the end of *Lady Isabel*. See, after the guy drowns, the girl goes home and has an argument with her parrot."

Braubinger laughed, his big harsh chuckle. Ray was sitting next to him, trying to hide a grin behind his goatee and shades. I guess I smiled too.

Katy was red in the face, losing her temper and knowing it. "It's part of the *story*, damn it. If you don't like the song, don't sing it."

"But which song, sugar?" Dean asked. "I admit I don't know *Child's Ballads* the way you do, but I did look up that one." He spread his hands wide. "There are dozens of versions. I mean, Christ, the title is *Lady Isabel and the Elf Knight*, right? But in the one I sing she's not a lady—just an inn-keeper's daughter. And her name isn't Isabel, and he's not an elf *or* a knight."

"But it does end with her returning home," Katy pointed out.

"And the parrot," Braubinger added gleefully. "Man, arguing with a parrot."

"I'm no scholar, Katy," said Dean. "I'm an entertainer."

"And I *don't* entertain? Is that what you're saying?"

"The song should end with the punchline, that's all I'm saying."

"A song isn't a joke," said Ray, thoughtfully.

"The song should end when the story is *over*," said Katy. "It's not your job to rewrite a tale that's hundreds of years old. If you can't sing traditional songs correctly, stick to writing your own stuff, and butcher it as you choose." Then she had gotten up and marched out.

Dean had sighed. "The purists are always with us."

•

Katy stood up and brushed some of Washington Square's foliage off her skirt. "I ought to be going anyway. I want to visit Seamus today."

"How's he doing?" asked Ray Hegg. "Still in the hospital?"

"Yup. Want to come with me to visit him?" asked Katy.

Ray shook his head. "Hospitals hold as much attraction for me as cemeteries and police stations. You may wind up in one, but what's the rush?"

Ray had a squeamish side. Sometimes I thought that his tough guy persona—the shaved head, the shades, the beard—were mostly there to hide it.

"What about you, Joe?"

"I was there yesterday," I told her. "Getting mugged doesn't seem to have improved his disposition."

Truth was, I had hardly recognized the poet. The doctors had shaved Seamus' beard to work on a cut on his cheek. He lay in bed, swaddled in bandages, looking smaller than I had ever seen him.

"What do *you* want?" he asked when he saw me.

"Just thought I'd see how you're feeling."

He snorted. "Three refugees from Cromwell's army take me apart in the street. How do you *think* I feel?"

"Not good," I guessed.

"That's the style," he agreed. "By God, I feel naked without my beard. I haven't been clean-shaven since I was a boy. Joe, is my memory playing tricks, or was it you who rushed to my rescue?"

"I helped scare them off," I told him. "Would you recognize those clowns, Seamus? If the cops caught them, I mean?"

He frowned. "Ah, I doubt it, lad. Most of what I saw was their boots as they kicked me. I think one pair might have been snakeskin."

"Not much help."

"I suppose not. But I am forever grateful for *your* help, Joe."

"My pleasure, Seamus. Do you know when they're letting you out of here?"

"A few more days. I should still be able to get up to Boston for St. Paddy's Day. His hand rose to his naked chin. "And that reminds me, have you seen Dean Coffey?"

"He's visiting his family in California."

Seamus had nodded gravely. "I need to see him. Tell him that, would you, my boy?"

"Sure, Seamus. I'm glad you're going to be all right."

"Ah, it's hard to kill an Irishman, Joe. Not by kicking us, at any rate. The English have been kicking us for a long, long time."

•

"Sounds like he's back to normal," said Ray.

"How about you, Carol?" asked Katy. "You want to come?"

Carol made a face. I suppose she was thinking of her last encounter with the poet, in the alcove of the Riding Beggar. "Look who's coming," she said.

Hustling through the Arch was a short, chubby man wearing a button-down shirt and a blue tie under a checked hunting jacket. He looked every bit as out of place among the people relaxing in the park as he did everywhere else.

"Braubinger," I said. "What's he doing here? His idea of the great outdoors is a subway station."

"Someone dropped a penny in the fountain," said Katy. "He's gonna dive in and rescue it."

Bob Braubinger dressed like a junior partner in a failing advertising firm. I don't know if his hair looked bad naturally, or if he was too cheap to get a good haircut. Bob had no job, although he always had half a dozen half-baked projects in the oven, each of which he was convinced was going to land him on easy street. His money came from his wife, who worked in one of the jewelry stores her daddy owned. What she saw in him was one of those mysteries best left to the philosophers.

Lately Braubinger fancied himself a budding show biz manager. He had singled out Dean Coffey to become the first victim of his talent.

"Hi, people," he said. "How's it going?"

"Not bad," I said. "Heard anything from Dean?"

"Nah. He never calls when he's out in L.A."

"You looking for someone, Bob?" Ray Hegg asked. He tugged down his sunglasses for a better look. "I only ask 'cause your head is swinging around like a flag in high wind."

"Yeah? Sorry." He turned toward Ray, but his watery eyes continued to shift. "Heard a rumor, just a whisper, that ABC might have somebody in the Square today."

"Ben Casey?" Carol asked, straight-faced.

"Nah. I'm not talking about an autograph session. I mean a talent scout. Looking for people for the new show."

"Really?" asked Katy. Her hands fumbled with the cord on her dulcimer bag and her green eyes began to wander, just like Braubinger's brown ones.

"What show?" asked Ray.

"Must be *Hootenanny*," I told him. "It's supposed to start this spring. A folk music show filmed on a different college campus every week."

"Very trendy," said Ray. "It really ought to sell the product."

"Meaning what?" asked Carol.

The bald man grinned. "I thought you folksingers sang for truth and beauty. And for just causes of course: end the cold war, ban the bomb, integrate lunchrooms. Now to hear that you're willing to go on TV just to help ABC sell detergent...." He shrugged in eloquent dismissal.

"Detergent is useful," said Braubinger. "Try washing clothes without it."

"Ray has a point," said Katy, tinkering with a dulcimer string. "The network is sure to pick and choose what goes out over the air. You lose the purity of the material if the songs are censored."

"Censoring purity," Ray murmured. "Interesting concept."

Katy didn't seem to hear him. "Of course, a sensitive performer could pick songs that didn't need any changing. Selectivity, that's the key."

"Sure," said Braubinger.

I looked at him. "You don't mind censorship?"

"Nah. It's their money, Joe. Why should they risk it to let some wild-eyed radical show off? Be sensible."

"Darn right," said Ray. "To hell with truth and beauty. Let's sing a hymn to the almighty dollar."

"Oh, shut up, Ray," I snapped. "What's wrong with singing for the money you need, if you sing well?"

He put on his sunglasses and grinned some more. "What's wrong is you always need more money. 'Money doesn't fill a vacuum. It creates one.'"

"Where's that from? A fortune cookie?"

"Benjamin Franklin," said Carol.

Braubinger made a face. "Since when are you an expert on American history?"

She shrugged and looked away.

"Don't pick on her for knowing more than you do," said Katy.

I tried to ignore them all. "Okay, Ray. I've seen some of your jazz heroes on TV. Some on Ed Sullivan, even. Do you have a problem with that?"

"Hell, no. More power to 'em."

"But it's wrong for a folksinger?" asked Katy. "You're not making sense."

"What you people ignore," Ray said peacefully, "is that folk ain't jazz. Jazz grew up in bars and whorehouses. It's supposed to be played for money. Tips and dinner, or a million bucks, whatever the market will bear."

"But folk isn't?"

"Folk music, so you keep telling me, is the music of the people, whoever they are. It's what the common folk sing to entertain themselves, right? Lullabies, worksongs, stuff like that. If you're singing it for money, then it's just popular music that didn't happen to start in Tin Pan Alley."

"Folk revival," said Katy, sounding like a doctor making a diagnosis. "There's nothing wrong with it, in principle."

"You think we're hypocrites?" I asked Ray.

"Hey, I have no problem with a little honest hypocrisy. Sincerity is *your* hangup."

"If somebody can get on TV and make an honest buck," said Braubinger, "I say, God bless 'em."

I frowned. Being on the same side of an argument as Bob made me uncomfortable.

"If you find that talent scout, then what?" Carol asked. "You aren't going to perform, are you?"

"Me? Hell, no." Braubinger seemed a little horrified. "I'm a manager, not a singer. But I'd like to talk to the guy about Dean Coffey. He'd be great on *Hootenanny*."

"As long as he doesn't try and sing his own songs," said Carol. "The networks would never allow that civil rights and anti-war stuff to go on the air."

"Are you Dean's manager?" I asked. "Officially?"

Braubinger waved it away. "Nah, not yet. Deano's waiting to see what I can do for him, and I respect him for that. I've been talking to a record company about him, and they're eager to hear his demo tape. Chafing at the bit. I think once they do we'll be closing a deal."

"That's terrific," said Katy. "Who is it, Bob? Vanguard? Elektra?"

Braubinger tugged at his tie. "Broker Records."

"Never heard of them."

"I have," said Ray. "In the *Wall Street Journal*, I think. Two stockbrokers started it as a tax dodge."

"That's how it began, sure," said Braubinger, rapidly. "But those guys have big plans, huge plans, I mean it. And you know how much moolah there is in the stock market. They're signing up a full roster of artists."

"Doesn't sound like much of a deal to me," said Katy.

Braubinger shook his head. "You guys wouldn't know a good thing if it ran over you. Folk music is a growing market, and you won't climb on the bandwagon. It's a crying shame."

"Oh, I'm convinced," said Ray. "Sign me up. I'll play the bongos on *Hootenanny*."

"Oh, *please*," muttered Katy. The drummer was still pounding away at the other end of the park.

"Ray Hegg," I added. "The singing chemist."

"Jazz giant of the test tubes," he agreed.

"Who's a jazz giant?" said a new voice. "I'll size up the talent in that field."

Ronald Von Ehmsen had come up behind me. He was a tall bearded man, the owner of a Bleecker Street joint called Café Rafio. In the Village, where eccentricity was as common as jaywalking, Von Ehmsen managed to stand out as an eccentric. He owned a large collection of limousines and old sports cars, plus the old motorcycle he was walking through the Square. There was a photo on the wall of the Rafio that showed him made up to look like Jesus Christ.

"We're debating jazz versus folk," Ray told him.

"Well that's easy," said Von Ehmsen. "When Anglo-Saxons steal from the Celts, it's folk music. When they steal from the Africans, it's jazz. Glad I could clear that up for you." He looked at me. "Hey, Talley. Is your boss at home?"

"Max is at the Beggar, yeah."

"Cool. I need to palaver with the boy. Tag along."

"Maybe I should come," said Carol. "It must be nearly time to set up."

"No," I said. "Stay and enjoy the sunshine for a while. Keep an eye on Bob, too. Make sure he doesn't sell the arch."

"No market for it," said Braubinger. His head was turning back and forth like a periscope, hunting for *Hootenanny*.

CHAPTER 8

This town is going down the pipes," Max said. Then, as if the word *pipes* had given him the idea, he went into a coughing fit. He glared at Von Ehmsen's cigar.

"Well, sure," said Von Ehmsen, scratching his beard. "So is everything else. Entropy increases, as Einstein always told me, back when we used to double-date."

"I mean the Village," said Max. Von Ehmsen was one of his best friends so Max had gotten pretty good at ignoring him when he started to rave. "I've lived here for thirty years, and I tell you the place is getting worse by the hour. The slums, people who don't care about each other—"

"Can it," said Von Ehmsen. "You talk like an old man. You've listened to too much of the hillbilly trash they play in your joint, all about the good old days when people shot each other with muskets and froze to death in horse-drawn carriages. The good old days is hog-crap."

Max grinned, a sure sign that he was losing his temper. "So everything is getting better, Candide? How come Seamus is in the hospital? How come we're sitting here talking about armed guards?"

It turned out that Von Ehmsen had come over to talk about organizing a meeting of club owners in the Village to discuss security measures. Half a dozen clubs and cafes had been broken into around Valentine's Day, and everybody was jumpy.

"I don't say armed guards," Von Ehmsen said, with exaggerated patience. "Maybe burglar alarms would be enough. If we all join in we could get 'em wholesale. At least we can find out if any of the club owners have security ideas the rest of us haven't thought of. What do you say? Will you come?"

Mac turned to glare at me. "Well?"

I was at the far end of Max's narrow, overstuffed office, sitting on a worn-out ottoman. "Sounds good to me. I'll go if you don't want to."

"So be it." He turned back to Von Ehmsen. "Discuss it with Mr. Talley. He's in charge of all our security precautions, up to and including sending in Marine advisors."

Von Ehmsen frowned. "That's your best offer?"

"Thanks a heap," I said.

He waved a hand. "No offense meant, kid. You're clean and you don't stutter, but Karzoff here is a respected man among the club owners. If I can say he's coming it'll bring others. But you...."

"I'm not a headliner."

"Lucky thing," muttered Max. "Headliners cost too damned much."

Von Ehmsen got to his feet and headed out. Those two never said goodbye to each other—just turned away as if in a huff. If there was a reason for the ritual, it was beyond me.

I followed Von Ehmsen to the front door and let him out. "Have you talked to Les Newcomer upstairs?"

"Yup. He's coming." Von Ehmsen turned to face me. "Do you believe what Karzoff said? About everything getting worse?"

"Nope. This country has been stuck in concrete for years. Things are shaking loose and all Max sees right now are the broken pieces. He doesn't see the progress."

"Bingo." He punched me on the shoulder. "*Progress*, man. The Village is a magnet, Talley. People, money, ideas, are pouring in. You have to make plans, move ahead. This is no time to let cheap hoods take over the place and scare people away. You dig?"

"I do. See you at the meeting."

"Great." He hesitated. "And Joe? Take care of our friend in there." He nodded toward Max's office. "When you get old and decrepit like him those twenty-hour days catch up with you."

•

Max was scowling at his paperwork when I got back to his office. "Don't try to talk me into going to that meeting."

"Okay." I sat down.

He looked up, reluctantly. "So?"

"I want to talk you into something else."

He sighed. "Naturally. What is it?"

I handed him a record album I had brought in two days before. "I've been waiting for a chance to show this to you."

He frowned, holding it at arm's length. I never figured out if he was far-sighted or had just never got the hang of his bifocals. "Tom Paxton. *I'm The Man That Built The Bridges*. Lousy title. So?"

"Look who put it out."

"The Gaslight. Huh. So Clarence Hood has gone into the record business?"

"More or less. Tom is one of their top regulars and he hasn't found a record company yet. So Clarence put out a disc and sells it at his club. Tom makes a buck; the Gaslight makes a buck. The publicity and airplay help everybody."

Max dropped the album on his desk. He sat back and folded his hands on his substantial gut. "God bless free enterprise. So?"

He knew damn well where I was headed, but he was making me work for it. It looked like I had caught him in a bad mood, but who could wait six months for a good mood to show up?

"Dean Coffey," I said. "He finished a demo tape in January. He put a lot of time and money into it, and it's good."

"Swell. So?"

"He hasn't found a record company deal yet. He's our top regular and it would be as easy as pie to put him in a studio and turn the demo songs into vinyl."

"Uh huh. And how much would this easy pie cost us?"

"We'd make it up in album sales, Max. Riding Beggar Records. It would be great."

"It stinks."

My jaw dropped. "Why?"

"We ain't the Gaslight. We don't have their rep, yet. And Coffey ain't Paxton."

"Dean is damned good, Max."

"Oh, he's going places, Joe. But he ain't there yet. Hell, even *I* know some of Paxton's songs. *The Marvelous Toy*, for instance. What does Coffey have to compare to that?"

"No fair. Dean doesn't write children's songs."

"I'm not talking about the *subject*, Joe." He ran a hand through his comb-over and sighed. "It's the commercial thing. I haven't heard any songs by Dean that, say, the Kingston Trio would record. Or that would get much airplay if Dean recorded them himself. Maybe in a year or two he'll be ready to record, but right now, no."

I tapped a hand on his desk, impatiently. "Bob Braubinger thinks he's ready."

"Oh, Braubinger." Max shrugged. "If he's your expert witness...."

"He's trying to get a record company to sign Dean up, but the company is a bunch of jerks, a couple of *stockbrokers*, for God's sake. What do they know about folk music?"

"What stockbrokers know about," said Max slowly, "is how to make lots of money. They don't generally know how to share it with the people who work for them."

"So Dean is gonna get hijacked. Come on, Max. You can't let this happen."

"I'm Robin Hood all of a sudden? Forget it, Joe. I'm a businessman. Convince me I can make a buck off this and I might be interested. But don't expect charity."

He ran a palm across the papers on his desk. "And as for saving Dean from the stockbrokers, he hasn't been in here asking for help. What you really mean is save him from himself, and I gave up *that* game before you were toilet-trained."

"Is that your last word?"

"Absolutely. For now anyway." He pushed Paxton's album gently across the desk to me. "Do you really think Von Ehmsen's meeting might be worth a visit, or were you just trying to butter me up?"

"I think one of us should go, Max. Look at it this way: let's say the other club owners agree on some security idea and we *don't* participate."

"They won't agree on anything. I *know* these people. But assume away."

"If the idea is any good, the burglars will look for clubs that aren't using it, right?"

"Damn." Max shook his head. "I never thought of that. You're a sneaky son-of –a-bitch, Talley. You'll go far."

I held up Paxton's record. "Will I go into the record business?"

He turned back to his paperwork. "Sneaky and stubborn."

CHAPTER 9

I didn't have a chance to visit Seamus again until Tuesday, and when I called the hospital they told me he had been released the night before. So, late that morning I found myself ringing the front bell at his apartment house on Christopher Street.

"No answer?" asked a familiar voice.

I turned and saw a short man with a sandy crewcut and perennially squinting brown eyes. Frank Renard had a face made for radio, as he put it himself, and that was exactly where he made his living.

"Looks like nobody's home. How you doing, Frank?"

"Not bad, not bad. They haven't fired me in over a month." Frank ran a late night radio show full of storytelling and social commentary, in the tradition of Mort Sahl and Jean Shepherd. Every year or so his wisecracks ticked off a sponsor and the station tried to can him. Protests from the fans always forced them to bring him back by the end of the week. So far.

Frank and I had a strange relationship, based on mutual benefit and frustration. I was always trying to get him to play folk music on his show, or interview some of my favorite musicians. He was always trying to get me to hire some of his favorite comedians to play at the Beggar. So far we had resisted each other's pleas.

"Are you here looking for Seamus, too, Frank?"

"Yup. I wanted to get the crazy Irish poet on my show for St. Patrick's Day. He hasn't been answering the phone."

"He told me he was going to Boston next weekend. But the reason he hasn't been answering the phone is that he's been in the hospital." I gave him a brief version of Seamus's troubles.

"No kidding. Ain't that something?" He scratched his crew cut thoughtfully. "You wouldn't think an Irishman would have to come all the way to the New World to get in a brawl, would you?"

"Maybe you could have him on the show to talk about that."

"Maybe I could. A whole panel of crime victims. Not a lot of laughs there, you think?" He looked at the apartment house door. "I don't like this, Joe. Where the hell is he?"

I frowned. "What do you mean?"

"I mean Seamus gets out of the hospital and the next morning he gets out of bed early—I know, 'cause I called him here before nine—and goes off somewhere. Does that sound right?"

"No, it doesn't," I admitted. "Seamus doesn't strike me as an early riser."

"Where's the super?" Frank looked as the list of intercom buttons. "Here's the joker." He leaned on the button.

The super, an old Puerto Rican, came up swearing in Spanish. "No here," he snapped, once he understood who we wanted. "He gone."

"Gone?" Frank repeated. "Gone where?"

"Gone." The super turned and we followed him down the hall. The door to Seamus's place was open. "I'll be damned," said Frank. "Gone is right."

The place was empty. It had been stripped to the walls.

"He got out of the hospital last night," I said. "How in hell did he move his furniture out this morning?"

Frank scowled. "He must have made arrangements in the hospital by phone. The better question is where did he go."

"And why."

"Yup. Let's go to my place. I'll make a few phone calls."

Frank lived on LaGuardia and as we hoofed it over there Frank started a sales pitch for his new favorite comedians. "There are two guys playing in the Village this month you just have to see, Joe. They are both incredible. Funniest thing you ever saw, I mean it. First one is Woody Allen—" He glared at me. "What was that noise supposed to be? A snort of disdain?"

"I've heard about that one. He's the guy who turns his back on the audience and talks to the wall."

"That's part of his shtick. Jewish neuroticism. The crowd eats it up."

I shook my head.

"The other guy is at the Bitter End this week. A Negro named Cosby. He's really going places, Joe."

"We don't have comedians at the Beggar, Frank. We do folk music, remember? You ought to try some of them out on your audience."

"Like who for instance?"

"Phil Ochs, Tom Paxton, Dean Coffey...."

"Uh uh. Not that guy." Frank spoke with a coldness I had seldom heard from him.

"Dean? What do you even know about him?"

"Never you mind." Frank's eyes were almost shut. "He's off my list, that's all."

Then he laughed. "Hey, I just figured out why Seamus ran out. He spends a lot of his time in Boston, right?"

"Right."

"Maybe he's the lady-killer they've been looking for up there."

I immediately remembered Seamus crowding Carol the waitress into a corner of that alcove. "You mean he got some girl in trouble?"

"No, Joe." Frank grinned, enjoying himself tremendously. "I mean maybe he's the famous Boston Strangler."

"I'm guessing not, Frank."

"Yeah. But it's a cool thought."

We were silent for the rest of the trip to LaGuardia. Frank was living with an actress, or so I heard. I'm not sure I ever met her. I know she wasn't there when we hit his place that morning.

He was reputed to have the biggest book of phone numbers in Manhattan and he put it to work that day. I watched, fascinated, as he sat hunched over the desk, the phone jammed into one ear, and dug in.

"Hey, Miguel! How's it hanging, kid? Yeah, it's Frank, your favorite culture maven. Listen, I'm trying to track down Seamus O'Hanlon. Yeah, I know you published one of little pamphlets. What? A chapbook? If you say so. Sounds like something you put on your lips to me...."

"No, he's out of the hospital. But it looks like he has moved on. I thought maybe he told you where to send the royalty checks." Frank grinned at me, rolling his eyes to show how unlikely he thought it was that a book of poetry would produce any money. "Well, if you hear from him, call me at the station, okay? What's that? Well, the show's booked up for now, Miguel. Much as I'd love to have you on again. Everyone loved your explanation of why your stuff is so much better that that drivel Ferlinghetti and Ginsburg keep churning out.

"Sarcastic? Me? I don't know the meaning of the word, Miguel." He hung up and sighed. "Why would Seamus disappear?"

"Why would somebody beat him up?"

Frank's eyebrows rose. "Interesting. You mean it wasn't just a robbery?"

"Maybe so. Maybe Seamus had reason to think those guys would come back. That could be why he ducked out."

"He can't get away that easy." Frank picked up the phone. "If he's in the U.S. of A. Frank Renard will track him down."

But he didn't.

CHAPTER 10

The next time I saw Dean Coffey was at the Bag of Nails, the bar upstairs from the Riding Beggar. Max had tried to convince Les Newcomer, the owner, to put up a big sign outside like we had, but he had refused. It took me a long time to realize that publicity was exactly what Les didn't want. The niche he had found was that his bar was the one place in this part of the Village where the locals could be sure *not* to find tourists.

That Thursday I was telling Les about the English folksingers I was shepherding through a half-week at the Beggar. "Sovay recommended them. Out of the goodness of her heart, I guess, and I suppose their politics are right."

"You mean left," said Les.

"What I mean is their harmonies are definitely *not* right."

Les nodded. He was a thin, perpetually sour-faced man, maybe halfway between my age and Max's. He had a slight New England accent and was the best person I knew to tell bad news to: his face always looked like he'd been expecting it.

"I hoped to sneak out to see Phil Ochs this week," I said. "He's doing his first paying shows over at Gerde's. But these cockneys need someone to hold their hands."

"They must have something going for them if Sovay recommended 'em." Les had held Sovay in great respect ever since she told him that 'bag of nails' was British slang for a lousy poker hand. He bought the name with the bar and had never known what it meant. He had even let us come up for a free drink, to thank her. After hours, of course, because like most bars in New York, his didn't permit women.

"It's one of the problems with running a café," I told him. "You can't get to see nearly as many concerts at other places as you'd like."

"Suits me," said Newcomer. "I was a school teacher in Massachusetts for fifteen years. One of my jobs was thinking up assembly programs. If I never see a stage again I won't shed a tear."

"Just how I feel about California," said a voice behind me.

"Dean! When did you get back?"

"Late last night." He yawned and scratched his bushy blond hair. "Plane delays...Don't ask. If man were meant to fly, airplane seats would be big enough to sit in. Hi, Les. Gimme a beer."

He took off his familiar gray corduroy jacket and hung it on the seat behind him. Some people accused him of using that coat as a gimmick, like Dylan's Dutchboy hat, but he always claimed it was just to keep off the cold wind that blew through the New York streets six months of the year.

"How's California?" I asked.

"Sunny and dull, two qualities this burg never achieves. How are things around here? Any news on *Hootenanny*?"

I filled him in on Bob Braubinger's latest rumors about the show.

"Yeah, that's great." Dean raised his beer mug in a toast. "May it run so long they run out of talent and come looking for people like me."

"Hey! Hey, you!" A voice was calling from another table. "You from California?"

The guy was sitting at a table not far from the bar. He was in his forties, bulky with fat, and needed a shave. When he swayed to his feet it was clear he had been drinking for quite some time.

"I used to live in L.A." he announced. "Man, I love that town. Were you in L.A.?"

He was close enough then that we could smell his breath. Dean and I instinctively stepped back.

"No," said Dean. "Not L.A."

"I was in a movie there once. They had—had an ad for extras, see. This big crowd scene. I was at a table…."

He raised his hand toward his mouth and seemed surprised to find no glass there. He frowned at his fist.

"Have a seat, Augie," said Les quietly. "I'll bring you something."

The drunk turned slowly around, spotted his table and moved unsteadily back to it.

"Christ," muttered Dean. "How do you stand it, Les?"

Newcomer shrugged. "Money in the bank to me." He began pouring another beer. "You can't worry about drunks like they're human beings. They don't care about themselves. Why should I?"

He walked around the bar to bring Augie his brew.

"What an attitude." Dean was red-faced, furious. "What a goddamn lousy attitude. The drunks can't help themselves, but people who sell them the stuff—" He stopped and looked at the beer in front of him.

"If it isn't Les, it'd be somebody else," I told him.

"That's a familiar line, isn't it, Joe? Next you'll tell me he was only following orders." He closed his eyes, raised his head, and loudly sang the chorus of an old song:

Are you shingling the rumseller's roof?
Are you shingling the rumseller's roof?
While your own house decays are you spending your days
Just shingling the rumseller's roof?

I let a moment pass after he'd finished. "Well, you're in a rotten mood."

"Yeah." He slouched in his seat. "Goddamned California."

I raised my eyebrows at that non sequitur. The trips out to the sunny west usually put him in a dark mood. I assume that there were problems with his family, but he never talked about them—although he certainly *sang* about a troubled family from time to time.

Suddenly Dean smiled and changed the subject. "Any progress with that idea we had? With Max, I mean?"

I shook my head. "I keep bringing it up but so far no luck. He doesn't want to go into the record business."

"Christ." He sighed. "Sometimes I feel like I'm treading water and juggling anvils. It can't go on like this."

"Don't give up on Max. I'm still working on him. I think he's still in a bad mood over what happened to Seamus."

"Seamus?" Dean's eyebrows shot up.

"Oh hell. You haven't heard." I filled him in on the mugging. "Frank Renard says nobody in New York or Boston has heard from Seamus. Frank doesn't have such great contacts in Dublin, but he's trying."

"My God," said Dean, shaking his head. "What a crazy thing. He gets beat up and then he just disappears."

"That reminds me. He told me he wanted to see you."

"Yeah? I wonder what for." Dean frowned. "When was that?"

"In the hospital. The day after you last played at the Beggar."

"Jeez. It seems like a year ago."

"He was supposed to go off to Boston next week for St. Patrick's Day stuff. You know how many Irish bars they have up there."

"Yeah. He was telling me about it that night. Right here in fact." Dean looked at the bar in amazement. "Right goddamned here. Seamus and Ray and Bob and I sat here and schmoozed. Hey, Joe?"

"Yeah?"

Dean tugged at his moustache. "So the cops say it was a robbery, huh?"

Before I could answer I spotted a familiar figure in the doorway. "Phil, come and join us? Tell us how the gig is going."

Ochs hurried over. He was always full of energy but that day he was vibrating. "Have you seen it? Hentoff's column?"

"No, I haven't seen the *Voice* yet. Why? What's he got to say?"

"You won't believe it." Ochs was positively bouncing with his eagerness to tell the news. "Not in this day and age."

"Phil, what the hell's going on?"

"Joan Baez just refused to go on *Hootenanny*. Know why?"

"Obviously we don't," said Dean. "Are you gonna tell us or do we have to go buy the Voice to find out?"

"They won't let Pete Seeger or the Weavers on the show. After all these years, they're still blacklisted. Can you believe it?"

We just stared at him.

Augie the drunk stumbled to his feet. "Show biz," he crowed. "There's nothing like it."

CHAPTER 11

What's the nature of this conspiracy?" Max asked.

He gestured toward the table where a bunch of us had been sitting, drinking coffee. There were Tom Paxton, Dean Coffey, Bob Braubinger, Phil Ochs, and a few others.

It was near set-up time and I had just stood and told the others to pack up when Max walked in. "No conspiracy, Boss, just a little war council. We're planning our strategy."

"Still sounds pretty sinister. Who is the intended victim?"

"ABC."

"What, television? You got nothing better to do than pick fights with those schmucks?"

"Do you read the *Voice*, Max?"

"Only to see where they hide our ad every week."

"Read this issue," said Dean. He waved goodbye to the other committee members who were walking out. "Read Nat Hentoff's column. Do you know about *Hootenanny*?"

"Yeah. TV discovering folk music, ten years late. What else is new?"

"According to the article, the blacklist is on."

"Blacklist? Jesus." Max sat heavily on the edge of the nearest table. "Against who?"

"Pete Seeger and the Weavers, at least," said Dean. "The producer says they aren't good enough to be on his show, if you can believe that."

"Nobody believes it," I said. "That's the whole point. The Weavers practically *invented* modern folk music. *Kisses Sweeter Than Wine. Wemoweh. If I Had A Hammer.* If they don't belong on the show, who does? Obviously this is political."

"Jesus," Max said again. He shook his head, and the light from the stage reflected off his bifocals.

"Joan Baez has already announced she won't go on the show. Paxton and some of the others you saw here are lining up performers to boycott it."

Max looked at us, his arms folded over his pot belly. "And you two favor a boycott?"

"Sure. Everyone here did, except Braubinger, of course. He says ABC can run the show anyway they want, because it's their money. And he says one folkie on the air is better than none."

"Makes sense to me," said Max.

"Christ," said Dean. "You agree with ABC?"

"I didn't say that, pal. It is a rare day when I agree with a corporation about anything."

"But you're against a boycott?"

He stood up. "I'm in favor of a cup of java. Hope you clowns left the pot on." He walked into the kitchen.

Dean and I exchanged a glance. We followed him in.

"You knew them, didn't you, Max?" I asked.

"Knew who?" He frowned into the depths of a coffee cup. "Jesus. Richie must be cleaning these things in the East River."

"You knew Pete, Lee Hays, Woody Guthrie," said Dean. "Cisco Houston, Leadbelly. All the greats from the thirties. The Almanac Singers and the Café Society crowd. You were already hanging around the Village then, weren't you?"

Max snorted. "I've been here since Peter Stuyvesant had two legs. Not hanging around. Working. What's your point?"

"You never talk about them," I said. "Even though you run a folk bar, you never mention the folksingers you knew back then."

He pushed his bifocals up his nose. "I run a folk bar because that's where the money is today. Five years ago I had a hipster joint. This place is special to you, but to me it's just a meal ticket."

"But you knew those guys, right?" I persisted. "Were you in the labor movement?"

Max sipped coffee. He was leaning back against the counter, facing us, and he looked like a man backed into a corner. I guess that's exactly what we had done.

"Things were different in the Depression," he said at last. "That was as popular as the left wing ever got in this country. More popular than now by a long shot. Because when people are selling apples and shoelaces on the street to survive, and farmers are going out of business—Jesus. Communism seems to make a lot of sense then."

He was silent for a long moment. Then he shrugged. "Yeah. I knew those guys. Some personally and all by reputation. I met them at concerts, at parties, at rallies for the Spanish Civil War, and at meetings."

"What kind of meetings, Max?" Dean asked. "Communist party?"

He pushed his bifocals up his nose and gave Dean that fierce grin. "So who are you all of a sudden? Roy Cohn?"

A door opened and I silently cursed the intruder for breaking the mood. Carol Meisel and Al Perkins appeared in the doorway.

"Hey, Joe," said Carol. "Max. Welcome back, Dean. You're all here early."

Al stepped into the kitchen, a king entering his domain. We had hired him as a temporary replacement during the Asian flu epidemic and the spark he gave the Beggar's simple cuisine had boosted our business and made him the permanent cook. "I need room to work, Max."

"Of course you do," said the boss. He put down his coffee cup like a man making a decision. "Al, Carol. I'm leaving you two in charge. There's five bucks in it for you if the place is still standing and licensed when we get back."

Al grinned. Carol gawked. None of us could remember the last time neither Max nor I had been there for set-up.

"Get your coats and follow me, gentlemen."

"Where are we going, Max?"

"We're gonna take a field trip."

It was a chilly March day. Max wrapped himself up in a bulky overcoat, a scarf and earmuffs. He always dressed as if it were ten degrees colder for him than the rest of the world. Maybe it had to do with his constant problems with his chest, or maybe he really did see the world as hostile. He walked fast in spite of the get-up and Dean and I had to hurry to keep up with him.

"Where to, Boss?" I asked as we crossed Sixth Street.

"My apartment. There's something I want you to hear."

Behind his back Dean raised his eyebrows at me. He had never been to Max's place. I had been there once, to sign some papers. Max believed in keeping his business life separate from his social life. He was so true to this principle that I can't swear he even had a social life.

Max lived in an old apartment house on Carmine Street, on the edge of Little Italy. You cold tell at a glance that a bachelor had been living alone there for at decade or more. The place was cluttered from end to end. It had the artificial tidiness a cleaning woman produces as she moves stuff around to dust, without actually putting anything away.

The living room walls held half a dozen paintings, all purchased from local artists, most of whom sold their stuff on street corners. The farthest any of the pictures took you from Manhattan was a pastel of the Brooklyn Bridge.

A pen-and-ink of Washington Square, done by our friend Agustina Adler, held a proud position on the longest wall.

Max pointed to a cracked leather sofa. "Sit there. Don't move things around, just clear off a spot and wait. I'm going to put a record on."

The far wall was covered with built-in shelving, and most of it was packed with LPs, singles and 78s. There was no pattern to the collection that I could see. Jazz lay side by side with opera, folksingers rested between big bands and show music.

Had he purchased any of them, I wondered, or were they all the gifts that you accumulated from a lifetime in the business?

There must have been some organizing principle after all because it didn't take him more than a minute to find what he was looking for. ""Okay," he said, pulling out a dusty album from the bottom shelf. "Here we go."

"What is this mystery treat?" I asked.

"Shut up and listen." He fiddled with his turntable. "Let's see; we'll start with this."

There was a ghostly cough of old vinyl and then a song came on. I frowned. The voices were familiar although I couldn't tag them. The tune was easy: *Jesse James*, which Woody Guthrie had borrowed more than once. Only the words were new to me.

> *Oh, Franklin Roosevelt, told the people how he felt*
> *We damned near believed what he said.*
> *He said I hate war, and so does Eleanor*
> *But we won't be safe till everybody's dead.*

Dean was grinning. "Max, what *is* this?"

Max handed him the record cover, old and cheaply printed. "*Songs For John Doe*, by the Almanac Singers," he explained. "After the Spanish Civil War the Almanac Singers went around the U.S. singing a whole lot of isolationist songs. A lot of their songs attacked conscription—the draft, that is."

"Like this song," I said.

Max nodded. "*Ballad of October 16th*, by Millard Lampell. They sang a lot of songs like that. When England declared war, they urged the U.S.A. to mind its own business and keep our boys safe at home."

"A lot of people felt that way," I said.

"Sure," said Max. "The German bundists and racist scum like Father Coughlin. Plus a bunch of head-in-the-sand isolationists, and the diehard pacifists."

He sat down heavily. "It was also the official line of the Communist Party."

He pointed at the album cover, which Dean had passed over to me. "The Daily Worker gave this record a glowing review. FDR, that great pillar of freedom, asked his cronies if there was any legal way he could ban it."

Dean shook his head. "Come on, Max. You're just dragging up all those HUAC charges."

My boss was grim. "This went on for a year, until Operation Barbarossa. Do you infants know what that was? The Nazi bastards invaded Russia. And the Almanac Singers, being good pacifists and isolationists, kept singing that we should stay out of the war, right?"

We waited.

Max snorted. "Like hell they did. Most of them took a break from performing. The record was an embarrassment and their repertoire was suddenly all wrong for what they wanted to say."

"I know they started singing about the war," I said. "*Reuben James* and so on. Guthrie and Houston joined the Coast Guard. Seeger joined the Navy—"

"*After* Pearl Harbor. The sneak attack gave them the chance to change their views with dignity. They started singing about how the good old U.S.A., together with good old Russia, could beat the Fascists. And *Songs For John Doe* landed on the scrapheap of history. Good luck finding one now; it's a collector's item."

"So what's the point?" I said. Snapped, I suppose. "Why are you telling us all this? You trying to shock us to death with the news that a few musicians might have been Communist sympathizers thirty years ago?"

Max threw the record cover. It skimmed the coffee table and bumped a dining room chair. "Jesus. You kids have no sense of history. Thirty years ago I was a Communist. Not a sympathizer, not a fellow traveler. A party member.

"But on September seventeenth, 1939, I quit." He glared at us. "Either of you know what happened then? No? Okay, here's an easier one. September first."

I shrugged.

"World War Two started," said Dean. "Germany invaded Poland."

"Yes!" Max leaned forward, his shoulders high with tension. "And on the seventeenth, two weeks later, they got a partner. While Crazy Adolf was attacking from the West, Uncle Joe Stalin struck Poland from the East. The leader of world Communism had cut a deal with the fascist scum."

His rage was as hot and real as if it had all happened that morning. "When that news came over the radio I cut up my membership card and mailed it to Party headquarters with a note about what Stalin could do with the pieces."

Dean chuckled.

"Glad you're enjoying this. Some of my best friends, my *comrades*, wanted nothing to do with me after that. I was ostracized in places where I had always been welcome.

"After the war, when Khrushchev started to reveal what a bastard Stalin had been, I watched some of those characters leave the Party, quietly, back door style. Who me? I'm a Democrat, that's all. I never even *heard* of Henry Wallace."

Max looked at me. "So to answer your question, Joe: No. I don't condemn anyone for belonging to the Party back then. I don't even blame them for not having the sense to drop out when I did.

"But I am still waiting for an apology. I was right and I suffered for it, and I'm still waiting for some of those jokers to admit it."

"So you *do* approve of blacklisting people," I said.

"Did I say that? Damn it, *did* I?" He pushed his bifocals up his nose. "Hell, no. I don't believe you should keep a man from working because of his beliefs. I think everybody should work, even Rockefeller."

"What about the McCarthy years?" Dean asked.

Max was starting to wheeze. He pulled out his handkerchief and pressed it to his red face. "What—what about 'em?"

"They were looking for ex-Party members to name names before HUAC. How did they miss you?"

"You're *hearing* why." Max shrugged. "I've always had bad lungs. The Army wouldn't take me because of them. Well, in the late forties it turned into tuberculosis. I spent six months in a sanitarium upstate, drying out.

"When I got back friends told me some official-looking jokers had been in the Village looking for me. Back then, a lot of people assumed anyone with TB was a goner. My guess is they wrote me off and never checked back."

"But what if they *had* called back?" I asked. "If you were subpoenaed, would you have named names?"

"Not important," said Dean, yawning.

Max grinned at me. "Nobody asked me, Joe. So we'll never know."

"But you can—"

"What do you want me to say? That I would have been like Zero Mostel and waved five fingers at the congressmen to say I was taking the Fifth Amendment? Or like Elia

Kazan and named everybody I knew? Unless you've been there you don't know *what* you would do!"

I nodded slowly.

Max stood up slowly and tugged at his trousers. "Let's get back to the joint and see if the Board of Health has closed us down yet."

CHAPTER 12

We live in a wonderful country," said Dean Coffey. "Anybody here ever notice that?"

The crowd applauded, just a bit, not sure where he was going.

"Let me give you a for-instance," he went on. "Here in the U.S.of A. we've got freedom of the press, which means the government can't tell the papers what to print, or tell the television networks what to show us. I've been looking at the TV listings lately, to see what kind of shows our three beloved, free and independent networks have decided we should see this year."

He held up a long, narrow piece of paper. "I've jotted down a few samples. Take notes; there may be a quiz. *Combat. The Gallant Men. McHale's Navy.*"

The crowd was chuckling now.

He smiled back under his moustache, all California beach boy innocence. "Let's see. We've also got: *Ensign O'Toole. McKeever and the Colonel.*" Each name got a bigger laugh.

Dean let the list flutter to the floor of the stage. "If there's a show about a conscientious objector I must have missed it. They seem to like Irish names for their soldiers, don't they? Are we going to see one called *Lieutenant Kennedy*? Maybe they are saving that for next season.

"Well, it's a great country anyway, because I can stand up here and sing a song like this. I just can't sing it on TV." He started *Down By The Riverside*.

Gonna lay down my sword and shield
Down by the riverside
Ain't gonna study war no more.

The Friday Night Hootenanny was off to a good start. It suddenly occurred to me to wonder if the television show might make that name unpopular. Maybe we should go back to calling it Talent Night.

Dean was too good and too busy to be a regular at talent nights, whatever you might call them, but like a lot of the other folkies, he showed up occasionally to try out a new song or check out the competition.

He was doing a coffeehouse at Brooklyn College later that night and had decided to warm up at the Riding Beggar first. This would be his first performance since his trip to California.

I walked over to the prettiest girl in the room and put a free soda down in front of her. Irene Fox was a spectacular blond. She wore a man's white shirt over red stretch tights and half the males in the joint were gaping at her. She never took her eyes off the man on the stage.

It would have been touching to see that beautiful woman watching Dean so closely, except that her lips were pursed as if she was grading his act and not finding it up to her standard.

"He's in good form tonight," I told her. "He'll knock 'em dead at the college."

"Which pays more than he'll ever make for a night here," snapped Irene. "I don't know why he bothers with this dump."

It was rhetorical but I answered her anyway. "The coffeehouse at the college is just one night, Irene. We can hire him by the week."

"For all the good it does him. This place isn't going anywhere, and neither will Dean until he moves to a better gig. I want him to make a record."

"I've been working on that."

"Oh, sure. That dumb idea about you and your boss getting rich as record company executives. I don't see how—Darn it. Why does he have to play that song? It's so *depressing.*"

Dean was introducing one of his best songs. "This is about the Korean War. It's one of the most current songs I have.

"No, really. Folksingers are supposed to write topical songs, right? But me, I'm too darned slow. By the time I finish a song about a corrupt mayor he's a corrupt governor. By the time I finish a love song the chick has two kids already. Maybe she's even married."

Irene frowned but the crowd was laughing. Dean shrugged. "So here's a song about somebody's old man." He closed his eyes and sang.

My father died one April,
At a place called Pork Chop Hill.
The bullet took his life away
But lacked the grace to kill.
And now he sits on porches
That he does not recognize.
His family are strangers
And each morning's a surprise.

"God," muttered Irene.

"You don't like the song?" I asked.

"He'll never be a star playing this sort of stuff," she said. "The Birchers will blackball him."

"Blacklist."

"And even if they don't, who wants to hear it? Why can't he play something cheerful, like…like *Tom Dooley?*"

Before I could point out that the hit song *Tom Dooley* was about a man being hanged for murder, she added: "The audience doesn't like it. Listen to them."

I did. To my ear they seemed intensely interested. Dean was coming to the last verse.

And now my country's leaders
Say we need another war.
The more that they explain it all
The less I know what for.
Their voices rise like fire
But their eyes give me a chill
Like something took their lives away
But lacked the grace to kill.

There was some grumbling mixed in with the applause. *Tourists.* Irene was probably right about them, anyway. If they represent the great American middle class, then protest singers like Dean Coffey, Phil Ochs, and Bob Dylan, could never be much more than novelty acts.

I went up on stage to introduce a boy-girl duo who were terrified and seemed an even bet to knock over their microphones before their set was over. By the time I got them kick-started I could see a tornado forming halfway down the room.

Agustina Adler had stopped Dean as he left the stage. She had him by the arm and was talking a mile a minute, a big smile on her face.

What she couldn't see, but Dean and I could, was Irene Fox coming up behind her, double time, a look on her face that said: *we're going to settle this once and for all.*

Not again, I thought. I jumped off the stage, calling "Gus!" loud enough to be heard, I hoped, but not loud enough to bother my performers who were struggling desperately with the Riddle Song.

Gus said "Hi, Joe," and then Irene had her by the shoulder, spinning her around.

"Keep your hands off him!" Irene said, loud and shrill.

"Off who?" She meant it. Gus was a toucher by nature, and it didn't mean anything. She had no idea why the younger woman was upset.

"You know damned well who!" said Irene, and this time everybody at that end of the Beggar could hear her.

"Is that right?" Gus asked, still looking confused.

"Is that right?" Irene mimicked. "Is that right? I'll tell you what's right: You aren't ever getting him back. You're too *old* for him. He thinks you're a goddamned *harpy*!"

I was afraid Gus would ask *who* again, and God alone knew what Irene would do then. I grabbed Gus's arm just as Dean took Irene's and we steered them apart.

"Sorry," I told her, when we were seated a safe distance away.

"What's her problem, Joe?" She blinked her frank brown eyes at me. "What did I do?"

"You talked to her boyfriend, Gus. That's all. Irene is the jealous type."

"Talked to Dean?" She looked thoughtful. "But that was over long ago, Joe. Dean and I are just friends now."

"I know that," I told her. "But I don't think Irene believes in the idea of men and women being friends."

"Is that right?" Gus repeated the phrase, unaware or unconcerned that Irene had just been mocking her for it. She shook her head. "That's just sad, isn't it? If I felt that way, I think I'd kill myself."

Involuntarily I looked up, checking that Irene was out of earshot. She would surely think that remark was a deliberate provocation. Fortunately she and Dean were standing in the door to the green room.

"You just stay here, Gus. I'll bring you an apple juice."

"No time tonight, Joe, but thank you. I'm just here to meet somebody. There's an all-night yoga class at the Asian Culture Center. I have to be there by eight-thirty."

"It's almost that now."

"Is that right? Gosh, I better find him and go. Bye bye." She hurried off, her salt-and-pepper hair rolling around her head like a light fog.

I lit a cigarette, relishing a moment of calm. Then I walked back to the green room. Dean was there, packing his guitar, while Irene stood, arms folded, watching. He saw me and smiled. "Off to darkest Brooklyn. Thanks for the practice."

"Thanks for playing. You were great."

Someone tapped me on the shoulder. I turned and saw Matty Mark Oliver. He was wearing his blue blazer, ready to perform with his trio. I wondered what brought him over; it was unusual for him to go anywhere near Dean. "Hey, Joe. Your cook is ducking out."

"I know, Matty. Al asked for half a night off. He's got everything's set up in the kitchen."

"Yeah," said Matty, and the amazement on his face made him look more Arkansas than usual. "But do you see who he's leaving *with*?"

He pointed to the door. Al was walking out, arm and arm, with Gus Adler.

"Well, well," said Irene. She watched the Negro man and the white woman all the way out the door before turning to Dean. There was a triumphant smile on her beautiful face. "Your friend has such good taste, darling. Such good taste."

CHAPTER 13

Why do you do this to me, Joe?" asked Matty Mark Oliver. He had leaned his long frame over my table, startling me.

I had been thinking about that song of Dean's, *The Grace to Kill*, and wondering, not for the first time, if it was about his own father. My old man had been a feisty, loud-mouthed steelworker and it was hard for me to imagine growing up with a father who couldn't even take care of himself.

Dean would never say whether the war vet in the song was his father. He wasn't exactly like Dylan, who told a different version of his past to every interviewer. Instead he just made it clear that the past was off-limits. Yes, he grew up in California. Next question?

Last year Phil Ochs invited some people to join him on a trip to Greystone Park Psychiatric Hospital in New Jersey, where Woody Guthrie was suffering from Huntington's Chorea. Dean refused to make the pilgrimage. "He's just an old man, dying too slow," was what Dean had said. "I've seen that before. Leave him in peace."

But Matty Mark wouldn't leave *me* in peace. "Why do you make me do this?"

I looked him over. "Make you do what, Matty?"

He sipped soda. "Face the goddamn tourists every goddamn week. I am spitting sick of hoot nights. Tell the truth. What did you think of the Village Three's performance tonight?"

I thought about it as I looked at the stage where the last act played to a dwindling crowd. It was Sam Furrell, the scrawny college kid who had made his dismal world premiere at last week's hoot. To my surprise, he had returned for more punishment.

The Village Three had performed two hours before and then trekked upstairs to the Bag of Nails. Ben and Larry had eventually gone home but Matty Mark had wandered back into the Beggar to sit in the back and be quietly drunk.

"You were okay," I told him. "The crowd enjoyed you."

He straightened up, both hands flat on my table. "Then why won't you let us play here on a money night? As a goddamn opening act, anyway? I am sick to death of playing for tips and tourists."

"Keep your voice down," I told him. "You want the facts, Matty? You play for tourists 'cause you play tourist music. The suburbanites want to hear Kingston Trio stuff and that's what you give them."

He frowned. "What wrong with the Kingston Trio?"

I sighed. "Not much. If you're going to imitate someone it might as well be them."

"The Chad Mitchell Trio copies them. The Travelers Three—"

"Mitchell does a lot of political satire. The Travelers do all that Hawaiian styling. And neither band does covers of the Kingston hits. They roll their own."

"So what are you saying, Joe? You want us to write our own songs, like your big hero, Dean Coffey?"

"Damn it, Matty." I stood up to get my face closer to his. "Would you listen to yourself? I tell you to be original and you think I mean you should copy someone different. Why are you mad at Dean?"

That startled him. "Shoot, you know why."

"Tell me anyway."

"The snake stole my song. *Down Devil Creek.*"

"So, if that song is so important to you, why don't you ever play it? On stage, I mean."

"What? *Let Me Take Your Side?* I'd rather slit my wrists."

I shook my head. "No, I mean *Down Devil Creek.*"

"Well, shoot." Matty Mark looked astonished. "That's just a little ol' hillbilly tune. Nobody wants to hear that."

"Do you remember what the college professors say about folk music, Matty? It's supposed to be what you learn from *people*. Not from books, not from records. And especially the songs you hear from your own family."

"So?"

"So why not quit imitating whoever is the flavor of the month and play the stuff you grew up on?"

He frowned. "Ben and Larry wouldn't go for it."

"Then to hell with them. You're better than they are. When you're sober, anyway."

He was gazing off into the distance, licking his lips thoughtfully. "Find a new group, you mean?"

"Or go solo."

"Oh, no." He shook his head. "Not this boy. I could never get up there by myself. Shoot, I have to get half-mashed to go up with a group."

I patted his shoulder. "Well, you think about it. I gotta go. Max needs me."

The boss was standing by his office door, waving me over. "Joe, I've been thinking. Has Coffey said anymore about that record deal?"

That was a surprise. It was the first time Max had brought it up, as opposed to the five or ten times I had nagged him about it.

"Well, no. Braubinger is still pushing him to sign with those stockbrokers. If we don't make Dean an offer soon, we're gonna lose him."

"Lose him?" Max frowned over his bifocals at me. "What does that mean, exactly?"

"I don't follow you."

Max sighed. "I thought you wanted to make a record to push Dean's career. Now it sounds like you're trying to use it to tie him to the Beggar. Which is it?"

"Both, Boss. The record would be good for him, and good for us. He'll move up faster, and we'll be the place where he started."

"Hmm. That's all right, I guess. Just don't expect loyalty. When Elektra or Columbia bends a finger he'll forget he ever knew us."

I grinned. "Max. You're a goddamned sentimentalist. You're afraid my feelings are gonna get hurt."

Max grimaced, like he was tasting something sour. "Dean Coffey is on his way up. How long do you think he'll stay at this little joint, for God's sake? He can't make a decent living on the club scene. Bohemian life is fun when you're twenty, but sooner or later people want steak, not cheeseburgers. He'll be hitting the campus tours, or traveling as the opening act for one of the big names. But he sure as hell won't stay here."

"I suppose you're right, but—"

"No buts, Joe. Face it: he's too good. If you're gonna get attached to the performers and want to keep 'em around like pets, just hire the no-talents. God knows there's enough of 'em around, and they'll stay as long as you let 'em."

I made a face. "It's not worth all the trouble of breaking in new talent if they're just gonna drop you on the way up."

Max raised a finger, an Old Testament prophet in a cheap suit. "Ah, but remember the sweet part, Joe. If you stay in business long enough you can hire 'em again on the way down."

"You're a cynic, Boss."

"A realist," he growled, and then started a row of hacking coughs. "Jesus. I'm not feeling great. You close the place."

"Sure, Max. Take it easy."

He shrugged into his coat and struggled to get his ear muffs on without weeding his thin crop of hair. "And Joe? Tell Dean we'll do that record with him. What the hell. We've got nothing to lose but money, and everybody thinks I'm made of that."

•

Carol Meisel was wide-eyed. "Really? Max finally said yes?"

I had told her because it was closing time and I had to tell somebody. Matty Mark was the only other friend still in the place, and he was hardly the person who wanted to hear good news about Dean.

"Yup, we'll be making a record. I'll have to find a studio and set it up. This is gonna be great, Carol."

"It's fantastic." She scrubbed another table. "Dean is going to be ecstatic, Joe. It's so great that you were able to change Max's mind. You are just amazing."

"Ah, well. All in a day's work. Let's get this place closed up fast, okay? We're gonna have a busy day tomorrow."

"I've done all the tables except...." Carol nodded to my table. Matty Mark sat there alone, his head in his hands.

I took two steps in his direction and heard the phone ring back in Max's office. I hustled back and picked it up.

"Joe, you gotta help me." It was Dean's voice, so shaky I could hardly recognize it. "Somebody wrecked my apartment, top to bottom."

"What do you mean? Someone broke in?"

"I mean they tossed the place, damn it. It's a disaster area. Can I come over there, Joe? I gotta talk to somebody."

"Sure. Knock on the door. I'll be waiting." We hung up.

"Problem?" I turned around and saw Matty leaning in the office doorway, bleary-eyed.

"Nothing worth calling in the Peace Corps over. Can you get home okay?"

"Me? Sure? Easy as mama's pecan pie."

"Okay. Thanks for the show. And Matty? Think about what I said about the songs, okay?"

"Sure. Why not?" His Arkie accent suddenly went molasses thick. "Southern boy makes big money playing hillbilly music in the city. Tomorrow's headline." And he swaggered out.

Chapter 14

Dean Coffey picked up the glass of bourbon and gulped it.

"Hey, slow down," I said. "I'm not gonna grab it away from you."

He gasped. "Sorry, Joe. Sorry. I appreciate this. God, I didn't know how scared I was. I could barely walk out into the street."

"Scared of what, exactly?"

We were sitting at my table in the back of the Beggar. The only light on was the one directly over our table, and it made the place feel spooky.

"I was playing the coffeehouse at Brooklyn College. Got back around two and, Christ...." He shuddered.

I had never seen Dean so pale. Screaming girlfriends and right-wing hecklers had never shaken him up like this.

"Somebody wrecked my apartment. Destroyed it."

"A robbery? Hell, I'm sorry."

He shook his head. "This was no robbery. I have a guitar any pawnshop would beg for. It wasn't even touched."

I frowned. "Then what was the point?"

"Beats the hell out of me, Joe. They were looking for something, that's for sure. They opened every drawer and looked in every corner."

I poured us both more bourbon. "I'll be damned. What were they after?"

"How the hell would I know? Ask *them*."

I put a hand on his arm. "Take it easy, man."

He took another gulp. "I stayed long enough to check that the lock was working—not that it did much good, right? Then I ran out of there and called you."

"That's okay, man. You can come home with me. Nobody's camped out on my couch in over a week."

"Look...Joe." He put down his glass. "To tell you the truth, I don't want to go out again. I'll be okay in the morning, but...." He shrugged.

"You want to spend the night here?"

"Is that okay?" He smiled a little. "I won't do any harm. Just conk out on the couch in the green room."

"Yeah. That's okay. I guess. I better tell Max about it, though. If he comes in and finds you, he'll get royally ticked."

"Damn. You are a friend in need." He stood up. "This is embarrassing, man. I hate being scared. *Hate* it. The last time I felt like this was when I was eight years old. I was playing in my front yard in San Diego and three teenagers drove by in a car. One of them had a gun in his hand, pointed straight at me."

"So what did you do?"

"I just stood there, like a rabbit caught in the headlights. Then he pulled the trigger and squirted water on me. But I hadn't known it was a water pistol."

I laughed. "That really happened?"

"Christ, yes. And it wasn't funny at the time, lemme tell you." He shrugged. "Be nice to think these guys tonight were just kidding around, too."

"Who could have wanted to wreck your place?"

He half-smiled. "Maybe it was Matty Mark, looking for the song I swiped."

"Glad to see they didn't take your sense of humor." I scratched my head. "You know, Von Ehmsen has been making the rounds, trying to get the club owners to beef up security—Hell."

"What is it?"

I shook my head, trying to clear it. "I just remembered what happened to Seamus. First him, now you. You think somebody has targeted the Beggar? Dean?"

Dean was glassy-eyed, staring at something I couldn't see. "What? Yeah. I forgot about Seamus. I figured that was just a mugging. What do the cops think, Joe?"

"Beats me. What else could it be, besides a mugging?"

"I don't know." He managed a grin. "He's Irish Catholic. Maybe it was a bunch of Protestants."

"Gimme a break. Nobody's fought over that stuff since the twenties."

"True. You know, you told me Seamus wanted to talk to me. I've tried to find him but he really has disappeared."

I nodded. "Back to Ireland is the best guess."

Dean made a face, like the whiskey didn't agree with him. "This is all too damned strange, Joe. Seamus wants to talk to me and he gets beat up and vanishes. Now somebody trashes my apartment."

"You think there's a connection?"

"I don't know. But I have to find out, don't you think?"

I sipped booze. "Hey, was Irene with you when you discovered the mess?"

He winced. "We broke up tonight."

"You're kidding. Man, I'm sorry."

"Don't be. I could stand her jealousy and her bitching, but, Christ. Did you catch her little remark about Gus and Al?"

"Yeah, I did."

"That was the last straw. I can't date a *bigot*, for God's sake."

"I'm sure it'll all work out."

He laughed. "One way or the other. Hey, have I said thanks for letting me stay?"

"Nothing's too good for a budding star." I had an awful thought. "Hey, the burglars didn't get your demo tape, did they?"

"Nope. When I left for California I gave my copy to a colleague for safekeeping. And the other two copies, well…."

He smiled sadly. "That's something else I gotta tell you. Man, it's been a busy night."

"What? What else happened?"

Dean was looking away, toward the stage. "What do you think of those stories Max told us about the Almanac Singers and the rest of those people?"

"What do I think? I think they're basically true stories, but they've got Max's own point of view glued all over them. What does that have to do with anything?"

"He still hasn't forgiven those people for the mistakes they made, or that he thinks they made, decades ago. I mean, they aren't war criminals. There's got to be a statute of limitations, right?"

He sipped bourbon. "And God knows they suffered enough in the blacklist, some of them, when they weren't allowed to work. Meanwhile, a lot of the ones who were blacklisted will never forgive the ones who testified to save their skins. It just goes on and on…."

"Where's this leading? You gonna write a song about it?"

Dean laughed. "Probably. Everything important becomes a song, given enough time."

I started to relax, because he was sounding more like himself. "Good. You write it and we'll record it. Max may not be a forgiving soul, but I talked him into making your record. There ought to be a song on the album condemning him for being narrow-minded. Serve him right."

"Oh, Christ." He leaned forward. "*Damnation!* That's what I've been trying to tell you, Joe."

"Tell me what?"

He looked me straight in the eye. "I signed with Braubinger."

I gaped at him. "You did *what*?"

"Signed a deal with Bob. He's my agent, officially. And we signed with Broker Records."

He sat back, let out a breath. He seemed to relax, as if announcing that he was throwing away his career had taken a great burden off him.

I stood up without knowing it and bumped into the wall. "Well, talk to Bob. Maybe you can change it. Tell him you got a better offer."

"No can do, Joe. It's all down in black and white."

"Oh, Christ." My throat was sore. I suppose I should have been congratulating him, but I couldn't do it.

"*Light and Sweet.* That's what they're thinking of calling my first LP. Coffey, light and sweet. Get it?"

I got it. It was about as subtle as one of Braubinger's neon neckties. More to the point there was hardly a song in Dean's repertoire that matched the title. Or were they going to fix that too?

"You should have told me, Dean. You didn't give me any warning."

He slammed his glass down on the counter. "What the hell did you *want*, man? Was I supposed to hang around for the rest of my life waiting for you and Max to make up your minds?"

"They'll change your style. They'll change your *songs*."

"We'll see about that. Maybe they can get me some publicity, at least. I mean, what kind of distribution can I get from a second-rate coffeehouse?"

I could feel my hands turning into fists. "It would be a start."

"Well, so is Broker, Joe. And they've got money up front. How much of an advance was Max offering?"

"We hadn't talked about that. I was thinking in terms of a cooperative deal—"

"*Money*, Joe. That's the key word here. I've got expenses and I don't have a steady salary. California…."

I nodded. "Those flights are expensive."

"Damned right they are." He laughed. "You have no idea."

"But Dean. I mean, *stockbrokers*, for God's sake. They'll try to turn you into Top Forty stuff. Musical corn flakes!"

His blue eyes pinned me down. "And what do *you* want to turn me into?"

"You aren't a commercial singer, a pop star…."

"Christ, no. *You* want me to ride the rails. Starve in soup kitchens. Live in the goddamned dustbowl."

He pushed his glass away, so hard it slid off the table and broke on the floor. "I got news for you, Joe. The Great Depression is over. I'm not the next incarnation of Saint Woody. There ain't gonna be a second coming."

"Damn it, Dean. I just want you to be yourself." But I didn't sound convincing.

"Then you ought to be very happy. Because that's exactly what I'm doing." He looked thoughtful. "I'm not like you. I can't always do things the easy way."

That rocked me back in my seat. "And I do? What the hell is that supposed to mean?"

He didn't seem to hear me. Suddenly he smiled and I was looking at the same old Dean, back on earth. "Have I talked myself out of a place to spend the night?"

"You sneaky bastard. If I kick you out now that would prove that all I cared about was the record deal, right?"

He nodded, deadpan. "Liberal guilt. It's stronger than the H-bomb."

I punched him on the shoulder. "Stay. Drink all the booze in Max's office. What do I care?"

"You're a pal, Joe."

Any sincere reply would have made me sound as cynical as Max. "Wait a minute. I just had a thought. What if your new agent gets you a chance to be on *Hootenanny*? You wouldn't do it, would you?"

Dean smiled and shrugged. "As Max would say, if nobody ever asks me, we'll never know."

CHAPTER 15

I don't get it," said Max Karzoff. "We're a hotel all of a sudden?" Seven A.M. was awfully early to call him, but Max went to synagogue most Saturday mornings and I wanted to catch him first.

"Dean was all shook up and too scared to go out on the street. Somebody destroyed his apartment."

"Jesus, what is this town coming to?" He sighed. "Couldn't you offer a better hiding place?"

"He didn't want to go to my pad. Didn't want to show his face on the street."

"Well, if you had to, you had to. I hope he doesn't leave a mess."

"Thanks, Max. Oh, one more thing."

"What, more good news?"

"Dean signed a contract with the stockbrokers. And Braubinger is officially his agent."

"Well, crap." He paused. "That dinky little label?"

"Yeah. It doesn't seem like much of a deal to me, but they were willing, and they had cash in hand—"

"And I kept putzing around, not making up my alleged mind. Damn. I hate having my legs kicked out from under me when I finally make a decision. Maybe I'll have a talk with him. Who knows? You take care, kid."

I cooked up a big breakfast: bacon, toast, eggs. That was something I only did when I was feeling sorry for myself, usually after calling Sovay.

I set up one of her tapes on my reel-to-reel and reminded myself for the fiftieth time to try to talk Dean into giving me a copy of his demo tape. Sovay sang *The Factory Girl*.

Oh I have fine houses adorned with ivory
Gold in my pocket and silver as well
And if you'll come with me, a lady I'll make you
And no more will you heed yon poor factory bell.
Oh, love and temptation are our ruination
Go find you a lady and may you do well
For I am an orphan with ne'er a relation
And besides, I'm a hard working factory girl.

Every song she did was about labor or politics. At least this one was also a love song.

An unhappy one, naturally.

I wished I had a tape of her singing even one song about relations between people, instead of between classes and movements.

To hell with that. When the tape ran out I washed my dishes, put on my coat, and headed for Third Street. It was chilly, with a promise of rain. I felt as gloomy as the weather, but I was trying to work up a smile for Dean. He probably felt pretty bad right now—a residue of embarrassment, bad decisions and fear. Plus a hangover.

It was nine o'clock by my watch when I opened the door of the Riding Beggar and walked in.

No one was in sight. "Dean?"

The place looked just as I had left it. There was a full pot of coffee at the waitress stand, and it didn't smell stale.

I called again and got no answer. As I walked forward I realized there was one light on that hadn't been on when I left: the spotlight beaming down on the stage.

"Dean?"

There was something on the stage, lying too low for the spotlight to pick up. I took a few steps forward. I said something; I don't know what.

Dean Coffey was in the spotlight for the very last time. He lay on our little stage, chest down, face turned toward me. Blood had pooled up beneath him.

Nausea, shock, terror.

I couldn't move. If a thought made it into my head, I don't remember what it was.

A noise, somewhere behind me. I tried to turn and something flopped down over my head. Somehow I knew it was Dean's corduroy jacket.

I couldn't see a damn thing. I reached up with both hands, trying to pull it off. Something hit me hard, a glancing blow in the back of my head.

I screamed, stumbling forward, trying to pull the coat away, grab the aching spot on my skull and defend myself, all at the same time.

It didn't work, of course. I stumbled into some chairs and almost fell down.

Just as I pulled the jacket off the second blow hit my left shoulder and I thought: *I'm a dead man.* The last blow hit my left temple and I didn't think anything else.

•

Sovay was singing about the factory girl again. Her voice was too damned loud. I asked her to sing more quietly but she wouldn't answer. *It has to be a tape. I'll just get up and turn it down.*

It wasn't easy to get off my bed. In fact, it wasn't a bed. I was lying on a hard wooden floor and I couldn't move.

I opened my left eye. My right eye was pressed against the floor and I couldn't shift my head to open it.

I was looking at a mirror, seeing myself on the floor, gazing back at myself with a stupid unblinking expression.

Get up, you damned fool.

Sovay's voice was gone. I missed it; remembered it was an illusion, missed it anyway. What could be worse than losing your illusions?

I looked at my reflection once more. There was blood puddled under my cheek, under my chest....

It wasn't a mirror. I was seeing Dean Coffee in front of me, lying dead on the stage. His last performance.

I lay in front of him, his last audience, waiting for another song that would never start. Maybe I was dead too.

I closed my eyes. Nobody sang this time.

CHAPTER 16

Memory came back first. I didn't want to open my eyes because I didn't want to see Dean again.

My head hurt and I gritted my teeth. Something was different and it took me a moment to realize what it was. I was lying face up, and on a bed, not a wooden floor.

Someone grabbed my hand. "Joe? Joe, can you hear me?" I opened my eyes and looked up at Carol Meisel, her pale face twisted with worry under her blond hair.

I tugged my hand free. "Hospital?"

"That's right." A smile flickered and went out. "You're in the hospital. You're going to be all right."

Finding words was difficult. "Dean?"

Carol stood up. "You're going to be as good as new, Joe. I'll go get the doctor."

The lights made my eyes hurt. I closed them and waited, but the damned doctor didn't come. When I thought I had waited at least an hour I opened my eyes again.

A nurse stood at the foot of my bed, doing something hygienic. She smiled. "Well, well. Back among the living, Mr. Talley?"

"Where'd Carol go?"

"Miss Meisel went home hours ago. Poor girl was heartbroken when she came back with the doctor and found you asleep again. That's a very sweet girlfriend you've got there."

"She's not my girlfriend. She's my waitress."

The nurse frowned. Probably thought I was delirious. I tried to shrug and instantly regretted it.

"Take it easy. I'll be right back."

I sighed. Every time I became aware of someone they left. The story of my life.

The doctor was the ugliest man I had ever seen. He had greasy grey hair and pop-eyes behind thick black frames.

"Well, Mr. Talley. Good to see you awake. Got yourself a little concussion, didn't you?"

"How's Dean Coffey?"

The doctor fit his stethoscope into his ears. "Let's take a look at you."

"Coffey," I repeated.

"Not good for you right now," he said, prodding me with a cold, moist hand. "All that caffeine. You don't need the stimulation."

"Damn it, *Dean* Coffey. How is he?"

"Right now we just want to worry about you. Turn this way, Mr. Talley. Open those eyes wide."

I closed them instead. It was the only bargaining chip I had. "Answer the question."

He sighed. "Okay, sport. Your friend is dead. Multiple gunshot wounds in the chest and neck. The police want to talk to you, but I'm keeping them out until you're looking better."

"This is about as good as I ever look."

I watched him laugh. "Well, it's better than me, I'll admit that."

"What time is it?"

"Ten in the morning on Sunday. Saint Patrick's Day. You've been flying around with John Glenn and the other spacemen for a little over twenty-four hours. But—" He wrote something down with a satisfied air. "I think you're back in Manhattan with the rest of us now."

"Nice place to visit...."

"Your sense of humor is working, I see." He stood up. "That's supposed to be a good sign. I've never understood why."

•

Max Karzoff arrived in fine style late that afternoon. "God damn you, Talley. What the hell have you done? You let some jerk get murdered in my club. The cops have closed the place, do you know that?"

He stood at the end of the bed, glaring at me, arms folded. "And then just for *lagniappe* you get yourself half-killed, so I have to run the place by myself. Jesus! What in hell do you think you're doing?"

Carol had arrived during the tirade and stood in the doorway, her jaw hanging.

"Hi, Max," I said. "I missed you, too."

"How—how dare you!" Carol was sputtering. She was a small-town girl and sometimes Max was too much for her. "Joe is hurt and you stand there—"

"Carol," I said. "Take it easy. Max is just showing his concern. If he was really mad he'd be a bundle of charm."

"Oh, you think so," he grumbled. "How the hell am I supposed to run the place while you lie here eating bonbons?"

"If the cops won't let you open the club, there can't be that much work to do, can there?"

"Smart guy. Always the smart answer. What's the matter, Joe? Maybe it's not your end of the boat that's sinking?"

I sighed. "They'll let me out of here tomorrow, Boss. I'll be back then."

"That's more like it." His voice dropped.

"Anything you need?"

"Call Sovay in England for me. Tell her what happened, and make sure she knows I'm all right."

Max frowned at me and muttered something.

"What was that?"

"I'm just amazed anyone could dent that skull of yours."

"Max!" said Carol, angry all over again.

He sighed. "Call England, sure. Anything else?"

"No."

"Okay. Call me any time." He marched out the door, a pudgy old man in a hurry.

Carol watched him go and shook her head. "How do you *stand* him?"

"He's not so bad. In a lot of ways he reminds me of my father. The main difference is, I never much liked my father."

She came up to the bed and smiled down at me. She was easily the prettiest thing I'd seen in two days, wearing a bright red dress. Combined with her long blond hair it was good for cheering up an invalid. "You're feeling better today, I can tell."

"Yeah. I needed a vacation anyway."

"Well, don't take any more of this kind, okay? We were all worried sick."

"Sorry. Hey, is this the hospital where they took Seamus?" Carol nodded. "One nurse I talked to remembered him. I'll tell you about it when you're feeling better."

I suddenly remembered why she had had so much time to talk to nurses. "They tell me you were doing the bedside vigil routine. Not necessary, but I do appreciate it."

She smiled. "I wanted to do it."

Before either of us could speak again there was a knock at my open door.

"Talley, right?" The visitor entered while he knocked, a middle-aged man in a neat brown suit. His sandy hair was set in a crew cut and he had a foul-smelling cigar in the corner of his mouth. "I'm Sergeant Guareschi, NYPD. You and I have some business."

If first impressions count for anything I doubt that Guareschi had a friend in the world. I felt surliness settling in on me as soon as he'd started talking, and from the set of Carol's shoulders she was feeling the same. Since it was clear he was waiting for her to leave, she did so after bidding me a quick farewell.

Guareschi turned to watch her walk out. I saw for the first time that there was another man, standing behind the sergeant, like a shadow. He also turned to watch Carol's exit.

For some reason, that irritated me even more. "You wanted to talk?"

Guareschi dropped his cigar stub into a garbage can where it let out a last puff of foul black smoke. Be interesting if it caught fire, I thought.

"I'm investigating the murder of Dean Coffey. You claim you discovered the body."

"Claim? I haven't claimed anything. Unless I've been talking in my sleep."

I pointed to his shadow, a slim man of about thirty, whose dark hair was beginning to recede. He had a pencil in one hand and a notebook in the other. "Is that a policeman, too, or is he drawing still lifes?"

The slim man looked a bit startled, as if he weren't used to being noticed. "Detective Aaron Levy," he said in a soft, amused voice.

"I'm pleased to meet you."

He grinned down at his notebook. "Likewise."

"You through?" snapped Guareschi. "Can we conduct some business now?"

"Sure," I said.

"Tell me about Saturday morning."

"I went to the Riding Beggar to see Dean Coffey. It was around nine—"

"What was Coffey doing there?"

"He asked permission to spend the night."

"And you gave it just like that? Didn't check with the owner?"

"Ask Max."

Guareschi grunted. "I will. So why was Coffey so scared that he had to spend the night in your club?"

"His apartment had been robbed."

"Yeah? He didn't report it to the police."

Now, how had he known to check that? I caught on, a bit late. "You've *already* talked to Max. You already know everything I'm telling you. For God's sake, why are you bothering me?"

Levy was smiling into his notebook again.

Guareschi lit another cigar. "You figure it was the murderer who hit you on the head?"

"I assume so. Who else would want to?"

"Someone who didn't want to be found standing next to a corpse. There must be a few people in New York who match that description."

"I suppose so."

"But let's say it *was* the murderer. Coffey was alone from three in the morning on. Why did the killer hang around until nine o'clock when you got there?"

I frowned. "*Did* he hang around? I assumed Dean died not long before I got there. There was a fresh pot of coffee."

Guareschi tugged at the cuff of his suit jacket, getting it to lie right. Somehow, I hadn't expected a cop to care so much about his clothes. "The coroner tends to agree with you. He thinks Coffey died no more than an hour or so before you stumbled in." He took a thoughtful puff. "So, who do you think hit you?"

"No idea. I don't even know what he hit me with."

"Oh." He turned to Levy. "Bourbon? Yeah, a bottle of bourbon. We found it lying next to you. No fingerprints, of course."

"What about the gun?"

"Haven't found it." He frowned. "Did you see one there?"

I shook my head, then winced. It felt like my skull was about to snap off its stem and roll down the bed.

"Okay. Who had a reason to want Dean Coffey dead?"

I stared at him, I hadn't thought of it that way before. I had more or less accepted the idea that Dean was dead, but hadn't come to grips with the idea that someone had caused it, on *purpose*. That was a shock.

"No ideas?"

"None. I can't imagine it. He didn't have an enemy in the world."

The sergeant snorted. He called over his shoulder: "Levy."

The younger man flipped his notebook open to a different page and started to recite. "Katherine Poe. Argued with Coffey a week before the murder."

I blinked. "Katy? Where was that?"

"In your joint," said Guareschi. "When they performed together."

"Oh, for God's sake." These idiots were giving me a pounding headache. "They argued about the right way to sing *Lady Isabel and the Elf Knight*. You don't think anyone would kill a man over that, do you?"

Guareschi shrugged. "I've seen men killed over the color of their shoes. Levy?"

Another flip of the notebook. "Matthew Mark Oliver. He threatened Coffey last October."

"Over a song credit. That was what, five months ago?"

"So they've made up now?" Guareschi asked. "They're best buddies?"

"It's no motive for murder," I retorted.

"Oliver said, and I quote," Levy continued, calmly, "'I'll kill that snake and eat his liver.'"

"Figure of speech," I said. "He always talks like that. He's from Arkansas. And anyway, it was half a year ago. You think he sat around brooding about it? Not his style."

The big cop nodded. "So you think he'd strike as soon as he got angry?"

"I don't think he'd strike at all. Look, are we about through here? I'm a sick man, remember?"

"Agustina Adler," said Levy.

"Gus? Now, you're joking. Or else you've lost your mind."

"Formerly Coffey's mistress."

"*Mistress*? You think he was paying for her to live in a penthouse or something? My god, where do you get these words? Where do you get your *ideas*?"

"He dumped her for a younger woman," said Guareschi. "Maybe that ain't a motive?"

"For some people, sure. But Gus...have you met her yet?"

"We will, soon enough. What about Coffey's current chippy, this Irene Fox? You said Coffey told you they broke up that night. Is *she* another saint?"

I dropped back on the pillow exhausted. Was I going to have to sum up the case for the defense for everyone I knew? And if one plea was not as heartfelt as the others—imagine trying to claim that Irene Fox did not have a jealous side—would that be taken as evidence against them?

Once you start naming names, where do you stop?

"What's the point of all these questions?" I asked, hoarsely. "What do you expect me to tell you?"

There was a long pause. Guareschi shrugged. "Tell me about Braubinger."

"Bob?" I relaxed a little. "Now, there's a guy with no possible motive to kill Dean. He just that night signed a record contract with him." I told them about Broker Records.

"There was somebody else though, wasn't there?"

"I don't know what you mean."

"Someone else who wanted to record an album with Coffey?"

I looked up at him.

"No answer? Taking the Fifth?"

Take the First, I thought. *Like Pete Seeger*. "Max and I kicked around the idea of recording an album with Dean, like the Gaslight did with Tom Paxton. But we waited too long and Broker Records moved in."

"So how did Karzoff feel about being pushed out by these stockbrokers?"

My head hurt like hell. Was I getting Max in trouble? Was he in trouble already?

"He was disappointed. He said he'd try to change Dean's mind."

"So you called him at seven A.M. and he said he was going over right away to talk to Coffey." Guareschi scratched his chin, which needed a shave. "Two hours later Coffey was dead."

"Damn it, don't put words in my mouth. Max didn't say he was going over there right away. I figured he would see him later in the day, when he went to open the place."

"But you don't know that for sure."

"Look," I said patiently. At least I was trying to be patient. "I see where you're leading and it doesn't make sense. Max wouldn't kill Dean,"

"No?" He smiled. "Karzoff is too sweet and kind, like everybody else you know?"

"He's too sensible. He's a *businessman*. What good would it do him to kill the artist he hoped to make money from? If he was going to kill anybody—which he *wouldn't*—it should have been Braubinger, or the people at Broker Records."

"Maybe they argued," said Guareschi. "People lose their tempers, they forget what's in their best interests."

I sighed. "Sergeant, you just don't know Max."

Guareschi stood up and leaned way back, trying to unkink his spine. "Oh, I know him. I know his kind too damned well. He's one of the people who have ripped Greenwich Village apart."

I must have gaped. From the look on Levy's face, he had heard this speech before.

"This used to be a nice place to live." Guareschi was gazing out the window. "Before the artists and the cafes and the beatniks, this was a blue collar neighborhood. Now it's all *scrocconnes*, like you and your friend."

"*No scroccones*," I said. "*Solamente neofitos.*"

He looked down at me, startled. "You learn Italian in college?"

"At home. My father was born about five miles from Vesuvius."

Guareschi raised his eyebrows. "Talley don't sound *Napoletano* to me."

"It was Vitale until my grandfather hit Ellis Island."

The cop nodded, thoughtfully. "Yeah, they changed a lot of names there, didn't they?"

He buttoned his suit jacket. "Well, don't think you'll get any favors, just because you're a *paisan*."

"I don't need any."

"What?"

"I'm a victim, remember? I don't need any special treatment."

He grinned. It was the first human, likable thing I had seen him do. "Yeah, that's right. But making that speech has become a habit over the years, you know?"

Chapter 17

Max has been worried clean out of his skull," Al Perkins told me.

"Great. Maybe I'll hit him up for a raise. Are we gonna be open for business tomorrow?"

"So the man says."

Al was driving, I was passengering in his old red Valiant. He was one of the very few people I knew who owned a car.

"You got any idea who clobbered you?"

"'Fraid not. I was looking at Dean when I should have been guarding my rear."

"Well, I'm glad the jackass didn't finish you, too."

"Thanks, Al. So am I. Say, that reminds me. The killer must have been hiding in the kitchen, or else in the alcove where they store napkins and things. That's the only way he could have come up behind me. Was anything out of place in the kitchen?"

"Cops asked me that, too. I didn't see nothing missing. 'Course, I left early, so I don't know for sure what condition the place was left in." He shrugged. "Wasn't as nice as I leave it, but it didn't look trashed neither."

"Yeah, I'd forgotten you left. You were out all night at some party with Gus, right?"

"Not exactly." He stopped at a red light. "It was a yoga thing. Turned out I only stayed for the opening lecture. That Zen hoodoo ain't my plate of cheese."

"Yeah, I was kind of surprised to find out you were going at all."

"Favor to Gus, is all. She's a cool lady." Green light. He set the car in gear. "She didn't want to go alone. I can dig that. But when we got there, turned out she saw a dude there she knew."

"Who was that?"

"Old baldy. Ray Hegg."

"Oh, Ray."

"Yeah. So I figured they would hang around together and it would be okay with her if I split. I hit a couple of uptown bars and went home to flop."

I sighed. "You got any feeling for what happened to Dean?"

"Just that it was a goddamn shame, is all. He was a good dude. Better than his music."

That intrigued me. "What was wrong with his music?"

"Not my meat, is all. All from the head, nothing from the heart. Always watching the audience like the gauge on a furnace."

I had never heard Al talk about music before. Come to think of it, I had hardly ever spoken to him outside the Beggar.

"Now, that chick Katy Poe. She's more my style. She means every damn song she sings. Every time."

"I wouldn't think British ballads would be your kind of thing."

He grinned as we pulled up to the curb. "Because my people don't come from old London town? Do yours?"

I nodded. "Touché."

"Ain't the story but the *style*. Katy's got heart. You need help with the door?"

"No, I can get out by myself. Thanks." I did so, and with only a little difficulty. The doctor said I would be as good as new in a week if I stayed away from booze, especially in the bottle. "So, what is your kind of music? Jazz?"

"Not so much. I like blues. Lightnin' Hopkins, Big Joe Williams. Sweet, sweet stuff."

"Well, the folkies are catching up with you on that. Rural blues is getting pretty hot." I opened the door of the Riding Beggar and we walked into an argument.

Max was bellowing rage in his office. Before I headed over there I glanced over at the stage where two men were on their knees, scrubbing at a stain. Then I realized it was Dean's blood they were washing away and a wave of dizziness hit me.

I turned away. "Who is Max yelling at?"

"Not us, I hope," said Al.

A tall broad figure was blocking the office door. I recognized the crew cut before I heard the voice.

"Don't give me that crap," said Sergeant Guareschi. "You start cooperating or this joint will stay closed until hell freezes over."

"Cooperating?" Max yelled. "I can't believe what you're asking. You don't even *know* what you're asking."

He spied me behind the cop. "Joe, get a load of Senator McCarthy here. He wants me to name names."

Guareschi was wearing a blue suit today. It didn't compliment the red in his face. "Someone broke into your place. Robbery wasn't the motive. It's common sense to find out if you had any enemies, and it turns out you had a rat's nest full."

Max turned to me, grinning fiercely. "Can you believe this? He's decided that the *Communists* killed Dean, as vengeance because *I* left the Party twenty years ago. Makes a big stinking heap of sense, doesn't it?"

"*You're* the one who isn't making sense," said the cop. "I ask you for a list of people who might do you harm and you claim there are none. You say you've been doing business for thirty years in New York City and never made an enemy. Gimme a break. The Commies were just one example."

"Why Max's enemies?" I asked. "Why not Dean's?"

"We're looking into Coffey's past, too. But nobody knew he was here except you and Karzoff."

"Maybe someone followed him from his apartment," I suggested. "Someone broke into his place, remember. Doesn't that prove he was the target?"

The cop shrugged. "Maybe. But that robbery could be unrelated, too. Stranger coincidences happen every day in this city."

"Speaking of robberies," said Max. "What about all the goddamned robberies of coffeehouses and bars this winter? Isn't *that* the likely explanation? Somebody tried to rob the place and Dean surprised them."

"Then why wasn't anything taken?"

"Maybe he scared them off."

"Why did the robber wait until eight in the morning to break in? Scared of the dark, maybe?"

Max opened his mouth, then shut it.

"It was no robbery," I said. "Someone tossed Dean's apartment. They couldn't find what they wanted, so they came here looking for him, and killed him."

The cop looked at me, one eyebrow cocked. "Yeah? What were they looking for?"

"I don't know."

"Did you ask Coffey?"

"He didn't know either."

Guareschi shook his head. "Then why didn't they torture him to get what they wanted? There was no beating. No cigarette burns."

"Jesus," muttered Max.

"Maybe he told them where it was," I said. "Whatever the hell it was they wanted."

"Maybe, and maybe they shot him anyway, but I don't—" He stopped to look at Al Perkins who had appeared in the doorway.

"What is it, Al?" asked Max.

"The kitchen's ready, but I gotta buy some supplies if we're gonna open tomorrow."

"Do it. We'll see you later."

"Wait a second," said Guareschi. "You Perkins?"

The cook gave him a wary look. "Uh huh."

"You left early on Friday."

Al stood silently.

"Answer me."

"Didn't know it was a question. Yeah, I left early."

"When did you start working here?"

"Middle of February," said Max. "I already told you—"

"I want to hear it from him. Well?"

"Middle of February," said Al, straight-faced.

"Where'd you work before?"

"The Limelight."

"So you were there when it got burglarized."

"Jesus," said Max. "Are you accusing Al? You're nuts."

"What about all the places he *didn't* work that got robbed?" I threw in.

Guareschi ignored us. "On the night of the murder you were out on a date with Coffey's ex-girlfriend. A white girl."

"Oh, that's enough!" said Max, red in the face. "You are *way* out of line, Sergeant. If you think you can come in here and pick on one of my employees just because he's a Negro—"

"He's a *suspect*," snapped Guareschi. "He's also an ex-con and I'll ask him anything I damn please."

"Ex-con?" repeated Al. He looked astonished.

"You thought we wouldn't find out?" asked Guareschi. "We got your record from Alabama. What's so damn funny?"

Al was grinning. "Shit. Trespass and malicious mischief. That was last summer when I was down there with the Freedom Riders. I forgot all about it."

"That's not a criminal record," I said. "That's a merit badge. They've still got segregated schools down there. And restaurants. And buses. And—"

"I don't give a *damn* about Alabama!" yelled Guareschi. "There was murder done *here*: Manhattan, County and State of New York."

"You brought it up."

He looked at Al, ignoring me. "Get your coat if you've got one, son. We're going to talk about it downtown."

"*I'll* talk about it," said Max. "I'll talk to my lawyer. You cooperate, Al, and we'll get you out of there as fast as we can."

Perkins shook his head, amazement showing more than anything else.

As I followed them to the door, he looked at me over his shoulder. "Glad you're back, Joe. Hope I'll be back too."

Back in the office Max was already on the phone, and waiting by the look of it. I sat down heavily on his old hassock.

"Guareschi doesn't know if he's skating on ice or swimming in shit."

Max winced. That made his bifocals slide down his nose and he pushed them back up. "If that colorful metaphor is supposed to mean that the sergeant doesn't know what he's doing, I agree with you."

He yanked on the phone cord. "It's interesting how that class always falls back on their biases when logic fails them. You notice? He tried every angle he could think of, and when none of them worked he looked again and saw a black man dating a white woman. Obviously guilty of *something*, right?"

"Look at the bright side," I said. "At least picking on Al was his last resort. It could have been the *first* thing he did."

"My staff optimist. I guess you're right. I ought to—" He held up a finger. "Hello? This is Max Karzoff. Is Mr. Yasner available?"

I walked out as he was giving instructions to his attorney.

Someone was banging on the door. For a club the police had closed we were keeping awfully busy.

I opened the door and let Bob Braubinger in. The pudgy little man looked like hell. I'd say he slept in his clothes but the bags under his eyes suggested he hadn't slept at all.

"Bob," I said. "I'm so sorry. I know how much Dean meant to you. You must—"

He waved it aside. "The demo tapes, Joe. Do you have a copy? The damned things have disappeared."

CHAPTER 18

My God," said Harry Hays, "I'm still in shock." He was in his late twenties, and all of his careful combing couldn't hide his bald spot. A year ago he and his cousin had taken some of their Wall Street profits and founded Broker Records. We were sitting in their office, two large rooms in Flushing.

"I mean, it was bad enough that Dean got killed, and on the very day he signed a contract with us. But on top of that, to realize that someone busted into our office and stole the demo tapes...."

He shrugged. "I mean, crap. We figured we could salvage *something*. Make a record out of the tape or get other people to record the songs. But now, we're not gonna make a penny out of this."

"Tragic," I said. Bob Braubinger murmured agreement, but I think he meant it.

"You have any idea when the tape was stolen?" I asked.

"We closed up here at five P.M. on Friday. Opened Monday at nine. So it could have been any time over the weekend."

"Were the tapes locked up?"

"Of course not. Who'd want a bunch of demo tapes?" He laughed sourly. "We have a hard enough time giving them away."

"Dean died early Saturday morning," said Braubinger.

"But his apartment was robbed Friday afternoon," I reminded him. "I think we can assume they were after the tapes."

"So where is the other copy?" Hays asked me. "Did you ask him about that?"

I nodded. "He told me he had given it to a colleague for safekeeping."

"A colleague?" Braubinger muttered. "Another singer?"

"I don't know. He didn't explain."

Hays started to speak but he was interrupted by a door opening behind us. "Walter, come on in. This is Joe Talley, from the Riding Beggar. Joe, this is my partner, Walter Costigan."

The second stockbroker was shorter than his cousin, pudgy and spectacled. He didn't offer to shake hands. Instead he leaned against a wall with folded arms and stared at me. He had mean eyes, eyes that saw profit and loss instead of people.

He said: "This is the guy who wanted to make a record with Coffey?"

"That's right," said Hays. "We were just—"

"You take the tapes?" Costigan asked me.

"What?" asked Bob. "Walter, man, what are you saying?"

"Come on," said Hays. "Get serious."

Costigan ignored them both. His dark cold eyes never left me. "You wanted to make a record with Coffey, but you sat on your thumbs too long and he signed with us. Right?"

"That's right," I agreed. I could see where this was going.

"So you figured to steal the tape and presto, you're back in business."

"*Presto*?" I said.

"That's dumb," said Braubinger. "*You* owned the tapes, it's in the contract. Joe couldn't have done a thing with them."

"Possession is nine-tenths of the law," said Costigan. "We would have had to fight him for it. He probably thinks we'll settle for a fifty-fifty split. But we won't. Make it clear to your pal, Bob. No deals. If he doesn't give us the tapes we'll turn him over to the cops."

I crossed my legs and looked at him. "Let me get this straight. You think I stole the tapes *before* Dean was killed? That's asinine. Dean could have just recorded the songs again. The tapes only became irreplaceable when he died."

"So you stole them *after* the murder."

"Joe was in the hospital then, Walter," said Braubinger. He sounded mystified by his friend's behavior.

"Try it this way," said Costigan. "Talley argues with Coffey because he signed with us. He kills him."

"With the Colt .45 I carry everywhere," I said, helpfully.

The stockbroker ignored me. "He calls up a friend and tells his friend to steal the tape, and then he fakes the injury for an alibi."

"You ever try to bash in your own head with a bourbon bottle?" I asked.

"I want that tape," said Costigan.

"And believe it or not," I told him, "I want you to have it."

"You do?" said Hays. His voice was a surprised squeak.

I turned to face him. "If you got your hands on it, what would you do?"

"Turn it into a record, if the quality if good enough. We've put out a bunch of records, already. You know the Gentrelles? A doo-wop band?"

"Never heard of them."

"You never listen to anything but that hillbilly crap," said Costigan.

"Like Dean Coffey?" I asked.

"Dean was *special*," said Hays. He sounded unhappy about it. "We could have made him a star."

"I don't think you could have made anything out of him but a mess," I said. "I don't think you gave a damn about him or his music. You just wanted to scratch a buck out of him."

"But not you," snapped Hays. "You're Dr. goddamned Schweitzer."

"You're out of character, Harry," I told him. You're supposed to be the *nice* guy. Your cousin is playing the heavy today."

"Screw you," he said, red in the face. "You've got no business talking to me like that."

"That's right. *You're* the one with the business." I stood up. "Come on, Bob. We're wasting these gentlemen's valuable time."

Corrigan took a step to the left, as if he had half a mind to block the door. Something in my face must have told him how much I would have welcomed that, because he stopped where he was.

Even though he was frozen in place, he still tried to look menacing. "We want those tapes, Talley."

"Then find the killer. He must have the damned things."

"It was *you*. *You* killed him and took 'em."

"Sure I did. Wake up, fellas, and smell what you're standing in."

"What about your partner, the Jew? He could have done it. He could have—"

"Shut up." I had opened the door, but I turned back to look at them. "I've got one more thing to say to you two and then I hope I'll never have to share breathing space with you again. I think Coffey was a damned fool to have anything to do with you, but he was old enough to cut his own meat.

"Dean was one of my best friends and I don't want his music to disappear. If and when I find the tapes I'll give them to you, because you're the only one with a legal right to make a record out of them, and that's what I want to see happen. Even a record that makes money for you clowns is better than no record at all."

I looked at Braubinger. "You coming, Bob?"

He muttered something apologetic to the broker boys and followed me out. I was mighty glad he did, because he was the one with the car.

In his Thunderbird convertible, heading back to Manhattan, Braubinger was contrite. "I'm sorry, Joe. They acted like major jerks. They had no right to talk to you like that."

"Yeah, well. If people only did what they had a right to do...." It had gotten cooler and Bob still had the top down. I didn't mind. I felt like the cool wind might clear up the throbbing in my head.

"I want you to know, Joe; I had nothing to do with the game they played. If I had known—"

"It's okay, Bob. Forget it. By the way, where did Dean sign that contract?"

"Right at the coffeehouse in Brooklyn. I convinced Harry to come out and see Dean live, and it worked out great. Damn. I thought we were moving at last."

We drove in silence for a while. "Now, *that's* gonna make a killing," said Bob. I followed his pointing finger. Off to the side of the highway I saw a large construction zone. One large collection of metal pieces looked like a shattered egg from some impossibly large bird.

"What *is* that?"

"It's gonna be the World's Fair. Opens next spring. Man, would I like to have a piece of that."

I watched the streetlights go by. Between Al Perkins' giving me a ride from the hospital and this trip to Long Island in Bob's chestnut-colored T-Bird I had been in a car more in one day than I had in the past two months. When you're already in Greenwich Village, why leave?

Bob grunted. "I just remembered something Dean said when he signed the contract."

"What was that?"

"He said that now he could quit his day job. What was his day job, Joe?"

I scratched my chin. "I didn't know he had one."

CHAPTER 19

Is that you, luv?"

"Just barely," I said, and yawned straight into the phone. "Sorry, Sovay. This time *you* woke me."

"You still in bed, ducky? It's tea time here, which makes it—bugger. I never got my A-levels in maths."

"Elevenses here. Time for a little something. I overslept."

"Well, no wonder. Did old Max tell me true? You were in hospital?"

I was shivering. The covers had come off in the night and it was a chilly day. I was not in the mood to go through the whole story again, not even for Sovay. "Yeah. Somebody tried to crack my skull. Luckily, that's my least breakable part."

She laughed, a wonderful throaty sound. "As long as they didn't damage your other parts, luv."

"Watch it, darling. The FBI is probably listening in. If they think you're a bad influence on me, they'll never let you come back."

"Oh, Joe, it's so good to hear your voice. I've called and called, waiting for you to get out of your sick bed and come home to talk to me."

"Where are you, by the way?"

"Charing Cross. About to take my life in my hands riding British Railways. Got a date in a skiffle club up North."

"Well, knock 'em dead, kid."

"Thanks, luv, we try. Oh, wait. There was more."

"What?"

"Max said someone got killed. A singer?"

"That's right. Dean Coffey. I don't think you ever met him. He hit town about the time you left on your little excursion home."

She laughed again. "Quite a holiday it's turned into, eh? Bloody eternal."

"Like Lee Hays said about the Weavers during the blacklist. The sabbatical turned into a Mondical and Tuesdical."

"Oh, Joe, I wish I were there with you."

"I miss you too, Sovay."

"Take care of yourself, my crazy beggar-man. I've got a train to catch."

"You be careful, too."

"And give Max my love. The bloody slave driver."

I hung up the phone and sighed. Damn the State Department and their idiotic medieval rules about undesirable aliens who might, God forbid, encourage the peasants to think. Why the hell couldn't JFK and brother Bobby do something about it?

The great Democratic thaw we had been promised was moving at a glacial pace. Dean had written a song about that—

And Dean was dead. Hell. A sudden nausea encouraged me to my feet and I headed for the bathroom. I felt better by the time I got there and decided to take a shower.

The doorbell rang while I was getting dressed. I buckled my belt as I opened the door and found Matty Mark Oliver slouching against the far wall. He was dressed like a long rangy cowboy today, with blue jeans and a straw hat. I guess it was a reaction to having to wear that blue blazer when he played with his band. "Get your shirt on, son. We're treating you to lunch."

I looked at him, standing there with his hands in the pockets of his jeans. "What if I say no?"

He blinked, as if seeing me for the first time. "You don't want lunch?"

"I'm out of the army, Matty. I don't follow orders anymore."

He held up his big bony hands, surrendering. "Shoot. Is that how I sounded? I'm sorry, Joe. Too much on my mind. Forgive the country manners."

I let out a breath. "No, *I'm* sorry, Matty. You didn't do anything wrong; you were just available. And yes, I could use some lunch. Give me a minute."

We walked up Washington Street, heading for Keats, a burger joint that was popular that year. I didn't ask who was going to be there, partly because I was embarrassed by my rudeness, and partly because just then it felt like everyone I *wanted* to see was either dead or out of the country.

Besides, it was one of those days when the streets of the Village were so crowded you could barely push your way through the sidewalk. It was days like this that made you feel Gus was right: New York City was the center of the world and everybody was being drawn here.

Phil Ochs and Katy Poe were waiting for us at Keats. "Hey, Joe," Phil said. "How you doing? How's the head?"

"In one piece, I guess. It's down from a New Year's Eve hangover to a regular Saturday night one."

Katy was smiling. "You look a lot better than you did on Sunday."

She was the only one of the three at the table who had visited me in the hospital, and I saw Matty looking uncomfortable now. I didn't want any apologies; I hated hospital visits as much as anyone.

So I turned to the other guest at the table. "Phil, how was your week with John Hammond? Everybody says you were great."

Phil grinned. "Thanks, Joe. I had a lot of fun. It wasn't a protest song audience, you know? But I put it across, I really did."

"He was terrific," said Katy. "And here come the cheeseburgers. You wolf one down, Joe. You're looking scrawny."

I laughed as I wrestled with the food. Keats' burgers were small and flat but they came covered with grilled onions, tomatoes and enough sauces to make you wear them if you weren't careful. "This concern over my health is touching, but you guys didn't bring me down here to watch me stuff myself. What's going on?"

Matty Mark laughed too. "Talley-man, you're too many for us. Too damned many."

"Okay," said Phil, leaning forward, all business. "As long as *you* brought it up, Joe. What do the cops think they're doing? I know they love to hassle us, but my God, they all act like they're J. Edgar's favorite office boys."

"What? They're after you guys?"

"Like hounds after a fox," said Matty. "That Mafiosi sergeant. And his shadow, Levine."

"Levy," corrected Katy. "They've been investigating the three of us, Joe. And maybe everyone else who ever played at the Riding Beggar. We thought maybe you knew what they were thinking."

"Yeah," said Matty Mark. "It must have been a robber who slammed you and Dean, so why are they picking on us?"

I spread my hands. "As near as I can tell the cops don't know a damned thing. Guareschi even suggested it might have been done by people Max knew in the Communist party."

"You're kidding," said Katy. "That was, what? Twenty years ago?"

"Cop thinking," said Phil, rolling his eyes. "Find a Marxist, find a murderer. Typical."

"But why *us*?" asked Matty. "We aren't Commies."

"Speak for yourself," said Phil, grinning.

"Idiot," said Katy.

I'd ordered coffee with my burger, and now that the burger had been dispatched, I lifted the cup and took a sip. Then I sighed and said, "Okay, remember this is what the cops are saying, not me. Right?"

They nodded.

"Katy, you had a big argument with Dean a week before he died. That makes you a suspect."

She frowned. "An argument? When?"

"Remember *Lady Isabel and the Elf Knight*?"

"You're joking." She pushed her chair back. "That was a *discussion*, not an argument. And who would kill anybody over a *folksong*?"

"That's what *I* said. And you, Matty Mark. Everybody knows you were mad about *Let Me Take Your Side*."

He blinked. "Well, I'll be good goddamned."

"Hey, what's wrong with *Let Me Take Your Side*?" asked Phil. "I saw it in *Broadside*; I thought it was pretty good."

Matty wasn't answering. Instead he glared down at his bowl of chili—which for some reason he'd barely touched—as if a song-thief was swimming around in it.

I shrugged. "Dean used a traditional fiddle tune for it. He learned it from Matty here—"

"*Down Devil Creek*," said Matty. "And it wasn't just *any* traditional tune. It had been in my family for fifty years. Hell, I used to *swim* bare-ass in Devil Creek when I was a pup. That snake went and *copyrighted* it."

"He copyrighted the arrangement," said Katy.

"Which he stole from me in the first place, the skunk. I tell you—"

"You told *everybody*," I reminded him. "Told them you would kill Dean for that."

"Well, shoot." Matty slumped back in his seat, glaring at me. "I'm just a country boy. That's a goddamn figure of speech where I come from. I didn't mean I was really gonna blow the guy away. You didn't think I meant it, didja Joe?"

"If I did, you wouldn't have ever worked at the Beggar again."

"If a man can't say he's gonna kill somebody, shoot. What's this country coming to?"

"Amen," Phil said, laughing. "This country was built on threats made and threats carried out."

"Anyway," said Matty Mark, "that was months ago. I mean, how long can you hold a grudge?"

"Some of your Southern cousins," said Katy, "are supposed to have feuded for a hundred years."

Matty Mark threw down his spoon, making a mess of his side of the table. Katy got hit on the arm with flying chili. "So that's it. Pick on the goddamn Southern boy again. Why didn't I use a good ol' coon gun on him, while I was at it?"

"Probably too heavy with your jug of moonshine," said Phil, gravely.

Matty Mark sighed. Sheepishly, he handed Katy his napkin with which to wipe the chili off her arm. "Sorry."

Then Phil said, "Hey, what about me, Joe. Don't leave me out. What did the boys in blue say about me?"

"They didn't mention you, Phil. Better ask them yourself."

"I did. They asked if I have an alibi. Good god, I was playing to a full house at Folk City."

"That isn't enough witnesses for them?" asked Katy.

"They said I could have robbed the apartment before the show and killed him after." He shrugged. "What could I do but confess? I said sure, I always warm up for a big show with a little breaking-and-entering."

"They're grasping," I told them. "You people are just the straws."

Phil smiled. "What do you think, Joe? Did it feel like me when you got hit on the head?"

"All concussions feel the same to me. How about you, Matty Mark? Did the cops buy your alibi?"

"'Fraid not. I met Ben and Larry around seven; we practiced and had dinner. Been working on that new Kingston Trio song *Greenback Dollar*. The cops say I could have robbed Dean's apartment before that, so they didn't care much for that alibi. But they plumb hated my explanation of where I was the next morning."

"Why? What was it?"

He smiled sadly. "I was home alone. Sleeping off a drunk. Shoot, Joe. You saw me that night. Did I look like I was planning a murder?"

"Can't say you did."

The three of us all looked at Katy. "The thing I can't understand," she said, "is how any of us were supposed to know that Dean was at the Beggar at all. Only you knew that. Right, Joe?"

"I told Max," I said, "an hour before the killing. He didn't tell anyone else."

"So, Katy," said Matty Mark. "What's your alibi?"

"Go to hell," said Katy, but not with any anger. She blinked her bright green eyes. "Let's just say the cops didn't think it was air-tight."

I puzzled over that one. It sounded as though she had spent the night with someone she didn't want to advertise. A married man? Or maybe she just wanted us to think she hadn't slept alone. In Greenwich Village chastity wasn't necessarily good for your reputation.

"The cops are looking at other angles, too," I told them. "Don't think you're the only ones."

"Like what?" Katy asked.

"Irene Fox. Dean broke up with her that night, so naturally—"

"Hold it," said Katy. "Where did you hear that?"

"From Dean. Why, does she deny it?"

"I haven't talked to her. Has anybody?" We all shook our heads. "God, that poor girl. She must feel like hell."

"Juicy motive, though," said Matty. "Why haven't the cops taken a hose to her?"

Katy made a face. "Don't be grotesque."

"He's got a point," I told her. "They dragged Al Perkins in with no better reason than he and Dean both dated Gus. I would think—"

"Stop," said Phil. "They busted Al? Your cook?"

So I told them all about that, assuring them that Max was doing everything he could to get Al away from the heat and back into the kitchen.

"What about other girlfriends?" asked Phil. "I hear Dean had a lot of chicks."

"A few," agreed Matty Mark. "Some of his fans were, well...." Letting his Arkansas twang stretch out, he said, "Inclined towards affection on short notice."

"That was mostly before Irene," I reminded him. "She kept a pretty close eye on him."

"But she wasn't there every night," said Katy. "And there were still a lot of girls who set their caps for him, as my grandmother would have said. Not me, thank God. He was never my type." She smiled wryly. "And I wasn't his, I suppose. 'Be handsome, boss, and let who would be clever.' But I saw others. Even some who worked at the Beggar."

"Really." I thought over the ever-changing list of people who had worked at our café. "Rhonda Kelly, the singer?"

"She was all *over* the boy," said Matty. "But she's gone back to Chicago, so as a suspect, she ain't much."

"Who else at the club?" Phil asked.

Katy shook her head of red hair. "I should probably mind my own business. I don't want to rope anyone into a murder investigation."

But now I was curious. "The waitresses, maybe? Janet? Carol?"

"Oh, for Pete's sake." Katy pushed her chair away from the table, wrinkling her nose, as if she had just found a bug in her French fries.

"What's wrong?" I asked. Matty Mark was laughing.

Katy was standing up, digging money out of her purse. "I don't believe you, Joe Talley. Honest to God, I don't."

"You owe me, Katy," said Matty. "Don't forget now! You owe me five bucks."

Phil looked as confused as I felt. We watched as Katy dropped her share of the bill on the table and marched out of the restaurant. She glared at me the whole way.

"What *is* this?" I asked. "Are we on *Candid Camera*?"

"Nah," said Matty, grinning from ear to ear. "Miss Poe is just a poor loser, is all. We've had a bet going since, I dunno, December, and she's just mad 'cause she lost."

"What kind of bet?" asked Phil.

"All about the Talley-man." He shook his head. "She's right about one thing, Joe. You are somethin' else."

"Goddamn it," I said. "*Tell*, you hillbilly."

He looked over at Phil. "You know Carol Meisel? Cute little blond waitress at the Beggar?"

"I think so," said Phil. "If there's only one blond."

"There is and she's it. So, do you think it's likely she'd be sniffing after Dean Coffey?"

I frowned. What the hell was he talking about? What could there be about Carol that I didn't know?

Phil sipped coffee and considered. "Well, I don't hang around the Beggar as much as you do, but I sorta thought she was Joe's girlfriend."

"Me?" I said. "What?"

"Well, the way she hangs around you, Joe. And she's always got an eye on you. I just figured...." He shrugged.

I felt tired and stupid. The knot in the back of my head began to ache again. "What was the bet, Matty?"

"Oh, that. Katy thought you knew Carol was in love with you. I mean, it's plain as mud. Even Phil could tell and he isn't in the place more than once a month."

"Hell," I said. I felt myself turning red.

"Yeah. Katy said you were just being nice, pretending you didn't know so as not to embarrass the little lady. But I said, *Shoot* no. Talley-man ain't *pretending* to be as thick as two yards of cow-dung. He really *is*." Matty Mark grinned. "Today she lost her bet."

I looked from one to the other: Matty triumphant, Phil bemused. "Damn it, Sovay—"

"We all know about you and Sovay," said Matty Mark. "Carol does too, but she's still nuts for you. Only the good Lord knows why."

"It's a puzzler, all right," said Phil, and he was grinning too.

I pushed my chair back. "Let's get out of here."

Carol?

I remembered her sitting at my bedside in the hospital. All night vigil, the doctor had said. I remember the nurse calling her my girlfriend.

I remembered asking Max to call Sovay for me, while she stood there, and Max getting mad at me for it. Dear God.

They were right, I was thick. No wonder a crack on the head hadn't killed me. It takes more than a bourbon bottle to break solid concrete.

Out on the street I thanked Phil and Matty for lunch, but my mind was elsewhere.

"Our pleasure," said Matty Mark. "And if the cops tell you any more about what they're thinking, let us know."

"Gladly," I told him. "I hope they catch the bastard soon."

"Oh, they won't," said Phil, still struggling into his black pea coat..

"Why not?"

He raised his empty hands. "All this motive and opportunity stuff is crap. They're just marking time. It wasn't a jealous girlfriend who killed Dean Coffey."

I turned and looked at him. "No? Who was it then?"

Phil smiled. "The same people who clobbered poor Seamus, natch. The CIA. Had to be. You don't think they can let us walk around forever, do you?

"Dean won't be the last, Joe. They'll go after me. Against Bobby Dylan. Anyone who tries to get people to think is a danger to the puppeteers."

Phil Ochs looked toward MacDougal Street. He raised the collar of his pea coat against the wind. "They'll kill us all. I promise you that."

CHAPTER 20

Paul Clayton was a fine singer, dulcimer player, and collector of folk songs. He deserved a better audience than he got that night.

It was Tuesday but it felt more like a bad, bad weekend. "Tourists," I complained to Max. "The place is crawling with them."

"Naturally." He was trying to clean his bifocals with the end of his neck tie. "There's nothing Middle America loves more than gaping at a murder scene. We should have left the chalk marks on the stage for them. The goddamned ghouls."

"Maybe I should show them the bump on my head."

"At a dime a pop? Why the hell not?" He turned and headed toward his office.

"Max, any word from your lawyer? About Al, I mean? "Yeah. They sprang him a couple of hours ago. I hope he shows up soon. Richie ain't much of a cook."

Richie was our chief dishwasher and his cooking leaned heavily toward what he called old army favorites. If armies travel on their stomachs, then his must have gone nowhere fast.

"There's a bright side to that," I told Max. "The tourists expect everything to be weird in the Village. Richie's food may have found its audience."

I walked back into the main room.

"Hi, Joe," said Carol Meisel, smiling. "Good to see you."

Carol. A pretty blond waitress with exceptionally bright blue eyes.

"Something wrong?" she asked. "You look kind of funny."

When was the last time someone whispered in my ear that a girl liked me? It felt like junior high school all over again.

I hadn't known what to do about it back in Pittsburgh, and I didn't know what to do about it now. After all, I was engaged to Sovay. More or less engaged.

"Nothing's wrong," I lied. "Just contemplating the nature of the universe."

"A smoke-filled coffeehouse is no place for that," she said. "The answers won't hold up in the great outdoors."

"So I'll stay inside. It doesn't—Oh, lord. Look who just walked in."

It was Irene Fox and she had been crying. Her carefully applied make-up was a mess. She wore a black blouse and skirt that were probably supposed to be mourning clothes. On her they looked like proper gear for a cocktail party.

I got there in a hurry, patting her hand and steering her to an empty table. "Irene, I'm so sorry."

"Thanks, Joe. God. I still can't believe it."

"I know, honey." I waved Carol over. "What will it be, Irene? Want a tea?"

"That would be swell." She slurred the last word and I realized she had been drinking before she got here.

She looked at the stage where Paul was singing. "God. That's where it happened, isn't it?"

"Irene, this isn't doing you any good."

She pressed her hands on the table, palms down, as if it were about to fly away from her. "I can't believe he's gone. Can you believe it, Joe?"

"Sometimes. But other times I expect to see him walk through the door."

"That's just how I feel. I went to the crematorium today, hoping that would make it seem real, you know?"

She was having a hard time focusing on my face. Definitely too much booze. It was one of those times I was glad we didn't have a liquor license.

"I hadn't realized the service was today."

"It didn't get any publicity. This newspaper strike...." She shrugged. "I never went to a *burning* before. All my relatives were buried."

She made a face. "Sounds awful, doesn't it? All my relatives...like I'm alone in the whole wide world."

"Who else came?" I said. She looked like she might start crying again, and I didn't want to give the tourists more of a show than they had paid for.

She rolled her eyes, trying to remember. "Let me see. The minister. Bob Braubinger, he arranged the whole thing, bless his heart. One of those awful policemen was there. Oh, and Ray."

"Ray Hegg?" I had heard the old beatnik talk about funerals and I hadn't thought he would be caught dead at one. So to speak.

"Yes, Ray Hegg. He looked awful."

"Very upset?"

"No, I mean *awful*. He didn't even wear a tie, can you believe it?"

I nodded. "I don't think he owns one, Irene. But it was nice of him to come anyway."

"I guess you're right." She smiled for the first time since she walked in. "I pay way too much attention to clothes. It's what they call an occupational hazard, right? Dean always said so...." The tears were coming.

I jumped in. "Relatives?"

"What?"

"Were any of his relatives at the service?"

"No. I knew everyone who was there." She frowned. "His family lives in Southern California, right? He never talked about them much, but he visited them every few months. God, I wonder if anyone has told them."

"The police probably did. I'll check with them."

"The police...." She frowned, her eyes suddenly calculating. "Joe, have you been talking to them?"

"What, the cops? Hardly at all. Twice in the hospital, and then today I stood around while that sergeant argued with Max."

"Oh." She paused. "What did you tell them about Dean and me?"

"Just what Dean told me that night. That you two had broken up."

Her pretty head shot back as if I had slapped her. "It was *you* who told them that, you bastard! It's a damned lie."

I stared at her. "You mean you two *didn't* break up?"

"We had a spat, that's all. We would have made up the next day." She finished her tea with a quick swallow. "If there had *been* a next day."

"You're probably right, Irene," I said. "But I had to tell the cops what Dean told me."

"Well, that's fine. That's just *great*." She dropped the cup. It rolled and I caught it before it went off the edge of the table.

I didn't tell her to calm down. That's never worked yet with anyone who has been drinking. It seldom does much good with people who are sober either.

"Irene, what's the problem?"

She leaned across the table, her face tight with anger. Her voice came out hoarse and low. "Those morons think I have a *motive*, thanks to you. They've gone to the modeling agency, asking if I have a violent temper. Can you believe it? *Me*? Violent?"

I thought about the times I had pulled her away from girls who paid too much attention to Dean. Sometimes she came away with a handful of hair. Her? Violent?

Hell, yes.

"The cops suspect everybody, Irene. They'd be chasing me around if they could figure out a way for me to have hit myself on the head."

She looked down at the table, brooding again. "It's bad enough that the man I loved is dead, but to have to deal with this crap, too. It's not fair, Joe. It is just not *fair*."

"You're right about that." I put a hand on her shoulder. "Are you okay for getting home?"

"I'll be just fine." She shrugged off my hand. She added, with venom: "So *nice* of you to care."

"I do care." What the hell, I figured. She was mad at me anyway. "Irene? Where were you when it happened? When Dean died, I mean."

She blinked, looking past me. "At home in bed. I need my beauty sleep, eight hours every night."

"Did Dean tell you he was going back to the Beggar that night?"

"No. He told me he was going home. Why do you ask? The police said he didn't decide to come over here until he found out that someone had broken into his place. That was after he left me."

"Of course. I forgot. Thanks, Irene. Keep in touch, okay?" I watched her go with a nagging sense that there was something else I should have asked her.

Someone place a hand on my shoulder. "Joe!" Carol was pointing at Max who standing near his office door, waving urgently.

I hurried to the back. "What's wrong, Boss?"

Max was red-faced. I thought he'd been having a coughing fit, but this time it was rage. "He's in the kitchen, damn it. Reason with him, Joe. He won't listen to me."

What now? I pushed the swinging door open. The kitchen crew was standing around watching a man who was bent halfway into a cabinet. He straightened out and I saw it was Al Perkins.

"Al! You're back."

"Not for long, man. Not for long." His handsome face was grim.

"Are you quitting?"

"Damn right." He raised three big soup pots he had pulled out of the cupboard. "These are mine. And I'm taking my knife set, of course."

"Al, what happened?"

"Cops got bored is what happened. They couldn't think of no more questions, so they tossed me out."

"Max sent his lawyer—"

"Yeah, well. I appreciate that, but I'll tell you. I don't think he had the cops shaking in their boots. He's more of a *tax* lawyer than a murder lawyer. You want the truth, I think I seen more police stations than he has."

"Are you out on bail?"

"No bail, man. What the hell can they charge me with? Dating a white chick is not a crime up here and that's what they're steamed about."

"Then why are you leaving?"

He glared at me. "You kidding? They got their *eye* on me now. It's just a matter of time till they see me jay-walking or something and then I'm off to jail."

"So where will you go?"

After a pause he smiled. "Alabama. Or 'Sippi. See what CORE is doing down there. Maybe join the Freedom Riders again. If the cops are gonna kick me around I figure I might as well earn it."

"Makes sense. You got your paycheck?"

He paused, looking down at the pots. "Didn't want to ask the man."

"Wait right here." I trotted down the hall to Max's office.

He was sitting at his desk, staring at the wall, looking like the winner in a lemon-eating contest. "You talk some sense into him, Joe?"

I shook my head. "He's leaving, Max. Another casualty of this mess."

"Jesus. *Damn* Dean Coffey. Why did he have to pick my place to get killed? And what the hell are you doing with my checkbook?"

"Writing a check for you to sign. Al needs his pay."

"That's *another* thing. Where am I gonna find another cook?"

"New York is full of them," I assured him. "Thousands of unemployed people. Half of them are folksingers, the other half are cooks."

He nodded. "And none of them can carry a tune or make a decent blintz. That's why they're unemployed."

"You know better than that, comrade. It's the lousy capitalist system that keeps people out of work. The bosses demand—"

"Oh, spare me." He had his keys out and was unlocking a drawer in his desk. "Just where do you think Al is going to cash a check tonight, especially while he's on the run from the police?"

I frowned. "Who said anything about running, Max? They let him go."

"And dollars to donuts that jerk Guareschi told him not to leave town, which is what he's about to do." He had the drawer open and was counting a pile of bills onto the desktop. He shoved them across to me.

"There. Give it to him in cash."

"That's more than he's got coming."

"Severance pay," said Max Karzoff. He was wheezing—a coughing fit getting ready to start. "I'm firing the bastard for trying to quit."

"Naturally. Makes perfect sense," I said, and started for the door.

"Joe?" He had slumped into his chair and was fumbling for his handkerchief. "Don't tell him the money's from me."

For some reason I lost my temper. "Hell no, Max. God forbid anyone thinks you have a heart."

He looked at me over the handkerchief—a tired man, old before his time. His eyes were wet and sad behind his oversized spectacles. "If they find out, they just try to break it."

CHAPTER 21

By the time Al Perkins left, Paul Clayton's first set was over. I hurried back to the green room to tell Paul what a fine job he'd been doing. I hope I was convincing, because I hadn't heard a note.

When I came out front the crowd for the late show was coming in and I saw two familiar customers wedged into a booth: Ray Hegg and Agustina Adler, both wearing sunglasses. That was normal for Ray but I had never seen Gus wearing shades before, indoors or out.

"Hi folks," I said. "How are you two—"

Gus's hands shot across the table and clasped mine. "Oh Joe, it's terrible."

I sat down, gently trying to work my hands free from her grip. "Gus, I'm so sorry. Let me buy you folks something."

Ray had an empty espresso cup in front of him and Gus had apple juice. I waved Carol down and ordered coffee for myself and another round for them.

"You're looking better," said Gus. "Then you did in the hospital, I mean."

"Well, I hope so. I'm sure feeling better. Thanks for visiting me there."

Ray cleared his throat. "You may have noticed I didn't. Hospitals and morgues just aren't my scene." He shrugged and drank espresso.

"I know that, Ray. That's why I was surprised to hear you went to the service for Dean today."

"He did that for *me*," said Gus. "I wanted to go to the funeral…." She frowned. "Is it a funeral when you cremate someone, or is that just for burials?"

"Makes no difference," Ray said shortly. He was in a bad mood, probably because he had been talked into going. "Makes no difference to anybody."

"Were you there too, Gus? I hadn't heard that."

She shook her head. "I was planning to. I even talked Ray into coming along." She patted his hand. "Moral support. But when we got there…." She trailed off, gazing at nothing.

"Irene Fox got there first," said Ray, darkly. "Queen of the uptown slummers. And Gus, with the good-natured self-effacement that makes her utterly unfit for modern life, refused to go in. She was afraid it would hurt the chick's feelings. As if La Fox ever gave a damn about anyone else's feelings."

"Come on, Ray," said Gus. Her ever-busy hands found a strand of her long gray hair and played with it. "Don't pretend to be mean."

She turned to me. "I couldn't risk upsetting Irene, so I asked Ray to go in. Sort of to represent me. I thought Dean might need some support."

I stared at her. "Support?"

"To get wherever he's going. That's the main reason every culture has mourning ceremonies, Joe. To give the person a push to his new life, wherever it may be."

I couldn't think of a reply. Theology was never my long suit.

"So," said Ray. "I didn't want to go, but I did. Gus wanted to and didn't. The things we mortals do in the name of mortality. What a load of horse sweat."

I sipped coffee. I knew better than to talk when Ray was speechifying.

"Did I see Al leaving a few minutes ago?" Gus asked.

"Yes. Leaving for good, too."

"For good? No."

"Perkins quit?" asked Ray. "You're kidding."

"No joke. The cops have been hassling him about the night of the murder and he just said to hell with it."

Gus took off her dark glasses. Her eyes were bloodshot and dark from tears. "Oh, that poor guy. And all because he did me a favor."

"You mean going to the yoga seminar?"

"That's right. I'm—well, I'm uncomfortable going to those things alone, and I didn't want to miss it." Her eyes sparkled with excitement. "They had this *swami* from Scotland who had studied in India. That's why it was an all-night session, because he could only be here for one day—"

"Then he had other people to rob," groused Ray. "If he'd ever been near India, I'm Harold Stassen."

"Now, *Ray*," said Gus, sounding like a den mother. "I thought he was wonderful."

"No offense, Gus, but you always do. Every new snake oil salesman…." He shook his head.

I decided to try to get them back on track. "You didn't want to go alone."

"Oh." Gus blinked, gathering her thoughts. "That's right. And I asked Al because Ray said he'd be too busy."

The bald man nodded, a little sheepishly. "The boss wanted me to entertain some out-of-towners with big research money in their pockets. I was supposed to show off the lab; tell them how we're just a few thousand bucks from winning a dozen Nobel Prizes. Instead they decided to knock off early and see the big city. The boss decided he'd rather play the host for that part himself, so I made it

over to the Center just as the yoga session was starting and
Perkins decided to bow out."

"Do you remember where you were earlier that afternoon?
Like five o'clock?"

"I was at home, taking a nap," said Gus. "I can't stay up
all night anymore, not without preparing."

"Now, wait a minute," said Ray. He leaned forward, his
bald scalp reddening all the way up. "Wait a goddamn
minute. Why are you asking her that, Joe?"

"Somebody robbed Dean's apartment that afternoon. I
was just—"

Ray slammed his cup onto the table top. It was a hard
evening for our glassware. "I *thought* so! I didn't believe
it, but I thought so. You were checking her alibi. Joe Talley,
boy detective."

Gus's hand found his arm. "It's okay, Ray. Please take it
easy."

"It's *not* okay." He glared at me, eyebrows rising toward
his bald forehead. "You want *my* alibi too, Sherlock?"

I sighed. "I'm sure the cops already have it. I just didn't
see any harm—"

"Damn right they do. I was at the Blue Note Record Shop
all afternoon, talking to the owner. You want the names of
some witnesses? Or will you just crosscheck my story with
your fellow officers?"

"Cool it, Ray."

He shook his head. "This is just so damned stupid. It's
unreal, man. You should have seen those cops tearing into
poor Gus."

Ray looked down at the table top until his breathing was
back to normal. Finally he raised his head and looked back
at Gus. "More of the same, babe?"

Gus nodded. Ray picked up the empties and walked off.

"Were they tough on you?"

Her attempt at a casual shrug showed me how fragile she really was. "Nothing I couldn't cope with, Joe. It just depresses me to see how their minds work. God, I would *hate* to have such a suspicious mind, wouldn't you? But I don't want to talk about them. Listen, I got to thinking at the service."

She smiled wryly. "Or *almost* at the service. As close to it as I got."

"Yes?"

"Do you know if the police have reached Dean's relatives in California? From the way they talked, I don't think they have."

"You may be right. Do you know where they lived?"

"No. But I have a key to Dean's apartment. Maybe there's an address book there."

"The cops have already been there, Gus."

"Looking for clues to the burglary, right? Not for the phone numbers of relatives. Someone ought to check, Joe." Her eyes were firmly fixed on me.

"Why not you?" I asked.

"I could never do it. Not so soon after his death. The vibrations…." She shuddered.

I was tempted to point out that the vibrations, whatever they might be, ought to be a lot stronger here, where Dean was murdered, than back at his home. Instead I said: "All right. I'll do it."

"That's wonderful, Joe! Thank you so much."

She fumbled in her purse and pulled out a small ring of keys. "My extra set. Dean's are the two marked with red fingernail polish."

"One question, Gus. Why not ask Ray instead of me?"

"Oh, I've already asked him for so much. Besides." She looked at me, all wide-eyed innocence. "It might be dangerous."

I was still looking for a response to that one when Ray got back with our drinks. He had forced a smile onto his face, trying to make up for his earlier mood, I guess. "Here we go. Please tip your waitress. Did Gus tell you why the police are fitting her for a ball and chain, Joe?"

Gus smiled but her juice glass trembled. "They seem to think I was jealous of Dean and Irene. And I made the mistake of telling them how yoga makes me feel full of power, as if I could do anything—"

"Which the literal bastards took as a confession that she *did* do anything, namely murder," Ray explained.

"They were checking schedules to see if I could have left the Asian Culture Center in time to—to—Dean...."

"Take it easy, Gus."

There were tears in her eyes. "I *loved* him, Joe. But not the way the police think."

"It's okay. Just—"

"Excuse me, Joe" said Carol, tapping me on the shoulder. "Paul is finishing his set."

I thanked her and hurried to the stage. I put a hand on the mike, looked at the audience—

And went blank. All those empty tourist faces. The goddamned enemy. I was standing on the spot where Dean had died, looking at all those tombstone eyes, come to gloat, come to stare. Who was the killer, which one....

I put down the mike and ran offstage.

Carol went wide-eyed as I shot past her, not slowing down until I was in the men's room.

I leaned over the sink, scrubbing sweat off my face and trying to calm down. My heart was booming like a bass drum.

The door opened behind me. Ray eased in and took off his shades. "You okay?"

"Yeah, fine." I swallowed. "I have to get back there and thank Paul Clayton."

"Don't sweat it. Carol got Max to do the honors. But what happened out there, man? You looked like you just spotted Martin Bormann at the front table."

I shrugged and tried a smile. "Call it stage fright, I guess."

"Bull. I've seen you up there a hundred times, and you never turned a hair."

"Yeah, but it was never the place where Dean got killed before."

"Oh." He scratched his bald head. "That didn't occur to me. You got a taste of the *gestalt*, huh?"

I felt sheepish and cranky. "Gibberish."

He laughed. "The truth usually is."

I grinned back at him; couldn't help it. "Let's go face the peanut gallery."

"Suits me. If you want my advice, tell 'em Richie slipped you some bad hamburger or something. His cooking might make anybody run for the roses."

I said I'd keep that in mind, but I wasn't going to get anyone thinking about food poisoning. Not with Al gone for good and God knows how long it would take to replace him.

"And Joe?" He stopped me with a hand on my shoulder. "Are you gonna keep looking for the killer?"

"I never *have* been, Ray. That's the cops' business. But I sure would like to find that demo tape."

"The what?"

"Dean's demo tape. Somebody swiped the studio copies on the day he died."

Ray frowned. "Weird, man. Every copy?"

"That's the weird part. He told me he left one copy with a colleague for safe-keeping."

"A colleague? That's a funny way to put it. Did he mean a musician?"

"No idea. And as far as I can tell, there are no surviving recordings of his voice or his songs. That's what I'm looking for."

"Can't blame you for that." Ray held the door open for me. "I wonder."

"What?"

His bushy eyebrows rose behind his sunglasses. "Think that could have been the motive for killing him? Pardon the cliché, but maybe it was something he said."

CHAPTER 22

Who's gonna clean this place up?" I asked. "And where will they send all his stuff?"

"I don't know," said Carol. "God, this is the worst mess I've ever seen. It looks like a tornado struck."

We were standing in Dean Coffey's apartment, looking at the wreckage the burglars left behind the evening before he was killed. It was a two-room pad on Ninth Street and, just as Gus had told me, it was right across from her place.

We had let ourselves in with her key and now we stood in the living room. I couldn't see the floor, so thick was the effluvia of scattered papers, slashed furniture and torn-up clothing. "No wonder he didn't want to spend the night here."

Carol was wide-eyed. "They were looking for something. I wonder if they found it."

I had walked Carol home from the Riding Beggar early on Wednesday morning, and told her about Gus's request. She offered to go along, offered so strongly that I couldn't have said no without being just plain rude.

I was still jumpy about Carol. Being told that someone was in love with me was a shock to my system. I figured Sovay was all the trouble I needed in the romance department.

Oh, well. Sifting through junk in a dead man's apartment hardly seemed like a prelude to romance.

"What are we looking for, anyway?" Carol asked.

"An address book. Or a letter with a return address in California. Something that would tell us how to reach his relatives."

We started to dig. We found his guitars, undamaged. We found his collection of records, ripped out of their sleeves, scattered on the floor. Someone had up-ended a reel-to-reel tape recorder, as if to unscrew the back.

"Have the police looked at all this?" asked Carol.

"Yup. Photographed it and checked for fingerprints. No luck."

In the bedroom, the mattress had been lifted off the double bed and dumped against the wall. We finally found Dean's address book in a corner of the dresser.

"That's funny. No addresses in California. Everyone's in New York."

"Maybe he had another one for home," said Carol. "Or maybe he had them memorized. I never bothered to put my parent's address down in my book. I know it by heart."

"You're depressing me."

She sat back and frowned. "If he visited people in California there must be bills, receipts...right?"

We found a shoebox full of papers in the bedroom closet. Or rather, the papers had been in the box once. Someone had scattered them on the floor of the closet while looking through them.

I pawed through the paperwork for ten minutes and lost patience. "Goddamn it, this is hopeless. We don't know what we're looking for, and we have to assume the killer already took anything he wanted—"

"The killer?" Carol frowned at me. "You think he wanted a list of Dean's relatives in California?"

I sat back on my haunches, trying to sort through my thoughts. They were as jumbled as Dean's paperwork. "No, that doesn't make any sense. I guess I half-hoped we'd find a clue to the killer here."

"Now, wait a minute." Her jaw stuck out in a way that was almost comical. "Are you hunting for the killer, Joe? That's the police's job, isn't it?"

Talk about déjà vu. I had had this same conversation with Ray the night before. I shrugged and looked back at the papers. "They're doing a lousy job."

Carol perched on the edge of the bed frame, a precarious roost. "Damn it, I don't want you to get hit on the head again. Or worse."

"I appreciate your concern, but—Look at it this way. I'm not really looking for Dean's killer. I suppose murderers belong in jail, but I've never felt any great passion for putting them there myself."

Her blue eyes stayed intently on me. "But?"

"Two buts. First, I promised Gus I would try to find Dean's relatives. Second, I want to find that demo tape. It's really all that we have left of him now."

She nodded and her shoulders relaxed. "Okay, I can understand that. Why don't you start sifting through the stuff in the living room? I'll take a look in the closets."

"I already did."

She stood up, dusting off her hands. "No offense, Joe, but I have never yet met a man who understood closets."

I opened every tape box. Each reel had been labeled and all the labels matched the boxes. Unless he had deliberately mislabeled—

That was crazy. You create demo tapes to be *heard*, not to be hidden. I was just spinning my wheels and making myself dizzy. I looked at the ceiling and considered giving the whole thing up.

"Troubles?" asked Carol, standing in the bedroom doorway.

"It's hopeless."

"Maybe not. This was wedged under the edge of the carpet outside the closet. I guess somebody missed it." She held out a scrap of yellow paper.

"Yeah? Let's see."

It was a receipt for a car rental, dated in January from Dublin Car Rentals in Willow Creek, California.

"Carol, you're a genius."

"Rubbish," she said, grinning from ear to ear. "But does it help?"

"It tells us where Dean went to visit his relatives. Now, maybe the cops can find them."

"Say, maybe his relatives have a copy of the tape."

"That would be great."

She looked around what remained of the living room. "Is there any point in looking around here anymore?"

"I doubt it. Somebody was sure searching damned hard for something."

"I hope so."

"What do you mean?"

"The other choice is that they wrecked the place just because they hated Dean so much." She shivered.

I said: "Someone hated him enough to kill him."

CHAPTER 23

The band that night was forgettable and I have long since forgotten them. All I can remember is that it was three suburban college boys trying to be the Clancy Brothers. They made a change from the Kingston Trio imitators, but that was the only point in their favor.

They were rendering—in several senses of the word—*Danny Boy* when Detective Aaron Levy arrived. I didn't recognize him at first. I had never seen him before without a notebook in his hand and Guareschi standing in front of him.

"More questions?"

He shook his head, smiling. "Off-duty. Just thought I'd drop by and see what the place look like when it's open."

"Fair enough. Let me buy you an espresso. If that wouldn't be bribing a police officer?"

His grin got wider. "My price is a little higher than that. Inflation."

I steered him to my table at the back and sat down opposite him. "You sure you aren't here to make more trouble?"

He looked startled. "Whoa. What have I ever done to you?"

"Well, for one thing Al Perkins quit yesterday."

Levy frowned. "Yeah? What for?"

"To get away from you jokers. What is it with Guareschi, anyway? Is his Klan membership up for renewal, or something?"

He snorted. "The Klan isn't that fond of Catholics. Jews either, if it comes to that."

"You know what I mean. Is Guareschi picking on Al because he's a Negro?"

"It's not that simple. Perkins had a motive and he knew the other suspects. He didn't cooperate when I talked to him so the Sergeant brought him in for questioning."

"The third degree?"

"Sure." Levy grinned. "You should see the Precinct House basement. Racks, thumbscrews, the works."

"Damn it, I'm serous."

"Okay, seriously then. You see any bruises on him? Was he walking stiff and sore, like a guy who had been beaten up?"

I thought about it. "No."

"Well, then." Levy sipped espresso. "Maybe we pushed him too hard. It's possible. We make mistakes like everyone else."

My mistakes don't go to jail, I thought.

"But that's how you do it, you know? You ask questions. If somebody doesn't answer, you ask again. If somebody lies, you check that out. Keep pushing, keep working away at it. This isn't *Perry Mason*. It isn't hunches that pay off; it's asking everyone questions until you ask the right person the right one."

"So, what have you learned so far?"

Levy shrugged. "A bushel of motives I'd trade for a stick of gum. Lot of people who could have been jealous of Coffey's lovers or his career. Jealous enough to kill him? Who knows?"

"Not me." I lit a cigarette.

"Now, how about opportunity?" He was enjoying the chance to lecture. I guess Guareschi did most of the talking. "On the one hand he was there all night, just waiting for someone to come shoot him."

"But who knew that?" I asked.

"Exactly. As far as we know, just you and your boss. Obviously you didn't hit yourself on the head. So that leaves—"

"Max? Be serious. He wouldn't hurt a fly."

"Yeah, well. I gave up the idea that some people were incapable of murder a long time ago." He licked foam off his lips. "Hey, this is really good. Want another espresso? My treat."

"I can't believe Guareschi seriously thinks Max could be involved."

"Well, Pete—that's Sergeant Guareschi to you. He's looking at all the angles."

"You sound like you have a lot of experience defending him."

"Do I?" I had surprised him again. "He doesn't need it. Believe this or not, Pete is not a bad cop. I have seen plenty worse."

"In Mississippi, maybe."

"Right here in Manhattan, my friend. You need to understand one thing about him, though. Pete is one thing that you and I are not. In fact, no one involved in this case is."

"What's that?"

"A native of Greenwich Village."

"Hell, Max has been here thirty years."

"Yeah, but Guareschi was *born* here. In Little Italy, which barely exists anymore. He can show you the NYU building that stands where he was born. You see Gerde's Folk City, but he remembers when Mike Porco was just running an Italian restaurant there."

Levy waved his hand toward the kitchen from which a familiar squalling noise was coming. "That cappuccino machine back there...Who do you think brought espresso to the Village? Appalachian folksingers?"

"So we're all interlopers, huh?"

"More or less. Your singer buddies moan a lot about the good old days, but they don't seem to have much sympathy for the poor schmucks who got run over by progress."

"Not true," I said. "I could introduce you to people who sing about that very subject."

"I'd like that," said Levy. "I'd like to meet some of those guys. Which reminds me? I know I promised not to ask questions...."

"Go ahead."

"How about professional jealousy as a motive? Are there any folksingers in the Village who might have killed Coffey to eliminate a rival; or because they envied his success?"

"He didn't *have* a lot of success."

"Yeah, but everybody said he was going places."

"True." I thought for a moment. "Have you asked anyone else?"

He nodded. "A couple of folkniks I know. They grinned and said 'Bobby.'"

I laughed. "Well, Dylan does come across kind of strong sometimes, but you know they were kidding. And anyway, he's touring England, I think."

"Do you know Bob Dylan?"

"We've met, sure. I've never invited him to play here. Talented songwriter, but that *voice*...."

"I've heard he's a *landsman* of mine."

"Jewish? I've heard that too, but it's hard to get a straight answer out of him. How do you know about him, anyway?"

Levy smiled. "My kid sister goes to NYU. Last time I saw her she was playing *Blowing in the Wind* on her six-string."

"Like I said, a hell of a songwriter."

"So, are there any other folkies who might want to bump off a rival?"

"I can't think of any. Frankly, I don't believe it."

"Too bad. It would tie in with the demo tape disappearing. The only other possibility is that there was something on it someone wanted to keep secret. But no one seems to know what songs were on it."

"You're kidding," I said. "Dozens of people must know."

"Yeah? Like who?"

"The engineers who recorded it."

"I talked to 'em. They say they do a dozen of the damned things every month. Can't remember anything about this one."

"What about Bob Braubinger? And the owners of the record company."

Levy made a face. "The stockbrokers? Those two boys... All they really remember about the songs is how they were going to *change* them. Make them more commercial. They wanted to add a song about surfing."

"Christ." I shuddered.

"Yeah. Braubinger is the best so far. At least he remembered a few of the titles."

"I can do more than that."

Levy's head rose. "You heard the tape?"

"Sure. Dean played it for everybody when he got it from the studio. I kept asking him to make me a copy, but he wasn't satisfied with it. Told me to wait and buy the LP."

Levy pulled out a notebook and a pen. "Tell me."

"Uh...." I felt like a contestant on a quiz show. "Let's see. The first song was *White Wolf*. Then came *The Grace to Kill*."

"The what to what?"

"*Grace to Kill*. It's an anti-war song. And there was *Let Me Take Your Side*."

"Hold it. Wasn't that the one Matty Mark Oliver was mad about?"

I nodded. "Dean based the tune on one he learned from Matty Mark. I'm not sure about the order but there was a love song called *Francesca*."

We went on for half an hour and I discovered that, while I knew the names of all the songs, and could briefly say what they were about, I had a lousy memory for lyrics.

"Damn. Let me talk to some of the singers. They're sure to remember better than I do. And I'll try to find the issues of *Broadside* with his songs in them."

"Thanks. I'd appreciate it. Hey, is something wrong? You look pale."

I made a face. "All of this talk about Dean just reminded of how much I miss the guy. And he ain't coming back."

Levy nodded. "Violent death is one of those things you don't get used to. Let's hope this country has had enough of it for a while."

We sipped more espresso. Then Levy pointed at the young men on the stage who were stumbling through a rapid-fire version of *Finnegan's Wake*.

"Are those guys average?"

"Low end of average, maybe."

"Good. I'd hate to think they were what all the excitement was about."

"It's an off-night," I explained. "Otherwise those boys would be lucky to play a baskethouse."

"Baskethouse?"

"The bottom of the folk hierarchy. Coffeehouse with no cover charge. They don't pay the performers, just pass a basket."

"Gotcha. But you pay here, I take it."

I nodded. "Not much, but something. The top of the tree are the nightclubs and restaurants."

Levy looked intrigued. "Yeah? Why is that?"

"Liquor licenses."

"Ah. Booze has a higher profit margin than espresso."

"Exactly." My mind was turning over an idea. "Aaron? Is anyone in the clear? Completely alibied, I mean."

"Among your crowd? Let me think. The key times are six to midnight, that's when Coffey's apartment was robbed. And between eight and nine in the morning. That's when he got killed, and you, uh...."

"Got my head examined."

"So to speak. There's also the break-in at Broker Records, but that could have been practically anytime over the weekend, so it's useless in terms of alibis."

"So is anyone covered?"

"Braubinger is out for the murder, if we believe his wife."

"I keep forgetting he's married. I don't believe I ever met the lady."

"Yeah, well. A wife's alibi for a husband is not something I'd bet the pension on. But she says he was home in bed till ten A.M. on Saturday."

"That sounds right," I told him. "Bob isn't an early riser."

"Huh. Katy Poe. No alibi for the robbery. She says she was with somebody at the time of the murder and that's all she'll say. We'd have to arrest her to squeeze the guy's name out of her, and barring a convincing motive there's no point."

"But you had enough reason to arrest Al Perkins."

Levy dropped his notebook. "As a matter of fact, we *did*. Give that a rest, okay?"

At least I had made him cranky on the subject. Not a major victory for the civil rights movement, but what the hell. "Who else?"

"Let's see. Matty Mark Oliver, the southern boy. He's loose at both ends, pardon the expression. He spent most of the evening with his trio, but he could have trashed Coffey's place before meeting them."

"I can tell you where he was at the time of the murder. Either sleeping off a drunk or nursing a hell of a hangover."

Levy shrugged. "Unless the hangover wants to come in and make a statement I'll have to call that unconfirmed. Next, welcome to the yoga gurus: Perkins, Hegg, and Miss Adler."

I waved Carol over for a refill. Levy switched to tea, saying otherwise he'd be awake all night. He told me Al had no real alibi.

"Hegg is definitely clear on looting the apartment. He went to that yoga thing straight from a jazz record shop where half a dozen people know him. His lady friend is open for the burglary, but it doesn't matter much since apparently they were both at the yoga thing until close to nine in the morning. They both have motives, but nothing I'd spend a nickel to phone in."

"Motives? Ray and Gus? Like what?"

Levy sipped tea. "Same motive, give or take. Gus used to date Dean Coffey. Ray used to date Irene Fox."

"Ray? *Irene*?" My jaw dropped. "Who told you that?"

"Several people. Why, isn't it true?"

"Ray can't *stand* Irene. He thinks she's brainless."

Levy raised his eyebrows. "In my experience men don't always pick their dates based on IQ, Joe. From what I hear it was only a couple of dates, just before she moved on to Coffey. I never said it was a *good* motive, but it's down in the ol' notebook."

I shook my head. Ray and Irene? Unbelievable.

"Speaking of Irene, she has no alibi, either. Same with your boss."

I had a thought. "What about Seamus O'Hanlon?"

"Who?"

"The poet who got mugged."

"Oh yeah," Levy rubbed a hand over his scalp, pushing back to the receding hairline. "I've checked the reports on that. Sounds like a pretty average mugging. Too bad and all that, but I don't see the connection."

"Maybe you're too optimistic there."

"Oh? In what way?"

"At the risk of bragging, I stopped those guys before they could finish whatever they had in mind. I think they wanted to kill Seamus."

Levy nodded. "Go on. Why would they do that?"

"I don't know. But he told me in the hospital that he wanted to talk to Dean. And I guess he never got the chance."

The detective frowned. "I hadn't connected that. They performed together that night, didn't they?"

"Well, not together. Seamus opened, then Katy played, and then Dean."

"Katy? Katy Poe?" Levy straightened up. He was suddenly all business. "Nobody told me that."

Hell. Had I gotten some one else in trouble? "You think that makes her a suspect?"

He was on his feet. "I'm thinking that three people performed that night and two of them were attacked. Maybe she's next."

"Oh, man." I stubbed out my cigarette and stood up. "Let me get you her phone number."

"I've already got it. Where's the phone? I'll get someone on this right now."

I watched him heading for the payphone near the restrooms. The phony Irish guys came off the stage and I told them how good they had been. I think they were convinced; I lie best when I'm thinking of something else.

Was Katy in danger? If so, what about everyone else who had been there that night? Max, me, Braubinger, Carol?

Carol. She hurried past as if called up by my thoughts. A fat tourist in a loud suit was leering at her as she served his espresso. Saying something rude by the look on his face. The other men at his table started laughing. She turned back to the kitchen, face reddening.

I wanted to go over and pour the coffee on the fat man's bald head—then throw the whole table out. Wanted to pound them all for being rude to Carol. I hadn't had that reaction last week when Seamus had done worse.

Life was too damned complicated.

"Got somebody on it," said Levy. He had returned while my attention was elsewhere. "Thanks for the help, Joe."

"You called Katy?"

"Called Guareschi. He's sending someone over to talk to her. Assess the situation; decide if we need to put a guard on her. We'll definitely be sending patrols around."

"Good. Thanks."

Levy nodded. "How much do I owe you for the drinks?"

"They're on the house. Since you're off duty."

He didn't notice the sarcasm. "Thanks. Nice place you've got here. And, hey, have your boss call my boss. He has a few more questions."

I frowned at him. "I hope Guareschi doesn't still have a bee in his bonnet just because Max was an old lefty."

Levy raised his glasses and rubbed his nose. "You know, Pete served in the navy during the War. When he was in basic training a lieutenant told him that they were certain to send him to the Pacific because nobody would trust a wop to fight his brother Italians. The lieutenant's name was Schmidt, by the way."

"What's your point?"

He shrugged. "There's only one world, Joe, but everybody sees it through his own personal window, and the windows are built in different times and places. Your boss's window was made by some Commies in the thirties—and the experiences that made him gravitate to them, of course. Pete's window was shaped by some pretty tough years on a destroyer in the South Pacific."

He looked thoughtful. "And as for your buddy, Dean. Well, I hear he was a rich boy from sunny southern California."

I thought about *The Grace to Kill*, Dean's song about someone's father rotting in a veteran's hospital. I didn't feel like bringing it up.

"What about yours?" I asked. "Where is *your* window from?"

"Me?" He grinned. "I grew up on the Lower East Side, youngest of four kids. The oldest was my brother, Daniel. When Daniel married a Gentile my parents sat shiva. Went into mourning, the whole nine yards. By the time my sister Rachel did the same thing—making it three in a row—they barely blinked an eye. And when I married a nice Jewish girl they thought I was just showing off."

"I'm not sure what you're trying to tell me."

"No?" He shrugged. "Maybe I'm better at asking questions then answering them." He was heading towards the door, but he stopped suddenly.

"You know, Joe, I'll tell you one more thing about Pete Guareschi. I once saw him threaten to quit, turn in his badge and gun and make a public stink. All because he thought the brass were railroading an innocent man."

"So? What happened?"

"He talked the bosses into postponing the arrest. They gave him twenty-four hours to investigate further."

"And did he solve the crime?"

"He sure did. He proved the guy really *was* guilty." Levy grinned. "Ain't that a kick in the head?"

CHAPTER 24

I walked Aaron Levy to the door. "I'm glad you came over."

"Me too. I hope to come back under happier circumstances, as the saying goes. Give your boss my regards."

I didn't say the same about his boss, but he didn't take offense. As we stood in the doorway a small group of men came down the stairs. They must have been partying pretty well, because they bumped into Levy, the walls, and each other as they walked out.

Levy stared after them.

"Aaron? Something wrong?"

"What's up there? Where were they coming from?"

"There's a bar. The Bag of Nails. Why?"

"Would it have been open that Friday night? I mean, late, when you left Dean in here?"

"I don't know. Probably. You think...."

Levy swung our door shut. Some previous owner had put in a one-way glass panel, which meant that we could see into the hallway, but people coming in faced a mirror. The cop was gazing at this glass now, his face brightening.

"Well, what do you know? The question has always been how did anyone know Coffey was here that night. What if someone was leaving the bar and Coffey saw him through the glass? All he had to was open it and invite the guy in."

"Nobody checked that out?"

"I assumed it was office space upstairs. There's no bar sign out front. It didn't occur to me that anyone might be tramping down the stairs at three in the morning." He looked at me appraisingly. "You know the manager up there?"

"Sure."

"Come up with me, then."

I asked Amy, our cashier, to tell Max I'd be right back and followed Levy up the stairs. The Bag of Nails was nearly empty.

I waved the owner over and we ordered two beers. "Les Newcomer, this is Aaron Levy. He's a cop."

"Yeah?" Newcomer puffed a camel cigarette. "We making too much noise up here again? The boys do get rowdy." Only the funereal atmosphere of the place suggested the Yankee was being ironic.

"Were you open last Friday night?" Levy asked him. "The night Dean Coffey got killed?"

"Last Friday? Sure. Closed at two, spent another hour cleaning up."

"When you left, was there anyone in the hallway downstairs?"

Newcomer gazed across the room, frowning. "Nope. Don't believe there was."

"When you passed the door to the Riding Beggar was it open or closed?"

"Closed. I always check it when I go by at night, just to be neighborly."

"You check it," Levy repeated. "You mean you try the door to see if it's locked?"

"Nope." He swiped at the bar with a rag. "I just mean that the door is shut and there's no light under the crack. Don't see any need to jiggle another man's handle."

"*Did* you see a light under the door that morning?"

"Nope." Newcomer turned to me. "But Dean was in there, huh?"

I nodded. "When I left him he was at the far end, by the stage, though. There weren't any lights on near the door."

Levy frowned. "Can you remember who was still here around three?"

"Well, Lemme think. There was Barney Campbell. I don't usually see him out that late."

"Who is he?"

"A businessman. Middle-aged. He lives a couple of blocks away, comes here two-three times a week to have a few. I think maybe he had a fight with the missus. Probably why he was out so late."

"Did he know Dean Coffey?"

Newcomer shrugged. "Not as far as I know."

"How about you? You knew him."

"Sure. He used to come up here for a drink now and again. He brought his guitar in once or twice and played a tune." Les frowned. "For free, of course. I don't have a license for music."

"Did you know Irene Fox?"

"Sure." He brightened. "Now, that's a doozy of a gal, don'tcha think? I knew she was a model before anybody *told* me she was a model. My, oh my. 'Course, I don't serve women in here, but she came up once or twice, looking for Coffey." He seemed to relish the memory.

"Uh huh," said Levy. "And just for the record, where were you around nine A.M. on the morning Coffey died?"

"Home asleep. I never get up until close to noon."

"Were you home alone?"

"Unfortunately." His mind still seemed to be on Irene.

"Do you happen to know Dean's address?"

Newcomer frowned. "It's in the phone book, isn't it?"

"Why? Have you looked it up lately?"

"Nope. I just assumed. What's the point?"

"No point. How about earlier that Friday? Say, between six and midnight. Where were you then?"

"Right here."

"Nobody relieved you?"

"More hands in the till, less money in the bank. I work as many weekend hours as possible."

Levy sighed. "Anybody else here late that night who didn't leave in a group?"

"Lemme think." Newcomer's gaze settled on someone at the far end of the room. "Huh. Come to think of it, yeah, there was one guy who came in, I don't know, after two, looked around and walked right out again. And there he is, over there."

Newcomer pointed to a group of young men at the far end of the room. They were engaged in earnest discussion over some beer.

"Which one?"

"The one in the blue jacket."

"Thanks, Les," I said. "Aaron, this is your lucky day."

"Why's that?"

"You wanted to meet some folksingers. That's one of the best in the business. Hey, Tom, you got a minute?"

He looked up, saw me, and said a few words to his friends. Then he picked up his beer and came over. He was a midsize guy in his twenties with warm eyes and brown hair that was beginning to recede. "Hey, Joe. How's it going?"

"Not bad. I want you to meet a policeman who likes folk music. He's investigating the death of Dean Coffey."

"Poor Dean. Man, that was a shame."

"Officer Aaron Levy, this is Tom Paxton."

•

"Did you know Dean Coffey, Mr. Paxton?"

"Knew him a little, yes. I met him, let me see, last summer, after that song of his came out in *Broadside*."

"*Let Me Take Your Side*," I filled in.

"Right. Good song. A little more subtle than a lot of the stuff that's been coming out, so I went out of my way to meet him. You remember, Joe? I came to your club one night."

I nodded.

"And when was the last time you saw him?" Levy asked.

"Saw him?" Paxton frowned and sipped beer. "Thursday. We were organizing the Boycott Committee and he joined up. We didn't—"

"What committee was that?"

Tom and I filled Levy in on the *Hootenanny* debacle. "By the way, Joe, there was a big meeting on the boycott on Sunday, while you were in the hospital."

"Yeah? Where was it?"

"The Village Gate. Judy Collins and Carolyn Hester set it up. Things are really beginning to move."

I started to say something but Levy interrupted. From the look on his face he was thinking that Guareschi was not going to be pleased to see left-wing politics popping up in his case again.

"So you saw Coffey at that *first* meeting."

"Right. I also talked to him on Friday afternoon, but that was on the phone. He called me with some ideas for the Committee. I said I'd talk to him later and he said he'd probably drop by the Bag of Nails after his show in Brooklyn."

"But you didn't meet him here?"

"I did." He put down his beer. "I mean, I *came* here to meet him, but he never showed. Some guys were expecting me…Well."

Tom gave Levy an appraising look, and then laughed. "I don't suppose you're looking to arrest any gamblers tonight."

Levy smiled back. "Not really."

"I was on my way to a poker game, so I didn't feel like hanging around on the off chance that he might show up. I probably stayed at the game until, I don't know, five A.M."

Levy asked him for the names of some other players and Paxton obliged.

"Where were you at nine that morning?"

"Asleep." He laughed again. "Dreaming I folded those three queens, instead of raising."

"When you left the Bag of Nails did you notice anything strange at the door of the Riding Beggar?"

Tom frowned. "Strange? Like what?"

"Any signs of life. Noise. Lights."

"Nope. 'Course I wasn't looking for them." He scratched his thinning hair. "Was Dean already in there?"

"That's right."

"I wish I'd known. I would have liked to have had another chat with him. About the Committee. About anything."

He raised his beer glass and shrugged. "That's the worst part, isn't it? Not getting to say goodbye."

CHAPTER 25

So, have the police contacted Dean's family?" Carol asked.

I was walking her home that early morning.

"Nope. Levy says they haven't had any more luck tracing down his relatives than we have."

"That doesn't make sense, Joe. We know he was visiting *somebody* in California."

"I know. Levy's gonna check out that Willow Creek stub we found, but I hate to have to wait—Hold it."

"What is it?"

"Maybe we can find out for ourselves. Would you mind stopping by my place while I make a phone call?"

Her blue eyes widened. "Sure."

We walked the extra three blocks to my place and went in.

"Nice pad," said Carol, and with unfailing instinct walked over to the one thing I would have hidden if I had known she was coming: a pin-up picture that hung on the wall beside all my news clippings.

She read the autograph on the picture out loud. "'To Joe, with all my love, Jane.'"

"That's Henry Fonda's little girl. An actress."

"She's very pretty. Where did you meet her?"

"I didn't. The caption is a joke. One of my army buddies in West Germany sent it to me. Forged the signature, too.

His regiment picked her as their pin-up girl of the year, so she sent them all copies of that photo."

Carol turned from Jane back to me. "I keep forgetting you were a soldier."

I snorted. "I'm not sure I ever was. The officers had their doubts, too. But I was in the army, I'll admit that."

She made a wide circle around the mattress on the floor. I had never bothered to buy a bed. "Who are you calling?"

"A cop I know in Los Angeles. Maybe he can help find Coffey's relatives. Want some tea?"

"That would be nice, thanks. Here, I'll put the water on."

I dialed the number. "No answer. It's around eleven there. He's out late, for him."

"Maybe you can call him in the morning."

"I guess I'll have to."

She had placed two of my unmatched china cups on the counter and now she shifted them around, as if there were some perfect arrangement to be found. "Where did you and Officer Levy go? If you don't mind telling me."

"I don't mind." I told her about our encounter with Tom Paxton at the Bag of Nails.

"Is Tom a suspect too, then?"

"I asked Aaron that. He's going to check that poker game, but, assuming it checks out, why would Tom return to the Beggar at eight in the morning? Plus, there's no smell of a motive there. He was more successful than Dean, anyway."

"Tom couldn't kill anyone," Carol said. "He wrote *The Marvelous Toy*."

I puzzled over that one for a moment. "Come again? People who write children's songs are automatically incapable of murder?"

Carol laughed, showing her pretty throat. "Oh, you know what I mean. He's such a sweet guy."

"What bothered Aaron more was that Dean had called Paxton earlier to tell him he'd be at the Bag of Nails. So who else did he call?"

"Oh," said Carol. "I see."

"And anyone who came there might have knocked at the door of the Beggar, or Dean could have seen them through the glass door and invited them in. If Dean spotted them on the way up the stairs they would have never reached the bar, so the fact that Les didn't see them wouldn't prove anything."

She frowned. "But no one would have come after two when the bar closed. So why didn't Dean die until morning?"

"Good question. I'll have to ask Aaron that."

"The water's ready. Tea coming up."

I watched her leaning over to pour water into the cups. At the club she had changed from her waitress uniform into a white and blue dress. Her blond hair tumbled down around the blue collar, looking so much prettier than when it was up—

What the hell was I doing?

There was only one chair at the miniscule kitchen table. I turned around my desk chair and, hey presto, it was a second kitchen chair. The place was that small.

We sat opposite each other and she smiled. "How's your head?"

"The bump is almost gone. It's as good as it ever was, which isn't saying much, I guess."

"Don't put yourself down, Joe." Her face and tone were serious. "You don't deserve it."

I fiddled with my teabag. "Did I ever thank you for visiting me in the hospital?"

"Yes, you did. I'm just glad you're all right."

"How about you? Are you okay? About the Dean Coffey thing, I mean. It upset everybody."

"It was awful," Carol agreed. "Dean being dead was bad enough, but what's worse is the way everyone is behaving now. Suspicion. And anger."

I nodded. "Yeah. If we only knew *why* it happened—"

"I've tried to figure it out," she said, and sipped tea. "Tried to think about whether the attack on Seamus is tied up in it. But I can't think while I work. Sometimes I think pinning up my hair shuts down my brain."

I laughed. "I don't know about that," I heard myself saying, "but your hair is a lot prettier down."

She smiled. "You think so?"

"You have beautiful hair. Didn't anyone ever tell you that?"

"Well, *you* never did."

Something popped into my head. "*Be handsome, boss....*'" I muttered.

"What, Joe?"

"Oh, something Katy said the other day. *Be handsome, boss, and let who would be clever.* She was obviously quoting someone and I meant to ask her who."

"That's Don Marquis. From the book *archy and mehitabel*. It should be written out without capitals and punctuation."

"Free verse?"

"Something like that." She studied me, her forehead wrinkling. Is something wrong, Joe? You're a million miles away."

Like hell I was. I was sitting a foot away from a beautiful woman, and I was acutely aware of the fact. I dropped my hand on the table and it landed on hers. It was a small table.

She didn't move it away. Neither did I.

"Carol...." My voice sounded hoarse and unnatural.

"Yes?"

"You know about Sovay."

"Yes, I do." Her calm blue eyes never left mine. "And I know that she's in England and I'm right here."

"I can't make any promises."

Carol smiled. "My mother always said that that's the mark of an honest man."

Chapter 26

Lord, I'm exhausted," I said. "Did you learn all that in Buffalo?"

Carol laughed. "What else is there to do up there?"

The morning sun pouring down on the mattress felt good. *Everything* felt good.

I leaned over and kissed her. "What brought you down from Buffalo, anyway? Other than the hope of meeting me, anyway."

"Isn't that enough?" She patted me on the chest. "Seriously, the only work I could find up there was waitressing. I figured if I was going to do for a living I could find someplace more interesting to do it. Also, my parents disapproved of New York. That was a big part of the attraction."

"Rebel without a cause. What were your parents like?"

She frowned at the ceiling. "Ever see the painting *American Gothic*?"

"Very funny."

"No, I mean it. They weren't farmers and they didn't look like those two, but they have that...stiffness. Not just in the way they stood, but the way they thought, and lived. My father is a teacher. Mom's just a housewife, of course. They think I should be married and having children by now."

I sat up. "Uh, that reminds me. I forgot to ask—"

"It's okay. I use birth control." She patted my chest. "But thanks for asking."

I thought I was a little too late to deserve any credit, but I didn't argue.

"What about you?" she asked.

"Did *I* use...."

"No, silly. How did you wind up in Greenwich Village? You grew up in Pittsburgh, right?"

"Just outside, yeah. I'm surprised you knew that."

"So, why aren't you working in a steel mill?"

"Well, let me see. I joined the army right out of high school. Landed in Berlin a few months before Khrushchev started to build the wall."

Her eyes went wide. "Really? Wow. What was that like?"

I gave it some thought. "Scary and stupid."

"Scary I get, but stupid?"

I shrugged. "That little slice of city is right in the middle of a different country. Four different armies run it, none of them belonging to the countries involved. The whole thing is nuts.

"And the weirdest thing is that whenever anything happened anywhere in the world, it changed the mood in Berlin. Like Berlin was a tiny scale model of the world."

Carol frowned. "I don't get it."

"If Kennedy dropped in the polls back home, security tightened. If Khrushchev condemned our policy in Southeast Asia, the checkpoints slowed down. Crazy.

"And all the time people kept hemorrhaging out of the East." I fumbled on the floor for my cigarettes. I hadn't talked about this stuff in a long time. I tried telling my brother once and we wound up in a huge argument. And the folk scene didn't exactly encourage swapping old army stories.

"Mostly I felt like I was living in a hallucination. Worse, it was someone *else's* hallucination."

"Were you there when the wall went up?"

I nodded. "In some places it isn't a wall, you know. It's buildings. I saw them bricking up the windows in an apartment house on Bernauer Street, blocking off the side that faced the west. While they bricked up the lower floors people were jumping out of the top windows, holding onto mattresses."

"God."

I looked down at my cigarette. "One day that summer, while the Berlin Wall was going up, my unit was called out in full combat gear. The middle of a bright sunny afternoon in that thousand-year-old city and we were charging straight into combat."

"Why? What happened?"

"The Russians tried to change the rules. The rules set up after the war—fifteen years before—said anybody in a military vehicle could cross to any part of the city. Our side sent cars into East Berlin all the time, mostly to challenge them, I guess."

"So one day they accepted the challenge?"

"Exactly. A U.S. military vehicle tried to pass through at Friedrichstrasse without showing their papers. The East Germans detained them. That's when *we* got called out in our tanks. Christ."

My hands were shaking. I put the cigarette down in the ashtray.

"I remember staring over the Wall and thinking: so this is how the world ends. A bunch of cavemen in fancy dress, throwing rocks at each other."

"But somebody backed down," said Carol.

"Yeah, the East Germans. It was a great victory, the brass told us. Our generals were walking on air."

"Generals," said Carol. She shrugged eloquently.

"Yeah. Well, some of my brother soldiers seemed to think it all made sense, too. Stupidity isn't confined to the top ranks, I guess.

"Me, I couldn't begin to make sense of it. My high school education hadn't given me any way to wrestle with the whole scene at all. Then, a week later I had dinner at a friend's place. He and his wife had a nice little flat in the married soldiers' quarters.

"We were drinking beer and playing some records. I wasn't really listening, and then suddenly I heard something that caught me, held me completely."

I closed my eyes, remembering. "These people were singing about American history, the Revolution and the Civil War, and tying it all to McCarthyism and the Cold War, too. They sang everything I was thinking. They saw all the same craziness I did, and yet they were *optimistic*."

I shrugged. "It was the Weavers singing *Wasn't That A Time*?"

"A great song," said Carol.

"It sure beat the pimply love songs on the radio. My buddy told me it was folk music. I said, no it wasn't. Folk music was *Jimmy Crack Corn*, and crap like that."

Carol laughed. "What did he say to that?"

"He asked if I had ever really *listened* to *Jimmy Crack Corn*. Because it's about a black slave rejoicing that his owner is dead."

Her pretty forehead wrinkled. "Really?"

"Oh, yes. And some versions hint that the slave had something to do with the death. Of course, they didn't teach us that in Penn Hills High. I guess they were afraid it might have made the songs too interesting."

"God forbid."

"So my friend Keith and his wife started to introduce me to Seeger, Guthrie, Gibson, Houston. It was all that kept me sane that year, while we watched the Russians walling us in. When I got out of the army, naturally I headed for New York."

"How did your family feel about that?'

"My mother passed away when I was a kid. My Dad died while I was in Germany. The only relative I have left is my brother Jack, and we don't get along too well."

"No? Why not?"

I sighed. "He's ten years older than me. Fought in Korea." I sat up, the better to face her. "Explain this to me, would you? Jack fought in the Korean War, which from everything I hear was a pretty stupid event from start to finish. I served in Berlin, which, from the outside anyway, looked like a decent and honorable thing to be doing.

"Yet Jack believes in the U.S. of A., the army, apple pie, the whole nine yards. He belongs to the John Birch Society, for God's sake. And me, I came to the conclusion that all the major players are fit only for straitjackets."

Carol nodded. "So your question is..."

"Why did each of us end up thinking the way we did?"

She frowned. "Ten years is a big difference in age."

"Yeah, but that big? Sometimes I feel like we're a hundred years apart. Anyway, Jack is on the West Coast now, so there's no family reason for me to go back to Pennsylvania. Instead, I came here to the Village, and I met Max just as he was getting ready to open the Riding Beggar. And the rest is show biz."

"That reminds me," said Carol. The blanket had slipped down over her pretty, pale breasts and she tugged it back up. "When Max visited you in the hospital he said something that confused me."

"Oh? What was that?"

"He was talking about the police keeping the club closed; you didn't seem to be concerned. He said: 'What's the matter? It's not your half of the boat that's sinking?'"

"That's an old left-wing joke. When the ship of state is in trouble the rich say 'Why should we help bail? It's not....'"

"I understand that," said Carol. "But in the context, it sounded as if he were saying you were his partner, not his employee."

I stubbed out my cigarette, giving me a chance to look away for a second. "You're pretty observant, aren't you? I'll have to be careful not to leave any love letters from Joan Baez or Liz Taylor lying around."

"Meaning?"

"Meaning you're right. When I got here Max was looking for capital to set up the Beggar. And Max being Max, he wanted a working partner, not a bank."

Where had the cigarette package gone? The problem with having the whole floor as a night table was the way things wandered around. Sometimes I thought the cockroaches— insanely large in the Village—carried things off.

"Remember, I told you my father died while I was in the service. He left all his money to me, essentially the value of the house in Pittsburgh. He explained in his will that my brother could take care of himself, but that I needed help."

Carol's eyes grew wide. "That must have hurt."

"No. Big brother Jack agreed with him. Told me to keep the cash and try to make something of myself."

"I didn't mean your brother. It must have hurt *you*. Didn't it?"

I looked at the ceiling. "I kept the money. Invested it in a half interest in the Riding Beggar."

"But everyone thinks you're just the manager and Max owns the place."

"That suits us both fine. Max likes to come off as absolute dictator. And this way, when some buddy wants special treatment I can blame my decision on Max. 'Sorry, but the boss says no.'"

"Okay," said Carol. "I can see that."

"Besides, if people knew we were partners, they'd run between us like kids between parents, you know? If Daddy says no, ask Mommy."

"Does anyone else know about this?"

"Only Max's lawyer. I haven't even told…." I stopped.

"Sovay. It's okay; you can say her name. But why did you tell me?"

"You tricked it out of me." I rolled over and kissed her. "Spy."

"Rubbish. You wouldn't tell me anything you didn't want to. You were just trying to impress me with how important you are."

"Did I succeed?"

She kissed me. "Oh, you're very important. To me, especially."

I looked into those sweet blue eyes and something made me move away. *Too fast, too fast.*

"Which reminds me, I was going to make a phone call." I got up and walked over to the wall where the phone hung.

"Oh, that's right. The L.A. policeman."

I got through to the LAPD and asked to speak to Sergeant Talley.

"How you doin', little brother?" he said, his familiar voice as nasal and breathless as ever. "Still hanging out with the beatniks and the ballet boys?"

"I'm just fine, Jack. How's Dolly?"

"Sweet as sugar. She's wondering when you're gonna leave pinko heaven long enough to visit us, but other than that, she's normal. Can't that kibbutz get along without you for a week?"

"I doubt it," I told him. "The crops are failing. We probably shouldn't have tried to grow pineapples."

"Hah. The only crops that flourish in Manhattan are the kind you smoke, and I don't mean tobacco. Is it true what I read about reefer back there?"

"Beats me, Jack. I stick to Pall Malls, like a good boy."

Carol was lying belly down, facing me, up on her elbows. I was suddenly aware that I was naked.

"I'll bet," said my brother. "You want something, kid, or are you just trying to help the bad guys get a head start on me?"

"I want something."

"Natch. What?"

"A friend of mine died here last week." I spelled Dean's name. "I think he had relatives in California but I haven't been able to find any. Think you'd have better luck?"

"Beats the hell out of me. These people are in L.A.?"

"No, Willow Creek." I thought about *The Grace to Kill.* "And I think his father may be in a V.A. home."

"Jeez. Where is Willow Creek? I never heard of it."

"It should be somewhere in Southern California. I know he grew up in San Diego. But if it's too much trouble—"

"Take it easy, Little Joe. It's no trouble. I know your hillbilly music doesn't pay you enough to fly out and do your own dirty work. Even though we have a spare room and Dolly would love to see you...."

"I hear you, Jack. Just see what you can do, okay?"

"Sure, kid. It'll be tomorrow, okay?"

"That's great. Thanks a lot. And say hi to Johnny for me."

"Will do. And hey, I'm sorry about your friend."

I hung up. Carol was still watching me.

"That was my brother."

"So I gathered. And Johnny?"

"John the third. My nephew. He's...." I calculated as I sat back down on the mattress. "Five years old. Time flies."

"Speaking of which, I'm going to be late. She turned away from me, reaching for her underwear, which was lying on the floor.

I put my hand on her hip. "Are you in a hurry?"

"Me? Oh, no." She cuddled back against my chest. "No hurry at all."

CHAPTER 27

About time you got here," Max growled. "Even the waitresses beat you."

"Sorry, Boss. I overslept."

"I guess you're still recovering from that crack on the head, but don't think you can use that excuse forever. Okay, I want you to—Hey, are you listening?"

I wasn't. Carol had passed by and I was grinning at her like an idiot. She gave me a small smile and walked off to set up tables.

"Sorry, Max. I'm all ears."

"You and the other donkeys. I want you to go see Von Ehmsen. He's been nagging me to send you over."

"Von? What about?"

"The security meeting, remember? You promised to go and then got yourself concussed to get out of it."

"Oh, lord. I forgot all about it. Do I have to do it, Max?"

"He'll be broken-hearted if you don't. Von says you're the mascot for the whole group now. After our little break-in a whole bunch of club owners decided they wanted to join the talk about security."

"Locking the barn door," I muttered.

"Well, at least part of the horse is still here." He patted me on the shoulder.

•

Walking south to the Café Rafio reminded me of taking that same route with Dean one Saturday morning a few weeks before. It was a chilly February morning and we had stopped at a pretzel cart for a couple of hot ones when Dean said: "Christ, what is that? A victory parade?"

About twenty NYU students were walking—no, marching—across Washington Square. All of the marchers were men, but a few girls walked beside the group, cheering them on.

I stared at the apparition for a minute, and then I got it. "It must be the Kennedy challenge thing."

"Somehow I missed this tidbit. What's a Kennedy challenge?"

"It seems JFK read about an army in Roosevelt's time— Teddy, not Franklin—that walked fifty miles in fifteen hours. Kennedy asked his army, which as far as I know is also *our* army, to try the same thing. And the idea has caught on."

"Caught on? How?"

"Like the hula hoop, that's how. Secretaries and executives and boy scouts have joined the party. Even little Bobby, the boy Attorney General. But this is the first time I've seen it in the Village."

"Man, what you miss not reading the newspapers." Dean threw his napkin into the trash. "I hope those strikers win soon and get back to publishing. I miss the *Post*. As Phil said, without the press, what are we gonna do for song material?"

"You think there's a song in that?" I asked, gesturing to the marchers, who were struggling back toward the NYU campus.

"Christ, yes," said Dean with a gleam in his eye. "Look at it this way, Joe. Three years ago we elected that spoiled Boston rich kid to get this country moving again. What happened to all those wonderful progressive programs of his?"

"Congress shot them all to hell."

"Exactly." He tugged on the front of his corduroy jacket, a little gesture he had when the juices were flowing. "So instead of moving forward, Jack's got us all marching in fifty-mile circles. Don't tell me I can't get a song out of that. I just hope I get it written before Paxton or Ochs does it."

"I didn't know you were so competitive."

He laughed. "I wish I *was*. Competitive, I mean. I can't keep up with those guys on the topical stuff. Ochs reads a news story and has two verses and a chorus before he turns the page."

Dean grinned and raised his hands in a helpless gesture. "I write too slow, that's my problem. I'm always a war late and an outrage behind."

•

I stood in MacDougal Street, thinking about it. He was never going to write that song about the marchers, or thousands of other songs, and I was never going to get to hear them.

Some bastard had turned off the mic in the middle of his show.

Why kill the singer, I wondered. Why leave me alive, a possible witness? There were plenty of people who would have said kill the club manager and let the artist live.

Von Ehmsen was waiting for me in the office of the Café Rafio, puffing on a rank cigar. "Joe! Damn good to see you. How's the head?"

"Throbbing. How are you?"

"Not bad, not bad. The Beggar's open for business again, right? I tried to talk your boss into keeping it dark for a while."

"For Pete's sake, why?"

"Improvements. Max had to bring in people to clean the stage, right? Why not tear out that rat-trap office at the same time and put in some more tables? A golden chance to improve the place. Golden, man."

"I take it you're bullish on folk music, Von."

"Hell, no." He waved the cigar for emphasis. "I don't give a fraction of a fig whether they hang Tom Dooley or not, Talley. I'm strictly jazz. But I believe in this crazy Village. It's booming and we gotta boom with it."

"So you're building?"

"You bet I am. I own the building next door and I've got walls to knock down, people to evict. Bigger and better bunkers for badder and bolder beats." He was lighting another cigar. "You want one?"

"No, thanks." The smell of his was making my head ache. "You called me here to talk about security."

"Bingo. Thanks for reminding me. I got so many ideas in this skull it's hard to keep 'em all straight."

He filled me in on Sunday's meeting, which didn't sound more productive than the usual group brainbust. I promised to show up for the next one.

"Cool. We can use you, Joe boy. Damn good thing they didn't crack your egg for good." He paused. "Have the boys in blue found those jokers yet?"

"Not as far as I know. But what makes you say *jokers*? More than one, I mean?"

Von Ehmsen raised his eyebrows. "Dunno. Guess I figured that burglars work in gangs. Isn't that how it works in the movies?"

"I don't think they were robbers. I think whoever it was came there just to kill Dean."

He stood up, shaking his head. "Not a chance, Talley. People don't rob cafés to commit murder. They break in to steal things. Just like has been happening all over the Village this year."

"Oh hell." The dawn finally broke. "You *want* it to be that way, don't you? And you don't want the guys to be caught."

Von Ehmsen's beard parted in an enigmatic smile. "Why would you say that, Joey?"

I liked being called Joey almost as much as I liked being called Talley-man. "Because if the club owners think the robbers are killing people more of them will be scared into joining your little committee."

Waving his cigar, Von Ehmsen said, "Never crossed my mind."

"Right. I suppose you want Seamus to join, too."

"I did. I asked him to come to the first meeting, but he said he was sick of the Village. So to hell with him."

I sat up straight. "You talked to Seamus? When was that?"

"A week ago?" Von Ehmsen frowned. "He was getting out of a cab at his apartment. Told me he'd just gotten out of the hospital. I asked him to come to our meeting but he said he was heading straight home to Ireland."

I thought about that. It confirmed what Frank Renard and I had suspected. "Was anyone with him, Von?"

"Nope. Why all this interest in Seamus?"

"Well, he disappeared without saying anything to anyone."

Von Ehmsen shook his head. "Nothing mysterious. He just lost his taste for the New World when he got beaten up. You see, Joe…." He leaned back, comfortably, ready to launch into his favorite subject. "That's what I've been telling you. Telling *everybody*. We need to protect the Village. Our customers will stay away if they think the place is too risky."

"Okay, okay. I'll come to the meeting. But humor me for a minute. If the killer was aiming for Dean, do you have any idea why?"

He fiddled with his cigar and looked at the ceiling. "You playing cop, Joey?"

"Just wondering who bopped me on the head."

"See? Just like Seamus. This sort of thing preys on your mind. But I still think it was a robber."

"But if it *wasn't*...."

"Yeah, yeah. If you had three apples and I had two oranges.... I was never good at hypothetical equations. I hardly knew the Coffey kid. He only dropped in here a few times."

"I'm surprised he came at all. Jazz wasn't his thing."

"Well, he always came with some of the old beat crowd, I guess."

That made sense. "Sure. Gus and company. He dated her for a while."

"Yeah, Gus. And Frank Renard, the radio guy." Von Ehmsen snapped his fingers. "That reminds me. If you see Gus, tell her Braubinger is looking for her."

"What for?"

"No idea. Maybe he thinks she knows Ed Sullivan. Ever notice how Bob thinks you are absolutely fascinating until he decides you don't have any important connections you can introduce him to?"

"He's a little transparent," I agreed.

"Window glass is concrete compared to Braubinger."

"That reminds me. What do you know about Dean's demo tape?"

"Didn't know he had one. Why?"

"It's disappeared."

"The hell you say." He looked at his cigar as if he could read the answer in the smoke. "That's peculiar, son."

I decided to make one last try. "So you have no idea who might have wanted him dead?"

Von Ehmsen grinned. "I never heard him play, but if he was like most of your crowd, maybe the killer was a music critic."

CHAPTER 28

I heard the door to the supply room open and then slam shut. I pushed away from Carol. "Was that—"

"Max," she said. "He saw us kissing, Joe."

"Hell. Now I'll be getting a lecture."

"I better go back to waiting tables." She paused at the door. "Want to come over tonight?"

"Love to."

I waited a minute and then followed her to the front room. Katy Poe was on stage, opening for Pete LaFarge, the excellent singer and songwriter Matty had been sneering about Friday. Pete did have a drinking problem, but he had looked sober as a judge when he walked in that night.

I had talked to Katy about the cops when she came in. "They wanted to *guard* me, can you believe it? Like I'm some Mafia parakeet."

"Canary. Remember, Katy, you played that night with Dean and Seamus. Seamus was attacked and Dean was killed."

Katy had shaken her head. "I just don't believe it, Joe. If anybody was after me, they had almost a whole week before Dean got back from California. I was around. Hell, I never go anywhere. Except on stage."

She was on stage now, singing *Blow Away the Morning Dew*:

If you meet a lady gay
As you go by the hill,
And if you will not when you may,
You may not when you will.

"Joe," said Max. "Can I see you for a minute?"

With a sigh, I followed him back to his office. He sat down at the desk and fiddled with some papers. All I could see was the bald spot in his gray hair. I sat in the old leather chair he'd picked up at some long ago rent party where someone was desperate enough to start selling off furniture.

"Who's the best Negro folksinger in the city?"

That caught me flatfooted. "The best? I don't know. Lou Gossett, Jr. maybe. Why?"

"Figure out who it is and hire 'em. I've been looking at our performer's list. The mayor of Selma, Alabama would feel right at home in this joint. Goddamn it, I miss Josh White. I miss Leadbelly."

My diagnosis was that he missed Al Perkins. "Okay, Boss. Will do. Anything else?"

"Yeah." He looked up and glared at me. "Can't keep your hands off the staff, can you?"

"Meaning what?"

"First a singer. Now a waitress. You gonna work your way through every female in the joint?"

I had known it was coming, but I lost my temper anyway. "Dammit, that's unfair and you know it. Sovay was more than a year ago. And Carol and I—"

"Yeah?"

"We're not hurting anybody."

Max slammed a drawer shut. "Didn't I tell you, back when we started this madhouse, *don't* get involved with the workers? The opportunity for exploitation—"

"Is that what's bothering you? Exploitation of the working class? You think Carol has to screw me to keep her job?"

Max stood up. He was red in the face and I thought he was probably counting to ten before he spoke. "At least once a week the waitresses disagree about who works which shifts. Am I right?"

"More or less. So?"

"So one day Carol is going to come to you and say she and Janet or Melissa are fighting over who works next Wednesday. Which is the night you and she are supposed to go dancing or something. And then what happens?"

I thought about it. "Hell."

"And if the girls find out, well. They can be cruel, you know."

I knew. I rubbed my forehead, where an ache was beginning to form. "Life is too damned complicated."

Max snorted. "You finally figured that out, did you? Better late than never."

And I had thought Sovay was my only worry. I stared at the ceiling for a while. "What do you suggest?"

"Break up with her."

I shook my head.

He sighed. "Didn't think so. Whatever rotten qualities you have, I never thought you were the overnight type. Well then, here's what we can do."

He leaned across the desk his voice urgent. "Fire Carol. You can make up an excuse, blame it all on me."

I was flabbergasted. "You don't mean that."

"Sure I do. She can get a job somewhere else; we'll give her a good reference. God knows there are lots of places around here looking for good waitresses. That way you can keep dating her. Like I said, Joe, blame it on the boss."

"She knows we're partners."

He raised his eyebrows. "How did she…Never mind. Pillow talk. Jesus."

"Look, I just don't think—"

"It could still work. I don't suppose you showed her our contract, did you? Tell her I've got exclusive rights to hire and fire. She'll work somewhere else and everybody's happy."

"No, Max. I won't do it."

"No? Why not?"

"I won't fire Carol—Hell, I wouldn't fire *anybody* just for my convenience. It stinks."

"So be it." Max waved a hand like a man weighing something. "Then it's up to *you* to protect Carol's feelings, and her reputation. *Also* to make sure the work gets done and the waitresses don't start catfighting."

I grinned. "Sounds like I'm doing all the work, as usual."

"Get out."

At the door I stopped and looked back at him. "If I had said 'sure, I'll go ahead and fire her,' would you have really gone along with it?"

Max peered at me over his bifocals. "What do you think?"

"Come on. Honest, now. What would you have done if I said it was okay to fire her?"

He shrugged and turned back to his desk. "Lost all my respect for you, for a start."

CHAPTER 29

That night, I discovered Carol's deepest secret.

It felt strange, walking back to Waverly Place with her after the club closed. We were talking about Pete LaFarge's wonderful song *The Ballad of Ira Hayes*, about the Indian who had helped raise the flag at Iwo Jima, and later drank himself to death. It was just like any of the other nights I walked Carol home.

Except this night I was holding her hand. This night I wouldn't leave her at the door and travel on to my place.

How many times in all those months had she asked me up for coffee or a drink? Katy and Matty Mark were right: I was an idiot.

We walked up two flights. She opened the door and I got my shock. "*This* is your place? My God."

She looked around. "What? What's wrong?"

"Wrong? Nothing. But it's not an apartment, it's a library."

"Oh." Her voice was soft. "Too many books."

Every bit of available wall space was filled with bookcases. Cheap do-it-yourself shelves filled with paperbacks, new-hardcovers, and crumbling leather-bound books.

She had more books than Max had records, and Max had gotten most of his for free.

"I just wasn't expecting it, Carol. Where did you get them all?"

"The city is full of used bookstores. Can I get you a drink, Joe?" She was flustered and I don't suppose I was helping.

"A drink? No, I'm fine. I just—how many of these have you read?" I looked at a few of the books lying out on a table: Heinlein. Camus. Chandler. Kerouac, naturally. Some names I had never heard of: De Beauviour. And a hardcover, obviously brand-new, called *The Feminine Mystique*.

Probably about make-up, I figured. I thought about telling her, gallantly, that that was one book she didn't need. In a rare moment of discretion, I decided to leave it alone.

"I've read some of them, most of them. I don't know." She was blushing. I guess *brainy* was not the adjective a girl wanted to be known by in 1963.

She put her arms around me. "Hey, did you come here to assess my collection?"

I grinned and kissed her. "No, lady. That's not what I came here for."

She should have used one of those books to prop up her bed frame. It wobbled.

•

The phone woke us at six A.M. Carol grunted and found the Princess phone on her night table. "'Lo?"

I was drifting back to sleep when she grabbed my shoulder. "Joe. Wake up!"

"What? What is it?"

"Its Gus. She sounds awful. Something's wrong."

I sat up, leaning over her, trying to hear. All I could pick out was music. Classical, I thought.

"Gus," Carol was saying. "Gus, it's me. What's wrong?"

"Damn it," I said. "Is there another phone?"

She shook her head. "She's not making sense, Joe. Listen, Gus. Turn down the music, okay? I can't hear you."

We were sitting on the edge of the bed, trying to hold the phone so we could both hear. That didn't work and I finally won the tug of war.

"Gus, this is Joe Talley."

"Killed him," she was saying. Her voice was slurred, like she'd gone off the wagon, big time.

Christ.

"Killed who, Gus?" I asked. Carol's eyes went wide.

"I killed…."

I held my breath.

"Everything is like that. Everything. Jealousy is at the root of it all. The dying and the killing. *Is that right?*"

"Gus, don't do anything. I'll be right over. Do you hear me?"

"Dean," she said. "Dean Coffey. Where was he? Where was Dean?"

And then she hung up.

CHAPTER 30

Dawn was showing its face over the roofs as Carol and I ran the five blocks up Ninth Street. By the end I was gasping and thinking of Kennedy and his fifty mile marches. Good for endurance, if nothing else.

Gus Adler lived in a brownstone building, almost across the street from Dean Coffey's apartment. I pushed the buzzer for her apartment. "No answer. Do I start waking people?"

"Wait a minute," said Carol, digging through her purse. "That key ring she gave us. She said it was her extra keys. Maybe—here it is."

The third key did the trick. We pushed into the lobby, which was done in shabby tile from the 1920s.

"Top floor," said Carol. She had been there before.

Gus's door was gray, which reminded me of her salt-and-pepper hair. I rang the bell, then knocked. "Gus? You there? It's Carol and Joe."

No answer.

"Maybe she was calling from somewhere else," said Carol.

"Maybe so," I said. "But—"

"We still need to find out," she finished.

This time the second key worked. The door opened into darkness. I slid my hand along the wall until I found a light switch.

We were in a wide foyer, facing an overstuffed armchair and an old-fashioned umbrella stand. There was a closet on the left and a small kitchen on the right. Beyond the kitchen was a living room full of Victorian furniture. More big wing chairs, tables with clawed feet. I felt like I had walked into a Charles Addams cartoon.

"Gus?" Carol called. "Anyone home?"

I was having a hard time breathing. The last time I had walked through a room calling and getting no answer somebody broke a bottle over my head.

"Look, Joe," said Carol. There was a line of light at the far end of the room, a crack under the door.

"What room is that?" I asked. We were both whispering now.

"The bedroom, I think."

"Okay, stand back."

I stepped forward and knocked on the door. "Gus?"

I turned the knob slowly, opened the door even more so. Another room full of antiques. The acrid smell of marijuana filled the air. A single bed lay against the far wall, and a reading lamp hung above it, providing the only light.

She lay on the bed, face up, head on her pillow. She wore a lacy white nightgown, romantic as one of Katy's old ballads.

Her right arm hung over the side of the bed. As I stepped closer I kicked something that was nestled against the sheets tangled on the floor.

It was a gun.

Footsteps behind me. It was lucky that Carol spoke up or I might have had a heart attack. "Joe, is she…."

"I think so. Let's look—Oh, damn."

Her long hair had covered the hole in her right temple. Squatting down I could see the drops of blood, blood and dark gray—

"Oh God," said Carol, and ran off to the bathroom.

I knew I should follow her, comfort her, but I wasn't sure I could walk. I could have used some comfort myself.

The phone lay at Gus's side, near an ashtray with the remains of several homemade cigarettes. I reached for the phone and thought better of it. Instead, I stood up, took a few deep breaths and went back to the living room. There was another phone on the wall. I called the police.

CHAPTER 31

Mother of God," said Guareschi. "It's a simple question. Did she or didn't she?"

I wanted to say that it was the questioner that was simple, not the question. I sighed instead. "I didn't hear her say it. If Carol says—"

"She didn't hear it either. Mother of God." Guareschi shook his head in disgust. He was wearing a brown checked suit today, neatly pressed, but with cigars bulging in the jacket pocket. "Somebody calls up to confess to a murder and you two are too busy playing telephone to notice."

"I told you what she—"

"Oh, yeah." He picked up a notebook. "I kill. We all kill. He was killed. This isn't a confession. It's—" He looked at Levy, who was slouched against the living room wall of Gus's apartment. "What do you do to a verb?"

"Conjugate it."

"Bingo. She called up to conjugate verbs at you. Is that your theory?"

"How the hell do I know why she called?" I asked. I was sitting in a wing chair that made me think of my Grandmother's house, back in Pittsburgh. Nobody had wanted the furniture when she died. The thrift shop had wound up with it all.

Who would get Gus's things?

Carol was still in the kitchen where Guareschi had been asking her questions while Levy grilled me.

It struck me as pathetic and futile. What could they ask us? What could we answer?

"Did she *say* she killed Dean Coffey?"

"No. She said she killed, that's all. I asked who, but she was talking about something else already. Then she mentioned that Dean was dead."

"What about hitting you on the head?"

"She never mentioned that."

"Did she say she was going to kill herself?"

"No." I hesitated. "But she spoke about jealousy."

Guareschi frowned. "What does that have to do with anything?"

"Gus was obsessed with the idea of jealousy. She thought it was the root of most of the world's problems. She—" I bit it off.

"She what?"

"She once said she would kill herself if she were as jealous as Irene Fox."

The cop snorted. Apparently he didn't think much of that as a motive. Neither did I, really.

"The music playing behind her call. What was it?"

"I have no idea. Something classical. There was an orchestra."

He dug back in the notebook. "Your girlfriend says it was Tchaikovsky's Fifth Symphony." He shrugged. "She probably read that off the top record on the stack when you got here."

I didn't bother to reply. If Carol said she recognized the piece of music then she had. I was trying to get over being surprised by the variety of things she knew.

Levy walked into the bedroom, which was still crowded with technicians. In a minute the record player started up.

"Was that what you heard over the phone?" asked Guareschi.

I shrugged. "Could be. Orchestral stuff all sounds alike to me."

Levy had stepped into the kitchen. Now he came back and nodded to his partner. Apparently Carol had confirmed that the music was the same.

"What's the point of all this?" I asked. "She killed herself, right?"

"Looks that way," said Guareschi. "She puffed a few sticks of reefer until she felt nice and rotten. She called your girlfriend and had a nice little chat with each of you—"

Levy grunted. He was back at his post against the wall.

The sergeant looked at him. "Something?"

"Maybe she didn't expect to find the two of them shacking up. If jealousy was her big hang-up, maybe that's what pushed her over."

"Now, wait a minute," I said. "That shacking up crack—"

"Could be," said Guareschi, ignoring me. "But none of it answers the big question: did she kill the folksinger?"

"Guilt would help explain the suicide," said Levy. "But it's not nailed down."

"Was it the same gun?" I asked.

"Don't know yet. It's the right caliber."

Guareschi got up without another word and headed toward the kitchen.

Levy sat down next to me on the couch. "I don't know about you, Joe. You keep walking in on death scenes. That's not good for your health."

I just looked at him.

"Did this Adler woman mean a lot to you? I keep hearing that she was eccentric, and to stand out as eccentric in the Village you have to be practically certifiable." He paused. "You take a vow of silence or something?'

"Shacking up?"

Levy grinned. "Didn't like that, huh? What shall we call it, then? Trysting? Pre-connubial bliss? I'd say free love but that's an oxymoron if I ever heard one."

"Goddamn it, Aaron. You had no right—"

"The hell I don't." His smile vanished. "You want me to go over to Miss Meisel's apartment right now? Check to see if there are sheets and pillow on the couch where you said you crashed for the night. Shall we do that?"

I shook my head angrily. "You act like this is some divorce case and you're a third-rate private eye hanging around a motel. What does any of this have to do with Gus's death?"

Levy shrugged. "It tells us that the two of you agreed to lie to the police. If you're lying about one thing we have to wonder what *else* you crazy kids have decided to fib to Mom and Dad about."

I thought about that.

"Either we can trust you or we can't, Joe."

"Hell."

"Protecting a lady's honor is nice, I suppose, but you should have thought of that before you went back to her place. We have to know what really happened."

"Okay," I said. "Forget the sofa. We were asleep in her bed when the phone rang. Everything else we said was true."

Levy nodded. "Good. I'll tell my boss that. It doesn't settle the main question, though."

"Whether Gus killed Dean."

"And herself, yeah."

I blinked. "Could this be anything but suicide?"

"You didn't hear the shot fired, did you?"

"No."

"Well, let's see." He folded up his notebook and tucked it carefully into a breast pocket of his white shirt. "Let's say there was somebody else here. I hear she shacked—Had a lot of gentlemen friends, right?"

"So I've heard."

"What about the bald guy? Ray Hegg. Wouldn't he be the most logical candidate?"

"They're good friends," I agreed. "But I don't think they've been lovers in years. If she has a current flame I don't know who it is."

"Well. Let's say she was here with somebody. She's stoned on reefer. Gets on this crazy jag about guilt and killing and calls you up…." He made a face. "That reminds me. We'll have to check to see if she called anyone else. If you hear that she did, let us know right away, okay?"

I nodded.

"Anyway, she hangs up on you and falls asleep. Just like we found her. But the other person takes the gun, puts it to her temple, and…." He shrugged.

"I don't believe it," I said. "Why would anyone—"

"To make it look like she killed Coffey. There's another way it could have happened too."

He pointed to the tape recorder on a table at the far end of the room. "Say she got stoned tonight, or *any* night in the past week and put her ramblings on tape, all about guilt and jealousy and Coffey getting murdered.

"Anyone who knew her habits could have come in while she slept and killed her. That little pistol wouldn't have made much noise against her temple. Then they stole the tape and played it over the phone to you and Miss Meisel."

"I don't know, Aaron. It didn't sound like a tape."

He was unimpressed. "You just woke up. Plus there was music playing. Did she answer any of your questions? Respond directly to anything you said?"

I tried to remember. "No. I thought she was in her own little world. She often was."

He shrugged. "Maybe she had already left our world."

"But why would anyone go to that trouble?"

"To set it up to be a murder/suicide by Miss Adler, rather than a double murder by someone else. Maybe to set a time for the death when they had an alibi, too."

I thought that one through. "The music we heard matched what was on her record player. Doesn't that prove the call came from here?"

Levy shrugged. "Tape recorders are wonderful things. The music could have been in the background when she recorded it, or the murderer could have recorded the music on a different tape. Even *after* the murder if his nerves were good enough. Or *her* nerves, of course. Do you know anyone who owns a tape recorder?"

I frowned. "Braubinger probably has half a dozen. He's always bragging about owning the latest gadgets. Katy Poe has none; she says she can't work the controls. Ray calls them soul-stealers; he doesn't own any. I have two."

"Yeah?" Levy had perked up. "Who knew you'd be at Miss Meisel's place?"

"Nobody."

He sighed. "Are we back to protecting her?"

"This is true, Aaron. Carol and I just started seeing each other."

"Is that so? Well, congratulations. Seems like a nice girl." He stood up. "I'll go see—"

"Detective." One of the technicians was calling from the other end of the living room. "You better take a look at this."

The technician had been sifting through a wastepaper basket from the bedroom, moving the contents into a bag, one piece at a time. Levy dropped easily to his knees and began examining something.

The two of them started talking. I couldn't hear what they were discussing but from the rising excitement it was clear they thought they had found treasure among the discarded tissues. After a minute Levy glanced back at me. "Take a look at this, Joe."

I walked over to Levy. He held out his own handkerchief, tightly wrapped around something small and flat. "Don't touch. It was stuck against the bottom of the can. Throwing out the garbage, you might miss it. Does it mean anything to you?"

It was a torn piece of cardboard, plain on one side. The other side was white and green, obviously part of a box of some kind. A page of typing had been pasted on the colored side.

Some of the words were legible:

White Wolf
The Grace to Kill
Let Me Take Your S
Lady Isabel and the
Francesca

I nodded. "I recognize it, all right. It's part of the cover from Dean Coffey's demo tape."

CHAPTER 32

No, I don't *recognize* it," said Carol. "But I can guess what it is."

Guareschi frowned at her. "Oh, you can, can you?"

"From the song titles, it has to be something to do with Dean Coffey." She looked at me. "Is it the cover of his demo tape?"

I nodded.

Guareschi turned around and started to drop his cigar butt into a trash can, then froze. The evidence he was examining had just come out of that can. He reached over Carol's shoulder and took an ashtray from the kitchen counter instead.

"That tape," he muttered. "How many copies of the thing were there?"

"Three," said Levy. "Two were stolen from Broker Records' offices on Long Island, and one was supposedly in Coffey's possession. He told Talley here he left it with a friend for safekeeping."

"Not a friend," I said. "A colleague."

Levy raised an eyebrow. "Does that make a difference?"

"There weren't a lot of people Dean would have called a friend. But he had plenty of colleagues. Almost any—" I stopped.

"Finish it," said Levy. "Any of the folksingers, right?"

I sighed. "Could be."

"How about the Adler dame?" asked Guareschi? "Could she have been a colleague?"

"I don't see how," I said.

He scowled. "Is there any way of knowing which copy of the tape that scrap was torn from?"

I shook my head.

"Then I guess I'm mistaken," said Carol. "I thought there was an autograph…."

"What?" snapped Guareschi. "What autograph?"

Carol was being delicate again, reminding me of something, while giving me a way out if I didn't want to mention it. Her tact was beginning to get on my nerves.

"She's right," I said. "Dean autographed the back of his own copy the day he got it. We were kind of drunk and he was practicing his signature for the backs of albums."

"So?"

"So we would see part of his signature if this were his copy. He wrote big."

The Sergeant sighed. "Well, that nails it for me. She stole the tapes from the offices of the record company. That could have been before or after she shot Coffey and busted your head. She destroyed the tapes and threw them away, but one scrap got stuck in the trash can."

"We're gonna have to search the trash bins in the basement," said Levy, sadly. "And me in my new sports coat."

"Do it." Guareschi turned to me. "Why would she destroy the tape? And what was she searching Coffey's room for?"

I didn't have to think long to come up with an answer. "If you assume jealousy was her motive for murder you can make it all fit."

"Meaning what? She was jealous of a tape?"

"There was a love song on it," said Carol. "*Francesca.*"

"Huh. And who was this Francesca?"

"I have no idea."

"Sergeant?" A voice called from the hallway. "We've got him, sir."

"Good." Guareschi showed a smile that was even nastier than Max's. "Bring him in here."

He turned back to us. "All right, you two. Make yourself scarce, but don't leave town. You out there, come in. Ah, it's the man of the hour. The star of *I've Got A Secret*."

Two cops in uniform had Ray Hegg by the shoulders. They pushed him roughly past us and into a chair in the living room.

CHAPTER 33

Carol and I passed Ray on our way out. He looked angry and confused.

When we reached the apartment's door I stepped aside and caught Carol by the arm. "Go on without me," I whispered. "I'll call you."

She opened her mouth, then thought better of it. With a nod, she stepped out and shut the door, loudly. I walked over to the big brown armchair in the foyer and sat down. My back was to the living room. I was out of Guareschi and Levy's line of sight.

A patrolman saw me. I gazed up at him, trying to look bored and irritated, a person being made to wait against his will. The cop didn't want to listen to me complain; he turned and walked on.

I could hear the voices in the living room.

"Where is she?" It was Ray speaking, but I barely recognized him. He sounded hoarse and tense, two qualities I didn't associate with the hipster chemist.

"You tell us, Mr. Hegg."

"Goddamn it, don't you play games with me. You mean she's missing?"

"You tell us," Guareschi repeated.

There was silence for a moment; Ray trying to think it through. "Is that why you dragged me down here, to ask me that? I don't know where she is."

"You have any idea why she'd run away, Mr. Hegg?"

"What? No. Hell, no. Why would she run?"

I heard the cop sigh. "When did you last see her?"

"Yesterday. Thursday. We had dinner together at the Keneret with Frank Renard."

"Who?" asked Guareschi.

"Frank Renard."

"He's on the radio," Levy explained.

"A disc jockey?" Guareschi asked.

"A raconteur," said Ray.

The sergeant sighed again. "And after dinner?"

There was a pause. "I don't know. We went home, I guess."

"You didn't go with her?"

"No. She said she was expecting company."

"Who?"

"She didn't say. Look what the hell is this about?"

"Did this other guy, Bernard—"

"Renard," said Levy.

"Right. Did Renard walk home with Miss Adler?"

"I don't think so. He was going off to do his show. Besides, Gus is a grown woman. She can walk home alone." His voice got higher. "Has something—something happened to her?"

Someone was pacing. Guareschi, from the sound of it. "Where did you go after dinner, Mr. Hegg?"

"I walked over to Christopher Street."

"What for?"

"The magazine store. I've got an article coming out in a chemistry journal."

"Was the journal in yet?'

"No, the owner thought it might be another week."

"This owner, would he remember you?"

"I don't know. I guess so. I'm a steady customer."

"So, where'd you go after that?"

"Home. Home to bed."

"Straight to bed?"

"What do you mean, straight? I wandered around. Who walks a straight line in Manhattan?"

"You didn't stop anywhere else? No more magazine shops?"

"No."

"And you got home when?"

"Around twelve-thirty."

"You sure of that, Ray?" Levy spoke up. "Sure you haven't forgotten an hour somewhere? It's been known to happen."

"Goddamn it, I told you—"

"You told us," snapped Guareschi. "You sure as hell did. First you told us that you and the Adler dame got home around nine A.M. on the day Coffey got killed. She agreed with whatever you said, but it was obvious she didn't know dawn from dinner."

"Now, just a—"

"Nine o'clock puts you both in the clear," said Levy. "Then it turns out an early riser across the hall here likes to spy on the comings and goings at Miss Adler's apartment. And she told us you were both there well before eight."

"I told you, that was an honest mistake."

"You told us," Guareschi repeated. "So, who were you covering for, Ray? Agustina or yourself?"

Silence.

Another cop walked in, frowned at me. I gave him the waiting room look and he walked on.

"Where is she?" asked Ray. His voice was a rasp. "I want to talk to her."

"We'll get to that," said Guareschi. "But first, talk to *us*. Who was she expecting to come over here last night?"

"I told you, dammit. I don't know!"

"Was it a lover?"

"I don't know!"

"Who is she seeing nowadays? Still you?"

"Not me. Nobody as far as I know."

"You sure?"

"Goddamn it, how many times do you want me to say the same thing?"

"Say something else," growled Guareschi. "Tell us why she hated Coffey."

"Hated? Gus didn't hate anyone."

"Then why did she tear up his demo tape?"

"She wouldn't...." Another pause. Then, softly: "So that's why...."

"What?" snapped Levy. "You just remembered something she said or did. You better come across with it. What was it?"

"Nothing." Ray's voice was stronger now. "Not a damned thing. What *is* this? Am I under arrest? What happened to lawyers and one phone call and all that crap? If you think I'm a crook, I want all the goddamned trimmings."

I had to grin. Ray was suddenly his old self. It sounded like he had decided to shut up and take whatever medicine they were ready to dish out, anything to protect Gus.

"You done talking?" asked Guareschi.

Silence.

"Too bad. I was hoping you could tell us where to find Miss Adler's next of kin."

"Next of—"

"She's dead, Ray. If you had told the truth she'd be safe in a jail cell, but thanks to you, she's dead. That's how much you helped her."

Long painful gasps, like a badly wounded man.

Levy spoke softly. "How did you know she killed him?"

"I didn't. I *don't.*"

"But you suspected?"

And Ray began to talk, at last. He had lied about the time, he said, to protect them both from annoyance. He knew he hadn't killed Coffey and was sure Gus hadn't, so what was wrong with a little white lie, to keep the cops away?

I shuddered, remembering the lie Carol and I had told about where we slept. We were lucky that one hadn't come back to haunt us.

"I was never sure she did it," Ray said. "I still don't *know*...Hell, I can't believe it."

I got up and walked out, not wanting to hear anymore.

Chapter 34

Goddamn it," Max said. "Gus? Oh, goddamn it." He was so choked up I could barely hear him through the phone. This time, it wasn't his lungs that were giving him trouble.

"Yeah," I said. I had called him as soon as I got back to my apartment.

"What a lousy thing." I didn't know whether he meant her death or the fact that she was a murderer. "Are they sure she killed him, Joe?"

"I think so, Max. When I left Guareschi sounded like he was playing the last chords."

"Jesus. I can't believe this. I knew her back in the forties. She used to come to Café Society. Hung around with Zero Mostel and Josh White…."

"I didn't know that she was that old."

"Old as me, you mean. No, she wasn't quite that ancient. She was something, Joe. Like they say, she didn't do much, but she did it well. She was never beautiful, but you couldn't take your eyes off her…."

I said nothing, just held the phone and let Max drift.

He sighed. "Then in the fifties she married a lousy beat poet. Name was Elson or Olsen, I forget. They went off to Frisco to live with that crowd."

"The marriage didn't last?"

"About two years. Not bad for that time and that crowd. Seems Olsen didn't trust her. He was always spying on her."

Jealousy again. It figured.

"So, there she was in a new city, trying to make friends, and her husband flying off the handle every time she spoke to someone…."

"Couldn't last," I said.

"And it didn't. And now…Jesus. She sure made a mess of things, didn't she? Dean, Al, you…."

"It's hard to hate her for it, though, isn't it?"

"Thank God for that. Hating dead people takes more energy than I can spare. The list would be too damned long." He sighed again. "Thanks for calling, Joe. I'll see you later."

The phone rang as soon as I hung up. "Joe? This is Irene Fox. I just heard—is it true?"

"Is what true?"

"The Adler bitch is the one who killed Dean."

"Irene, that's no way to talk—"

"Don't you lecture me, Joe Talley. I was in mourning *first*. Was it her?"

I sighed. "That's how it looks."

"And now she killed herself? God, I knew she was after him, but I never thought…."

"Nobody did."

"It's not *fair*, killing herself. She did it just to get away from us. It's like she's thumbing her nose at us."

"Who told you about this, Irene?"

"What? Oh, Officer Levy. He called up with some questions, and he told me you talked to her before she killed herself."

"That's right."

"Did she…." her voice dropped so low I could barely hear her. "Did she say anything about me?'

"You? I'm afraid not, Irene. She wasn't making much sense."

"That snake. That gray-haired old snake. I wish—"

"What?"

"How come *you* lived and Dean died? Why couldn't it have been the other way around?"

She hung up, and that was fine with me. I couldn't have answered her question anyway.

I decided to use the phone before it rang again. "Carol? It's me."

"Oh. Hi, Joe. Listen, there's—"

"After you left Ray told them—"

"Joe." Her voice had something in it I had never heard there before. Something hard. "*Listen to me.*"

"Yes?"

"I don't want to talk to you right now. I don't...I don't want to talk to you at all. Or see you."

I was stunned into silence.

"Okay, Joe? I'm hanging up now."

"Wait a minute! Don't hang up. Let me catch my breath. Is something wrong?" That last question was so stupid I could have kicked myself the moment it came out of my mouth.

I heard her take a deep breath. Whatever this was about, it was clear she wasn't enjoying it any more than I was. "I don't want to talk about it right now, okay?"

"Are you mad at me?" Another stupid question. Dear God. Why didn't I quit while I was behind?

"*Yes*, I'm mad at you. Can't you *tell* that?"

"I hear it. I just don't understand it. What did I do?"

"You don't know, do you?" And that made her even angrier. "You don't have the *faintest* idea." She slammed down the phone.

I sat down on the edge of my mattress, staring at the telephone as if it had turned into Elvis Presley. What in hell had I done to Carol Meisel? This was a woman who had apparently loved me without requital for six months. In a mere three dates I had her slamming down the phone on me as if we had been married for years. It had to be some kind of record.

My head was beginning to ache. I don't suppose I could blame the concussion this time.

The phone rang. Carol calling back to apologize. I jumped up, headache be damned, and grabbed it. "Hello, sweetheart."

Sovay laughed. "How did you know it was me, luv? You must be a fortuneteller."

I sat down heavily on the couch, feeling put upon. I was not cut out to be a Don Juan. I was a lousy liar, except when it came to business deals.

I told Sovay about Gus Adler, and she started to cry. "Gus? Oh Joe, it can't be. I don't believe it."

"I know, babe. It's a shock to everyone."

"And poor Ray. The man must have a broken heart."

"Maybe you should give him a call, Sovay."

"That's a good idea, luv." She chuckled. "I'm a guest of the son of one of Britain's leading industrialists. Young Colin tries to make up for his father's sins by helping out the trade unionists from time to time. So phone calls are free today."

The thought came into my head automatically and unbidden: was she sharing Colin's bed?

I felt shame coloring my face. What right did I have to even think the question? Not when I had been sleeping with Carol. I think some part of me missed having the right to be jealous. It felt like a lost innocence.

"That's great, babe. You call Ray."

"I will, right this minute. Ta for now. Take care of your sweet self, Joe."

I lay down on my mattress, expecting the thumping of my headache would keep me awake, but the interrupted night caught up with me. I drifted off to sleep, dreaming that Sovay had found out about Carol and was trying to kill me with a bourbon bottle.

Woke in a cold sweat, wondering how I could be stupid enough to cheat on a woman who had chosen that stage name. *Sovay* is an old British ballad about a female highway robber who disguises herself to test her man's courage and loyalty.

'If you had given me that ring,' she said.
'I'd have pulled the trigger and shot you dead.'

The phone rang again. It was *another* woman. This one wasn't in love with me; thank God.

"Joe, it's Katy. I heard about what happened. Listen, we're going to have a—I don't know—call it a wake. Something to bury the ghosts, if we can. Tonight. Everybody's going to be there."

"Where will it be?'

"The Beggar, where else? Max already gave us his permission."

"Is Carol coming?"

"Carol Meisel? Yes. I already talked to her."

CHAPTER 35

The sign on the door of the Riding Beggar read "CLOSED FOR PRIVATE PARTY." But it didn't feel like a party so much as an inquest.

I was a witness. The jury members were the friends gathered to drink Max's coffee for free. I couldn't figure out who was supposed to be the judge.

As I faced the room I had another weird sensation, as if I had never been there before. What's the opposite of déjà vu?

Gus would have known the name for it, but Gus was no longer with us. She had had her last glass of apple juice at my table.

Carol sat near the side wall, pretty as a picture in a conservative blue dress. She saw me looking at her and glanced away.

"Hiya, Joe," someone called.

It was Matty Mark, sitting across from Irene Fox. I was surprised she had shown up. One of them had brought a bottle of wine.

Katy Poe, the organizer of this event, sat at the table nearest the stage, wearing a black skirt and black turtleneck, an outfit she sometimes performed in. Was she in mourning, or about to perform? Or both?

212 • Robert Lopresti

Bob Braubinger was standing near the stage, drinking a beer. He saw me and grinned. "Well, there you are. I didn't know if you'd have the nerve to show up."

"What do you mean?"

"Turns out it was a middle-aged woman who put you in the hospital. That doesn't exactly make you Cassius Clay."

I looked at him: the idiot grin and the slippery suit. "If you think that's funny, you should have seen her with a bullet in her head. That was a real knee-slapper." I turned away.

"Hey, Joe," he called over my shoulder. "Don't be a party-killer. I just—Oh, man. Everyone's too sensitive these days."

I walked to the back of the room where Max sat talking to Von Ehmsen and Frank Renard, the radio man.

"Sit down, Joe. Von has a line on a good cook for us."

"Well, not a bad one, anyway," said Von Ehmsen. His shades glinted as he raised his wine glass. "Used to work for me and just got back to town. I'll send the cat over tomorrow."

"Sounds good," I said.

Von Ehmsen stroked his beard. "They say you and the Meisel chick were the last ones to talk to Gus."

"Right. And Frank here had dinner with her that night."

"Yeah?" said Max. "You didn't mention that."

Renard shrugged and sipped wine. "Ray and I had dinner with her. She seemed to be in a good mood, but dopers can fool you."

"You're taking it pretty cool," said Von Ehmsen.

Renard wore a little smile. "Trick of the trade, Von. I had to go on the radio one night five minutes after hearing that a buddy bought the farm in Korea. You learn not to show anything. I'm not sure it's a good thing to learn, though."

"Did you know Gus well?" I asked.

"I know everybody in the Village, Joe, and God knows she was part of the scene. I had her on the show once, years ago, hoping she could spin some stories about Kerouac or Ginsburg. All she wanted to talk about was Egypt and Tarot cards." His shrug showed what he thought of them as a topic for a radio show. He turned his squint on me. "I made the mistake of telling that to your buddy once"

"What? You mean Dean?"

"Yup. He ran to her and tattled on me. I think that was when he was trying to get her into the sack. It was months before she would even speak to me after that."

I frowned. "That's why you told me you'd never have Dean on your show."

"Yeah. He had no right to tell her what I said." Renard raised his wine glass. "Gossip should be left to us professionals."

"Amen to that," said Von Ehmsen. "And now a toast to Agustina Adler, gentlemen. She was one fine lady, she was."

"A fine *murderer*, you mean!" said a voice behind me. "And a goddamned tramp!"

I half jumped out of my seat. Irene again, the harpy at the feast. You couldn't blame her for being mad, but it was all one-sided, and it wasn't what anyone wanted to hear.

"Mind your manners, Irene," said Max. But he softened it by adding: "Have a seat, if you want."

"I told you she was after Dean," said Irene. She was none too steady on her feet. "I told you what that woman was like, but would anyone listen to me?"

"The lady's got a point," said Matty Mark, who had just appeared at her side. He patted her arm in a gesture that looked more proprietary than protective. "All of us misjudged Gus, all except Irene. Shoot, she even told me about the gun, and I didn't think anything of it."

"Who told you about the gun?"

"Gus. The Village Boys and me sang *Jesse James* here one night and she told me she bought a pistol once years ago to protect herself. But shoot, I didn't know she was gonna *use* it."

"You *should* have known," said Irene. "All of you jerks should have known."

She turned towards the door, swaying a bit. "I'm going home. I should have never come to this creepy place. Everybody's mourning for that *bitch*, instead of for the man she killed."

"Hold on, Irene. Lemme walk you home," said Matty.

We watched them go, Irene clinging to the arm of her new protector. Matty couldn't take Dean's place musically, but he was moving in where he could.

Von Ehmsen picked up a napkin and delicately wiped wine off his beard. "I knew Gus a hell of a lot longer and better than that hillbilly did and she never mentioned a gun to me."

"Well, she got one somewhere," I said.

The bearded man snorted. "So you buy the conventional wisdom, Talley?"

"Meaning what?" asked Max.

"The idea that Gus killed herself because she shot her ex-sweetheart because he done her wrong, or something, and clubbed your boy here on the noggin. I suppose if you say it often enough you can believe anything. But Max, you ought to know better."

"Oh? And why's that?"

Von Ehmsen shrugged. "Because Agustina Adler might possibly have committed suicide, but she would never have killed anyone else, not in a million years, and we all know it."

"I *don't* know that," said Max, frowning. "I don't know if I can be that sure of anything. Or anyone."

Von Ehmsen shook his head. "Spoken like a true Jewish atheist. What about Seamus?"

Renard leaned forward. "Yeah, what about O'Hanlon? He disappeared just before the killings started. You think that was a coincidence?"

"That's been bothering me," I admitted.

"Coincidences happen," grumbled Max. "That's why they have a word for 'em."

A hand landed on my shoulder and I jumped.

"Hey, Joe."

I looked around at Phil Ochs. "Aren't we gonna play some tunes? I mean, Dean was a musician. How can we remember the guy without a few songs?"

"Talk to Katy," I said. "She's running things."

I watched Phil walk off toward Katy. Soon their heads were bobbing up and down excitedly.

"What do you think they'll decide?" asked Renard.

"They're musicians and there's an audience." I shrugged. "What do *you* think?"

Von Ehmsen laughed. "I guess they're not rich enough to pass it up."

"That's true," said Max. "The best musicians get so successful they start performing less. But the bad ones are always ready to go, no matter how bad they are...."

"Or how drunk they are," said Renard. "I've had a few perform on my show who were too looped to stand."

Drunk. I looked over at Carol. She was talking to Janet, one of the other waitresses. Her back was toward me and I got the feeling it was deliberate.

Maybe I'd been too easy and she didn't respect me anymore. Damn.

I turned back to Max. "You need me for anything, Boss?"

"You? Jesus, no."

"Then I'm gonna find a bottle of booze and become intemperate."

Renard chuckled. Von Ehmsen nodded approvingly.

"Best of luck to you," said Max. He frowned. "Been a hell of a week, hasn't it? Thank God it's over."

I left just as a couple of musicians were stepping on stage. I don't know who they were because I didn't bother to look. I didn't want to see something that might tempt me to stay.

Thank God it's over, I repeated to myself.

A nice thought, but the worst was still to come.

CHAPTER 36

I didn't go far. The Bag of Nails was right upstairs.

Les Newcomer saw me coming in and nodded. "What'll it be, Joe?"

"Bourbon—no." I remembered my last encounter with a bourbon bottle and shuddered. "Make it an Irish whiskey."

"One Irish. That's a new drink for you."

"Maybe it's time for a few changes." I looked around the place. The bar was dark and gloomy, more like a cavern than a tavern. On the other hand, some people thought the Beggar's long tables made it look like a cafeteria, so who was I to complain?

If it was a cavern, there were not a lot of cave dwellers tonight. It struck me that these men brooding over their drinks looked much more like mourners at a wake than my friends downstairs did. Maybe celebrating a lost life with music made more sense than weeping.

"I hear you're closed downstairs," Les said when he brought my glass.

"Yeah. A little going-away party."

"For Al Perkins? I heard he was leaving."

"Already gone," I said, sipping whiskey.

"Too bad. Nice fella."

"Yes, he is. You remember the day I hired him? I brought him up here for a drink."

"It rings a bell."

"Braubinger was in here. I remember him explaining to Al that Martin Luther King was going about the whole civil rights thing the wrong way."

"Is that right? What was Bob's theory?"

I grinned. "He said there was a lot of money to be made in civil rights. All that liberal guilt waiting to be tapped."

"That's Bob," Les agreed.

I nodded. Braubinger had gone on to say that he had wanted to join the Freedom Riders the year before but his wife had stopped him. She didn't want to be left alone. "I ask you, Al," he lamented, "how can a man help the oppressed when his old lady is bitching at him all the time?"

My drink had vanished. I asked Les for a refill.

Dean Coffey had come into the bar that same February day and Braubinger had introduced him to Al as the next Bob Dylan. That was wasted on Al, who had never heard of Bob, but I remember it as the first time I heard that phrase used to describe some up-and-coming songwriter.

God knows it wasn't the last.

Dean had ordered a beer and unpacked his guitar. I asked him to play one of his songs for Al and he chose *White Wolf*:

> *Sometimes when you come to me*
> *You're more alive than anyone I've ever known*
> *Sometimes when I go to you*
> *I think I'm looking at a face of polished stone.*
> *Who's in the mirror when you drop your mask?*
> *Who hurries home after the show?*
> *Like a white wolf running through the snow,*
> *Like a white wolf running through the snow.*

I remember wondering who the song was about, assuming it was some past or present lover. Looking back, it seemed to fit Dean himself pretty well: a man who could dazzle you with his cleverness and passion, and then vanish when you try to look behind the surface.

How could I spend so much time with a man and know so little about him?

All the memories were closing in on me. And there was one stuck in the back of my head, something that I was forgetting.

Down the bar I heard Les telling a couple of men in gray suits how the bar had gotten its name. "Bag of Nails is British slang for a busted poker hand, you see. The guys who opened this place were a couple of Limeys, and after the War they were stuck in Singapore with just enough money to scrape home on. Instead, they decided to invest it all in a high-stakes poker game…."

I started to pull my wallet out of my hip pocket and the damned thing didn't want to come. When I bent over to ease it out the room turned at funny angles and I had to lean against the bar for support.

Apparently I had achieved my goal. I was drunk. Now, why had I wanted to do that to myself?

I couldn't remember. Probably a good thing. After all, I might have been drinking to forget.

But what was the other memory, the one that had seemed so important a minute ago? Something about Al? Dean?

Les came back and I pushed my money across the bar to him. "Every time you tell that damned story about the poker game it comes out differently. Are any of them true?"

He gave me his tight little smile. "For all I know, Joe, they might all be."

•

The cold March air hit me like a slap in the face. I stepped backwards, blinking hard and bumped into the opening door.

"Whoa, Joe. You okay?" It was Braubinger, coming out behind me.

"Yeah, Bob. I'm fine. How's the wake going?"

"Going fine. Phil just did a new song about the Freedom Riders. It's a killer. You sure you're okay, Joe? Let me walk you home, all right?"

Braubinger was smiling. His shoulders were hunched up in his trench coat and puffs of steam were coming out of his mouth.

If it's that chilly, I should be feeling colder, I thought. I must be really drunk.

"Okay," I said. "Let's walk."

Braubinger kept up a commentary as we went. He talked about his latest find, none other than that earnest college kid, Sam Furrell. "The boy's got talent, Joe. I may be able to make something out of him."

Like he was going to make something out of Dean, I thought. Was he going to hook Sam up with the stockbrokers? God help the kid.

There was something I wanted to remember. *Had* to remember.

"You aren't saying much, Joe. Something on your mind?"

"Just don't feel like talking."

Braubinger shifted his shoulders as if his coat was itchy. "Hey, I'm sorry about what I said before. About Gus hitting you with the bourbon bottle."

"Doesn't matter." I had forgotten about that. But it wasn't the *important* thing I had forgotten.

"So, what do the cops think, Joe? Do they think she was, you know, alone when she died?"

I frowned at him. "You mean, did she commit suicide?"

He blinked. "Yeah, I guess that's it. Did she kill herself?"

"You bastard," I said.

He stared at me. "What? What did I do?"

I felt sober. More sober than I had in days, maybe. I put my hand on Braubinger's trench coat and shoved, slamming him against the wall of one of 4th Street's brick townhouses.

His normally flushed face was suddenly pale. "Joe, man, what the hell—"

"You want to know if the cops think Gus was alone when she died."

"Let go of me, dammit!"

"I'll tell you, Bob. The cops know she was expecting a visit from somebody that evening. Now, who could that have been?"

The whites were showing, all around his piggy eyes. "I don't know! How should I know?"

I took my hand off him, but I didn't back up. "Ever since I saw Von Ehmsen tonight I knew I was forgetting something. I just figured it out. Yesterday Von told me that *you* were looking for Gus."

Braubinger licked his lips. "Why would he tell you that?"

"Because it was true." I smiled. "It makes sense. It even explains your sudden boy scout act, wanting to get me home safely tonight. You just wanted to quiz me about whether the cops knew you were there that night."

"I wasn't there, Joe. Why in God's name would I—"

"Cut it out, Bob. You told Von you were looking for her and a few hours later she tells Ray she's expecting company. You want to try to convince the cops that that was a coincidence?"

Braubinger licked his lips again. "Well, dammit," he said. He put his hands in his pockets and looked at the dirty sidewalk. "I didn't kill her, Joe. She was alive when I left. I swear it."

"Why were you visiting her in the first place?"

"You can't tell the cops about this, Joe. It would ruin me."

My head was swimming. I didn't really think Braubinger had killed Gus. If someone had killed her the motive had to be tied to Dean's killing, and why would he kill Dean? But I couldn't think of another reason for him to visit her late at night.

Not for love. I don't think his wedding ring would have stopped either one of them, but from what I knew of Braubinger his taste ran to those under twenty more than those over forty.

"It was for Sam." He spoke so quietly I barely caught the words.

"Sam? Sam Furrell? He went there with you?"

"No." Braubinger looked, for once in his life, embarrassed. "He wanted some dope."

I blinked. "Oh. You promised to get him some pot if you could be his agent."

"It wasn't like that. Not exactly." He shrugged. "The kid's like every newcomer on the scene, right? Wants to experience everything at once. An agent is supposed to know how to *get* things. Club dates. Money."

"Marijuana," I said.

"Yeah." Braubinger tried a grin. "I arranged to see Gus at ten last night and buy some reefer. She always has—had some. We smoked some and I gave her the money and left. I swear, Joe, she was fine then."

"What kind of mood was she in?"

He frowned. "She was stoned. You ever been stoned? She was staring at the walls, counting dust molecules. What kind of mood do you call that?"

"She didn't seem depressed?"

"No. Hell, no. She fell asleep, for God's sake."

The wind blew harder, bringing tears to my eyes. "I thought she was staring at the wall."

"That was before she went into the bedroom. You asked what kind of mood she was in. You're not in a mood when you sleep, are you?" He shook his head. "My God, what a conversation."

I took a breath. "Let's get this straight. You smoked some pot. You bought some more. She got tired and went to bed. You *saw* her in bed?"

"Yeah. When she said she was going to bed I thought maybe it was a come-on. But she's not my type, you know?"

"I know."

"But I guess she was just tired. People don't have good manners when they're stoned, you know? Anyway, when I was ready to go I stuck my head in to say goodnight. She was under the covers already. I locked the front door and left."

I was thinking hard. "Did she have the record player going?"

"No. Not while I was there."

"Did you see a gun?"

His eyes went wide. "A gun? Where?"

"Anywhere in the apartment."

"No. Man, that's how she killed herself, right? With a gun?"

Did she kill herself? Wake up in the middle of the night, put on a record, call us, and then pull a gun from under her pillow and—

It could have happened. And Woody Guthrie could be elected our next president.

But neither one was likely.

CHAPTER 37

The next to last thing I heard before I fell asleep was Frank Renard on the radio. He had been playing recordings of beat poets for most of his show: Ginsburg and Ferlenghetti, mostly.

"You may not feel it," he said. "You may not even have heard it. But this old town is a poorer place tonight then it used to be. Gus is gone.

"People come and go in this city. Jeez, whole neighborhoods disappear, torn down to make room for a hundred-story mousetrap for the winners of this week's rat race.

"But some people stick around. They may not be the movers and shakers, but the people I'm talking about change your lives too. Maybe in more important ways then the people who make laws and build buildings.

"Gus—Agustina Adler—was one of those people. She knew all the people the newspapers call the Beatniks. She was there when people started reciting poetry in coffeehouses, when audiences snapped their fingers to applaud because clapping bothered the neighbors. She was there, doing her eloquent little pen and ink drawings that earned her bread, but mostly she was just *there*, a permanent part of the scene, we thought.

"And now she's dead. The cops aren't sure why or how. Maybe that'll stay a puzzle like so much else about her.

I was lucky enough to have her on this show, and that's what you're gonna hear now. Gus Adler talking a little bit about what interested her most. Give her a listen."

And that familiar, too sweet, voice came over the speaker. "I came to New York just before World War II, Frank. Is that right? Yes, the late thirties. I thought I was going to be a great artist, but that wasn't the time or place for great artists. I got a job in a bookstore down in the Village, and started meeting all these darling writers...."

I drifted off to sleep with a dead woman telling me about her life.

•

"You sound like the living dead," said my brother. His call had dragged me out of a nightmare I couldn't remember.

"Thanks, Jack. Thanks a heap." I slumped on the couch, keeping a death-grip on the receiver. I don't drink often. I almost never get drunk. Now I was remembering why.

"How you doing, little brother?"

"Not great, Jack. I had one of those nights."

"What kind is that?"

"The kind you think I have every night."

He chuckled. "That bad, huh? Well, then, you deserve it."

I fumbled for a cigarette. "What time is it?"

"Seven A.M. my time. That makes it ten where your sorry butt is sitting. I was just about to leave on a fishing expedition but I thought you might want to hear about your buddy's relatives first."

"Oh, Lord." I closed my eyes, hoping the headache would recede. It did, but the room began to spin, lazily, clockwise.

"Uh huh." Jack's voice was flat. "So you're not interested anymore." *And you've been wasting my time*, he meant.

"I didn't say that. Tell me about it." I tried to speak with more enthusiasm than I felt. "What's the good word?"

"Well, for starters, you screwed up. No surprise there, I admit. You pointed me at the wrong end of the state."

"I did what?"

"You were off by five hundred miles. About average for you, I suppose. You goddamned easterners think California is about the size of, what, New Jersey? I had a Baltimore cop on the phone last week, wanted me to drive up to Sacramento to get a file for him, like it was a trip around the block."

It's not easy to be patient when your pulse is playing bongos on your eardrums. "Tell me what you found out, Jack."

"Well, if it isn't too much damned trouble for you to listen…. Okay, you guessed right about this bird's father. Dean Coffey, Sr. is living in a VA home, not much more than a vegetable, from what I hear."

"And this is up in Willow Creek?'

"No! Pay attention, kemo sabe. It's in La Jolla, just a taco toss from San Diego. Five hundred miles from Willow Creek. Your Dean Coffey is listed with the hospital as next of kin. They'll have to change that now, I guess. But he hasn't been there to visit his dad in more than a year, practically since the old man arrived there. Some devoted son."

I stubbed out my cigarette. "Damn it, that makes no sense. He went to California every few months. Why the hell was he going to Willow Creek?"

"Beats me. He was your friend, not mine. One thing I can tell you for sure was, he wasn't visiting his dad."

I didn't want him to get started on our obligations to family. "What's in Willow Creek, anyway?"

"Not a hell of a lot. Lemme see…. A lumber mill. Jones and White, that's a big fruit processor. Dessmond Pharmaceuticals. Axelrod…."

"What's Axelrod?"

"A private college. Snooty. Run by a church, I think. You figure he was taking courses on the side?"

"I doubt it. Anything else?"

"A juice company. Works with the fruit processor, I guess. That's about it. Okay, the fish are waiting. Take care of yourself, kid."

"You too, Jack. And thanks. Hey—wait a moment."

"What?"

I ran back over what he had said. "You said Dean has hardly visited his father since he went into the VA home."

"Right."

"But you made it sound like that was only a year or two."

"Right again. Early 1960."

"Huh. I heard that he was injured during the Korean War. Where has he been since then?"

My brother snorted. "Wrong again. Don't go around telling people this loser got his in the Frozen Chosin. Maybe he served there, for all I know, but that ain't what put him in the Home."

"Then what did it?"

"Drunk driving. He wrapped his Chevy around a tree in late '59."

•

After we hung up I lay down on the mattress again and let my head resume spinning. This time it wasn't entirely the fault of the hangover.

Dean had taken a tragedy in his life—his father's accident—and given it a political twist by writing a song in which the cause of the man's illness was a war injury. Making the personal into the universal; isn't that the nature of art?

But more specifically, when Dean was a teenager—and maybe with no other family, at least he had none now—his father had gotten drunk and taken himself out of the picture. Just when Dean needed him most.

I was thinking of Dean's furious reaction to the drunk that day in the Bag of Nails. Just after his last trip to California, where he hadn't been visiting his father.

Sweet God in heaven. It was beginning to make sense.

Chapter 38

I showered, dressed and walked over to Sheridan Square to buy a dozen roses at a florist that was open twenty-four hours. The florist was a skinny guy with bad teeth. He grinned at me. "Special occasion or apology?"

"Maybe both," I told him. I carted the foliage to Waverly Place and knocked on Carol Meisel's door.

Her eyes went wide. "Joe."

I held out the flowers. "Whatever I did, I'm sorry. I know you're also mad that I don't *know* what it is I did, but I can't do anything about that. Just tell me what it was and, I swear, I'll never do it again.

"Joe, I—"

"Carol, in the last twenty-four hours I've turned around five times to tell you something, just assuming you'd be there. I never felt that way about anyone. Never so much, and never so quickly."

She opened her mouth but I spoke up. "Don't tell me I'll get over it. I don't *want* to get over it."

She took the flowers out of my hand and smiled at them. Maybe at me, too. "First things first. There's something you need to know about me."

"What's that?"

"I'm allergic to roses." She threw them over her shoulder. Then she moved into my arms and we kissed. We kissed for so long that when she spoke again I had lost track of the first half of her sentence: "But you, I like."

As a hangover cure, it wasn't half bad.

•

"Let's see if I understand this," I said later. I was lying in bed, my arm around her. "You think I was pushing you around, treating you like a child, or a junior partner."

"Grabbing the phone," Carol said, nodding. "Shoving me out the door at Gus's apartment. Yes, that's exactly how I feel."

"I was taught that women were supposed to be protected. The caveman thing...."

She kissed me on the cheek. "If a saber-tooth tiger comes along, he's all yours. But until that happens, I don't want you trying to make decisions for me. Okay?"

"Okay." I looked at her thoughtfully. "If you want to be fully involved, this is your big chance. I got some news today."

"Yes?"

"Gus didn't kill Dean. She didn't kill herself either."

Carol's eyes went wide. Her hand clutched at the blanket. "She—Are you certain?"

"Well." I shrugged. "Close enough for folk music."

"Do you—who—" She sat up in bed suddenly, wrapping the sheet around herself. "Do you know who did it?"

"Not for sure. But I know where to find out. So, do you want to come with me?"

Chapter 39

Are you sure this is a good idea?" Carol asked me again.

"No. It's probably a rotten idea. Do you have a better one?"

We were standing in front of a brownstone on Great Jones Street in the East Village. The building looked as rundown and beat up as I was feeling.

"There's the police."

I nodded. "There sure are. So far they've driven Al Perkins out of town and closed the Beggar down for three days. You want to give them something fresh and see what they can do with it?"

She thought for a moment and shook her head. "Joe, I'm scared."

"All right, then. Don't go. Maybe it would better if I go alone and—"

"Damn it. Don't protect me."

I sighed. "Back to that again?"

"People have been trying to protect me all my life. I don't like it. I never have."

"Not me, sweetheart." I tried my atrocious Bogie imitation. "I may use you as a human shield, but I'll never try to protect you."

"Deal."

"Let's do it," I said.

It was a long walk to the fourth floor, but time seems to fly when you don't want to arrive at your destination. I spent the time thinking about the logic that brought us here.

For instance: someone had beaten Seamus, maybe tried to kill him. In any case, they had scared him so badly that he had fled the country.

After he was attacked Seamus said he wanted to talk to Dean. Dean was murdered a week later, on the day he signed a contract with Broker Records.

Coincidence? No.

I had been assuming that someone killed him that day because they didn't want him to make a record. That would explain the stolen tapes.

But maybe I had confused cause and effect. Maybe he had been killed for the same reason he had been willing to sign with Broker Records.

Dean settled for a contract with the stockbrokers because he needed money. He told Bob Braubinger he needed cash because he had just quit his day job. But what *was* his day job?

I was pretty sure I knew.

Fourth floor. I knocked on the door and we waited. Maybe I didn't really expect an answer. Part of me was expecting to find another corpse.

On the third knock I heard someone muttering inside. It sounded far away.

Carol and I looked at each other. "Where there's life," I said.

"What is it?" grumbled the voice on the other side of the door.

"It's Joe and Carol."

"Not interested. Come back tomorrow."

"Please," said Carol, "We've been so worried about you."

There was a shuffling sound and the noise of two locks popping back. "Door's open," said Ray Hegg.

Unlike Carol's apartment, or Gus's, Ray's pad did not surprise me. The walls were white, crisp cold white. There were no pictures or decorations to be seen. It could have looked empty and impersonal, but with those bright white walls, it looked more like a statement of some kind.

Ray was wearing black pajama bottoms, a heavy black bathrobe with a red Chinese print, and shades. The curtains were drawn tight and even with the reflective walls there wasn't enough light for him to need those shades.

"Why were you worried about me?" he asked Carol. His eyebrows rose toward his bald scalp.

"We hadn't seen you since yesterday morning at Gus's. The police were so awful to you, and you and Gus were so close...."

"She was a good friend to me," said Ray. "Maybe the best friend I ever had." He slumped into a leather chair and, in an after-thought, waved at the couch across the way. Carol and I sat down too.

"She was my lover once, too, a long time ago." He took off his glasses and pinched his nose with two fingers. "God, I'm tired."

His eyes were red. He had been crying.

"The cops decided she killed herself, because she killed Dean," I told him.

"Is that so?" He paused. "And why did she kill Dean, according to those masterminds?"

"Guareschi says she was jealous, because he was sleeping with Irene Fox."

Ray jerked his head back. He was grinning. "Man, what tiny little brains. Did they explain why she didn't kill him when he slept with a dozen other chicks? Do they know why she didn't just kill *Irene*?"

"So, what do you think happened, Ray?'

"Beats me. You're the one who's been playing Peter Gunn, not me."

Carol was looking at me and her eyes were saying: *we can still back out.* I looked away.

"There's one thing that puzzles me, Ray. I was talking to my brother in California today."

"Is that a fact? How's the weather out there?"

"We found out that when Dean flew out to visit relatives, he was going to northern California, to a town called Willow Creek. But he didn't have any relatives in that part of the state. So why did he go there?"

"Is this what you came here for?" Ray put his shades back on. "To ask these damned fool questions? God, Joe. You set new standards for insensitivity every day."

He turned toward Carol. "Can't you cram some sense into that skull of his, baby? You're smarter than he'll ever be."

I wasn't about to be distracted. "Practically the only business in Willow Creek is a pharmaceutical company. Why would he visit *them*?"

Ray sighed. "Probably to pick up some aspirin, if his head hurt like mine does."

"We think he was working as a courier," Carol told him. "Picking up something at that factory and bringing it to New York."

"Something illegal," I said, "or why all the secrecy? And that was his day job, the way he got his money."

"Fascinating stuff," said Ray. "Too bad *Dragnet* went off the air or you two could get rich making up their true stories for them. Why are you telling me all this crap?"

"You're a chemist, aren't you? I always think of chemists spending their days vulcanizing rubber or something, but they also make pharmaceuticals. I thought maybe you could think of something illegal he might have been carrying. Something available in California that can't be had in New York."

Ray yawned. "God, I am so exhausted. Didn't sleep worth a damn. Anybody else want some coffee?"

"Sure," said Carol. I nodded.

Ray walked off to the kitchenette. "Sugar, anybody? The cream has spoiled, so you'll have to drink it black."

"Ray," I called. He was still out of sight. "What could Dean have been bringing across the country?"

"I'm thinking, Joe. Gimme a break here."

Carol and I looked at each other. She shrugged.

When he came back out, Ray was carrying a black enamel tray. He placed it on the orange crate that served as a table.

He looked at me and sighed. "Joe, you are one of the world's most transparent men. You should have let your chick singer here take the lead if you wanted to play it this way."

"I don't know what you mean, Ray."

"All that crap about can I guess what he was bringing. Just ask me what you really want to know."

"Okay. Was he bringing the stuff to you?"

"That's more like it." He moved espresso cups from the tray to the crate, taking his time. He added napkins and two open enamel sugar bowls, one black and one red.

Finally he seemed satisfied. "Now, where were we? Yes, Dean was bringing chemicals across the country for me. Or, at least *to* me. Satisfied?"

"So what was it that—"

"Stop." I had been reaching for a sugar bowl. "Use the black one. The sugar in the red one is a little bit special."

"Oh, Ray," said Carol. "You don't mean it."

"Oh, Carol," he said mockingly. "Yes, I do."

"What are you two talking about?" I asked.

Ray picked up a sugar cube from the red bowl. "This is the crux, Joe. You're looking at the whole thing right here."

"Sugar?"

He shook his bald head, still grinning at me. "This is Dr. Hoffman's billion dollar baby. D-Lysergic Acid Diethylamide-25."

"LSD," Carol whispered.

"Right the first time, sunshine. LSD it is." He held the cube up to the light, as if examining a fine gem. "This stuff could put you waitresses out of business. All you need is one drop on a little sugar cube. No dirty dishes to pick up."

"That's what Dean was smuggling?" I asked. "Sugar cubes?"

"No, you idiot. The production equipment. Plus rye argot for manufacturing."

"But it isn't illegal," said Carol.

"Just wait, sweetie. The controls on it are getting tighter every month. You have to be a goddamned research scientist to get near it now, and even *they* are fired, just for doing experiments."

"Scientists up at Harvard," I said. "That's what Seamus was doing for you. Picking up something on his trips to Boston."

Ray nodded. "Information, mostly. He had contacts with lab technicians there. You might say he was part of our marketing research."

"Marketing research," I said. "You make it sound like General Motors."

Ray laughed and it was such a cheerful, easy laugh that for one fine moment I thought that everything was going to be all right, somehow. "Why not? We're all just capitalists, trying to fill a need."

He pointed at the red sugar bowl. "People on the west coast are already paying a dollar a cube. We're a little backwards over here. By the time demand on the east coast gets up to a reasonable level the people I work for will have a complete laboratory in operation."

"The people you work for," I said. "You don't mean your day job at the lab; you mean the mob."

Ray shook his head, smiling. "Well gosh, Joe, I don't think they call themselves that. They don't wear little lapel pins that say GANGSTER, either. But yeah, I guess you have the general idea."

"Why did they kill Dean?" asked Carol.

Ray sighed. "Ol' Dean-o had a good thing going. We paid him enough for those little jaunts to the Golden State to subsidize his musical career. God knows he wasn't making any money playing joints like yours."

"But if it isn't illegal—"

"*Possession* isn't a crime. Not yet. But the feds are supervising production, ready for the day the laws change and they can shut it down. We want to leave no trail linking us to a source that they know about. You dig? That meant we needed our messenger boys to have no mob connections and spotless records."

"So what happened?"

"That damn fool Seamus developed a conscience. My friends sent people to kill Seamus, and look who got in the way. You two clowns."

"Seamus had said he wanted to talk to Dean. I guess he wanted to talk him into leaving the courier business."

"He had already done that, damn him. But Seamus was the first one to tell our bosses he was quitting. I suppose he wanted to warn Dean that they hadn't been too happy about it."

"That's why Dean signed with Broker Records," I said. "He knew he'd need money in a hurry."

"Your bosses wouldn't trust them to stay quiet," said Carol. "Is that it?"

Ray shifted in his seat. "Would you? Seamus was a poet, and a drunk. He was bound to talk one way or another. And Dean—the guy was a *songwriter*. Spilling his guts was what he wanted to do for a living. Sooner or later he would try to get it off his conscience by turning it into three verses and a sing-along chorus. My people didn't want to hear some joker singing their trade secrets on *Hootenanny*."

"You told them about it?"

He shrugged. "They asked my opinion. They said, can we take a chance on this guy? My reputation was on the line, you understand."

"Oh, Ray," said Carol, soft and sad. "You told them to kill him."

"I sure did, honey." His brow furrowed. "Because sooner or later it was gonna be him or me. And that was an easy choice."

"Who did the mob send to kill Dean?" Carol asked. "Do you know?"

"Sure do, babe." Ray stood up and stretched. He turned away, heading back towards the kitchen for more coffee. "They sent the guy who recruited him in the first place."

"Wasn't that you?"

He turned back to us. He had a gun in his hand. "Right again, baby. Right again."

CHAPTER 40

Bad mistake.

That was all I could think. Bad, bad mistake.

I started to stand up and Ray swung the gun toward me. "Sit down, Joe. Stay close to your sweetheart. Now, what am I going to do with you two?"

My head was throbbing, pounding away at the place where someone, where *Ray*, had hit me with a bottle of bourbon.

"Well, now," I said. "That explains why Dean didn't die until the morning. You and Gus were at that all-night meeting."

"You got it."

"But how did you know Dean was there?"

"Easy," said Ray. He took off his shades. "Dean called about ten minutes after I got home from the yoga bash. Said he'd been trying to reach me all night. Somebody broke into his place and he wanted to know if it was our mutual friends."

"And was it?"

"Of course. Think, Joe. Once they ordered him killed they had to check that there was nothing in his pad that would lead the cops to them. Or to me. Just common sense."

"And stealing the tapes from the stockbrokers?"

"Insurance. In case he sprang a surprise, like saying he had a written confession squirreled away somewhere.

If he didn't cooperate we would destroy the tapes." He shrugged. "Didn't turn out to be necessary."

"And what happened to those copies?"

"My friends threw them in the river. I thought they were jumping the gun—" He looked down at the gun in his own hand and grinned. "Don't squirm like that, Carol. You're gonna make me nervous."

I nodded. "You planted the tape cover at Gus's pad. That was from one of the copies in the brokers' office, right?"

"Exactly. I got it from my buddies before they dumped the rest of the stuff."

"Dean told me he gave his copy of the tape to a colleague. Was that you?"

Ray laughed. "That's what you really came here for, isn't it, Joe? Not to find out who killed your best friend. Just to try to find his tape so you can make a buck off him."

Carol was squeezing my hand, reminding me to stay calm. I said: "Twist it anyway you want, Ray. It wasn't me who killed him. *Do* you have the tape?"

"Yeah. Not here, though. It's in my desk at the lab where I work. My day job, you might say."

I was thinking hard. "What are you gonna do with the tape?"

"I know what I *wished* I'd done with it. I should have mailed it to you, Joe. Just so you'd stop this witch hunt."

"But at least it's safe," I said. "Thank God there's something left."

Ray shook his head in mock wonder. "You have a twisted set of values, sonny. Now, what am I gonna do with you two?"

"Let us go," said Carol.

He didn't seem to hear. "I could call my bosses, I guess. They'll send someone to take care of you."

I took a breath. "If you have us killed, Ray, you better start running. My brother is a cop in L.A. He knows I was trying to find a connection between a dead man and Willow Creek. If I turn up dead, he'll come looking. Trust me, he's persistent as hell. It's one of his most annoying habits."

Ray scratched his smooth bald head. "That only matters if it *looks* like murder, Joe. My pals are good at arranging accidents. Or suicides."

"Suicides," said Carol. "Is that what happened to Gus?" Ray grimaced and looked away for a second, but the damned gun didn't move an inch. "Poor Gus. She knew something was wrong, God knows how. And when I lied about the time we got back from yoga class...I told her it was to protect her, but she started asking questions I couldn't answer."

"So you killed her?"

"Easy as apple pie, Joe. I still had a key to her place. I just slipped in when I knew she'd be asleep."

"And murdered her. Your best friend, for God's sake."

He stiffened in his chair. "You the judge and jury tonight, Talley? It's damned sweet of you, saving the state of New York all that money."

He picked up a cigarette, tried to work the lighter with his heft hand. "Let me tell you a few things about Agustina Adler. The first time she tried to kill herself—the first time I know about, anyway—was in 1952, after her marriage fell apart. She cut her wrists. Ever wonder about those long ruffled sleeves she always wore?"

"To hide scars," said Carol. "I saw them once when she was washing her hands."

"You are a shrewd one, girlie." Ray's hand was shaking too badly to light the cigarette. He yanked it from his mouth and threw it on the table. It hit the red sugar bowl and bounced to the floor. "It never pays to underestimate you. Rumor has it you even managed to wrestle this clown into bed."

I started to stand up. "Damn it, Ray."

He gestured with the gun. I sat back down.

"Relax, Joe," said Carol. "He's just calling names. It's his hate pouring out."

"Hate? Bull." He scowled at her. "How could I possibly feel any hate after all the hours I've spent in folk joints, listening to your chums singing about love and peace and goddamn beauty? All of you stinking phonies."

His rage astonished me. The original Mr. Cool was burning hot tonight.

"Do you know who took Gus to the hospital that time to get her wrists sewn up? Yours truly. Three years ago she tried again, an overdose of pills. I was the lucky dog who called the ambulance on that one, too."

"Why did she try to kill herself?" I asked.

"Boredom, she said. The real reason is anybody's guess. But the way I figured it, when I killed her I was just evening up the score. She owed me for saving her life twice already."

Jesus, I thought. *If this is how he treats his friends, what would he do to his enemies?*

And which are *we*?

"And the phone call to me?" Carol asked.

"Better than a suicide note. And easier. Whenever Gus got heavy into the hemp she liked to tell her troubles to the tape recorder. I was there two nights before when she made that tape. I just made sure the record on the machine matched what was on the tape and took off with it."

"Where to?" asked Carol. "You don't own a tape recorder."

"He went right across the street," I said. "To Dean Coffey's apartment. Dean had two recorders, and the phone wasn't switched off yet."

"Very good," say Ray. "You aren't a complete fool, are you?"

"That's *how* you did it," I said. "But why kill her at all?"

Ray grimaced. The way he was sweating you'd think we were holding the gun on *him*. "I told you. She was beginning to suspect me."

"She would have never told the police about you," Carol said. "Not even if you confessed."

Ray's eyes widened. "Damn it, don't you think I *know* that? But I couldn't bet my life on that. And even if I was willing, my employers weren't."

"So you killed her," I said.

He glared at me. "You got a point to make here, soldier boy?"

"My point is that you've killed two people already, Ray. And what about the drugs you help manufacture? They'll kill even more."

"Oh, will they? How much do you know about LSD?"

"Not much," I admitted. "Those Harvard professors got in trouble for experimenting with it. Some people on the West Coast went crazy using it."

"Crazy," Ray muttered. "Crazy according to the government, and we know how sane *they* are. Do you know how much money they spend on A-bombs every year? Do you know how much they pay farmers to grow food they plow back into the dirt?"

"Come on, Ray. You're changing the subject."

"I'm just showing you who is defining crazy here. LSD is like...." Ray smiled. "Like booze without the hangover. Communion without the priest."

"You're a chemist. You must know the stuff screws people up."

"As opposed to the booze they sell at the Bag of Nails? How many people go straight from the Beggar to the bar or the other way around?"

Of course that was the connection Dean had seen at last: that he was helping people ruin their lives with chemicals, just the way Les Newcomer was. Just the way some rumseller had helped Dean's father destroy his life.

Ray was still scowling at me. Was there any way to talk him out of what he was talking himself into?

"Do you know what the fatal dose is for LSD? No? Carol?"

She shook her head.

"Nobody does. They haven't found a dose large enough to kill someone. How much Scotch does it take to kill someone, Joe?"

"We haven't killed anyone at the Beggar."

"Not yet, maybe. But what about Pete LaFarge? He's working on it, isn't he? And don't you encourage him to get smashed, since he can't perform sober? Same thing with Matty Mark Oliver—"

"Ray," said Carol, "what are you going to do with us?"

Ray looked down at the gun in his hand as if someone else had put it there. He sat down heavily. "Christ, I am so tired."

"Look," I said. "Let's call the cops. Let them straighten this out."

"Sweet reason," Ray sneered. Every time I spoke he seemed to get angry all over again. "Sweet goddamn reason and faith in your fellow man. Isn't that what you folkies preach? Stop the war—unless, of course, it's the Spanish Civil War. You *liked* that one."

He snorted. "You people laugh at the Beats, but for wholesale phoniness you clowns are miles ahead. You preach love and universal brotherhood, but Coffey and Oliver were ready to slit each other's throats over an old song. You talk about universal brotherhood but when Gus holds hands with a Negro it's a topic of conversation for weeks."

"But we didn't kill her," I said. "You did that."

Carol squeezed my hand, trying to keep me quiet.

"I know that!" Ray shouted. "I know that better than anyone, damn it!"

He sat frozen for a moment and then jerked forward. He picked up handful of sugar cubes from the red bowl. They bounced in his left hand like Captain Queeg's marbles.

"No cops." His voice had changed again. Now it had the sharp hysterical note I had heard when the police told him Gus was dead. "A trial would be a farce. My bosses would kill me anyway, just to make sure I didn't talk."

I started to speak; thought better of it. Ray went on. "Calling my people won't work. They think I've been too much trouble already. They might decide that three bodies are as easy to dump as two. I think they would."

"So you can't kill us," Carol said.

"Oh, sure I could." He grinned again. "Shoot you both and disappear. Shave off the beard, buy a wig and split. How long would it be before the smell gave you away?"

My stomach tied in knots. "Come on, Ray. You don't want to do that."

I don't think he heard me. At that point I don't think he heard anything except the sound of his own voice and the rattle of the sugar cubes in his hand.

"But I am *tired*. Too damned tired to start a new life as a fugitive in stinking Ohio, or some other hell hole." He looked down at the cubes. "They haven't found a fatal dose yet. Did I tell you that?"

"Don't do it, Ray," said Carol. "Killing yourself won't solve anything."

I took a deep breath. "I don't know about that."

They both stared at me. I said: "Do you realize that if this gets out Dean Coffey is going to be remembered as a drug peddler instead of a songwriter? Maybe killing yourself is the best thing you can do for him, Ray. Maybe it would make up just a little bit for murdering him."

"Don't say that," said Carol, eyes wide. "That's horrible!"

"I love it," Ray said, laughing. "Talley's still in there pitching. Still promoting his hero to stardom. Too bad you couldn't get them to spread Dean's ashes in Yankee Stadium, Joe."

He stood up, sidled past his chair and backed away. The gun was still pointed at my face. "You figure when the tape turns up you can make a record and turn a few bucks, right? If everyone knows he was a pusher it might hurt sales."

"Put it however you want, Ray. It's still all you can do for him."

"So you want me to kill myself, leave no confession. Let the cops go on thinking that Gus killed Dean out of jealousy. You don't seem to care much for *her* reputation."

"Dean was *my* best friend. Gus was yours, for all the good it did her."

"Stop it!" shouted Carol. "Stop it both of you. Please, Ray, call the cops right now. None of this is worth dying for, or killing for. Ray? Do you hear me?"

His cold eyes were looking straight at me. The gun jutted forward.

Oh God, I thought. *I love you, Carol. I love you, Sovay.* It would be a shame to die not knowing who I would miss the most.

Then Ray's shoulders jerked, and his head bowed as if he'd made a decision. "Stand up."

I stood. My legs were numb, as if I had been sitting for hours in one of Gus's yoga positions.

"There's a bottle of Scotch over there, Joe. And some tumblers. Bring them over here."

I found them in a white cabinet and brought them to the table. "Pour some Scotch for me, please."

I poured. "Fill it, damn you. This isn't Newcomer's joint. We serve honest drinks here. Full measure every time."

His rage was still burning: high, hot and pointless. I poured more.

"Good. Now both of you get over against the far wall."

As I backed toward Carol I saw Ray sit back in his leather chair. He dropped his handful of sugar cubes into the Scotch glass.

"Ray, for God's sake," said Carol, "don't do this."

"You're probably right, Carol. Probably tastes like hell." The glass had overflowed a little, making a mess on the crate. He picked it up and raised it, dripping, to his face. "Booze and LSD. Think that'll do the trick? Maybe I can leave some research notes and science will know what the fatal dose is, at least for this particular combination. My last scholarly paper, huh?"

He was looking away, at some distant place beyond these walls. I thought about making a grab for the gun.

But how do you stop a would-be suicide at gunpoint? Threaten to shoot him?

He sipped and made a face. "Not a drink you'd recommend as a waitress, huh baby? Me neither."

He turned to me. "Okay, Joe. I'll do my bit for your pal's reputation. I'll do it for the only reason people ever do good deeds. Because right now anything else seems like too much trouble."

He looked at Carol. "Don't call the cops, pussycat. I'll shoot anyone who comes in after you leave. You don't want someone's death on your conscience do you?"

He took another sip of his unholy brew and shuddered. "Like I said, I don't recommend it."

CHAPTER 41

You really screwed up," said Max Karzoff. "You never—Jesus! Take it easy, Joe. You jumped a foot."

"Sorry, Boss. I'm a little on edge. What did I do wrong?"

"Scheduling a hoot tonight. This is the worst crowd we've had on a Saturday night in a year."

I looked at the dozen bored people watching a performer who had done all makeup and fashion could do to make herself look like Joan Baez—a common style that year. Unfortunately her singing voice suggested Jimmy Durante.

"Yeah, but it's better than bringing in a paying act to play to an empty hall. Chad Mitchell is at Town Hall and the Kingston Trio is at Carnegie Hall. All the folkies are at one or the other. And the police reports have kept most of the tourists away."

Max raised a handkerchief to his face and coughed hard. "What a week. Stabbings in the street, a goddamned *rumble* just blocks from here. Spring fever, New York style. A few more weeks like this and our weekend crowd will decide to stay in New Rochelle for good."

The next act was the Bleecker Street Boys, a new name for some familiar faces. Matty Mark and friends were trying a different *nom de folk*. They sang *Tom Dooley* in a way that made you wish someone would hurry up and hang the guy.

When they finished, to polite applause, I climbed onto the stage and thanked them, showing more enthusiasm than they had.

Not their fault. They had only shown up as a favor to me. Now they would rush off to see one of the famous Trios, as most of our audience had done.

"Now, let's have a big Riding Beggar welcome for one of the best new singers in Manhattan: Sam Furrell!"

Sam came up, grinning and brandishing his guitar. It was hard to believe that only two weeks ago he had been so afflicted with stage fright he could barely make his voice heard through the mic. Maybe Braubinger was right about that one.

He leaned forward and started a Fred Neil song. I was glad someone had his mind on the job, because mine was on Ray Hegg. What the hell was he doing right now?

I went back to my table, nodding at Carol. "How you doing?"

"Not great," she said. "Thank God it's not a busy night, because I've mixed up half my orders. Can't concentrate."

"I know what you mean," I said. "But I guess we won't know anything until tomorrow."

The outside door slammed. Bob Braubinger came in, a beast at full charge, right past Amy at the cash register. He looked around wildly, then spied us and headed over.

"Joe, Carol. Have you heard the news? My God, has *Max* heard the news?"

Carol squeezed my hand so hard it hurt.

"What news, Bob?"

"It's Von Ehmsen. Somebody shot the guy."

CHAPTER 42

What the hell are you talking about?" Max shouted. "I saw Von just last night."

"Well, you ain't gonna see him tomorrow," said Braubinger. "Somebody shot him dead on MacDougal Street this morning. They already caught the guy, is what I hear."

"Who was it?" I asked. If Ray had taken another life, it would be on me....

"Some little old man he was trying to kick out of a building he owned."

I took a breath, remembering Von Ehmsen's big plans for expanding the Café Rafio. *Walls to knock down, people to evict.*

"I tell you," Braubinger went on, "those old codgers are scary. You never know which of them has a Luger tucked away as a souvenir from his army days."

Max sat down hard. He was pale, eyes wide and staring, but I don't think he was seeing anything.

"This damned town." His voice was high and thin. It made him sound older than he was. "This damned town is going to hell on skates."

"Take it easy, Max," said Carol, putting an arm around his shoulders. She nodded at someone behind me and I turned to see Katy Poe.

We told her what happened to Van Ehmsen and Katy's green eyes squeezed shut. "Oh, Lord." She looked at Max, and dropped to her knees beside his chair. "Max, I'm so sorry."

He looked around, blinking stupidly behind the bifocals. Finally he spotted me. "Joe."

"Right here, Max."

"Jesus. This ain't gonna be good for business."

•

That night Carol came back to my place. We had nothing to say to each other, nothing that could make a bit of difference.

We made love anyway.

We had seen death and the pain of death first hand, and somewhere Ray was....

Doing what? Killing himself, just because I asked him to? Maybe getting his second wind and preparing to kill someone else?

Who the hell told me to play God?

We clung to each other like shipwrecked sailors. It wasn't love or even passion; it was desperation.

•

We got up early on Sunday and walked over to Ray's place, hand in hand. There was an ambulance in front and a police car parked beside it.

"Do we go in?" asked Carol.

"Of course we do."

The door of the apartment was open and cops were clustered in the living room. Officer Aaron Levy saw me and did a double take. "Well, I'll be damned. It's Talley again. Come here, you two."

"What's happened?" I asked. "Where's Ray?"

"You just…." He cut himself off. He was giving us that cop stare, the one that says he knows everything you're thinking now or might think in the future. My brother was born with it. "Ray Hegg is dead. I'm sorry."

"Christ, no," I said.

Carol didn't try to speak. She just sat down on the couch.

"What happened?" I asked.

"We're still trying to piece it together. Looks like suicide, or he was so smashed he didn't know what he was doing."

He led us further into the apartment. The simplicity of the rooms was destroyed. Furniture lay in pieces; a table lay on its back, one leg broken off. At first I thought the cops had torn the place apart looking for something. Then I thought of Dean's wrecked pad. "Did someone break in?"

"Don't think so. It looks like he did it all himself. We got a phone call from a neighbor. She thought she smelled gas and there was no answer at the door."

"He turned on the gas?" asked Carol .

"Nope. It was something else that smelled. You'll find it in the bathroom. Hegg is in the bedroom, but you'd better not go in there." Levy made a face. "He cut himself up pretty badly with a knife. I don't know what he thought he was doing, since he didn't aim at anything vital. Finally he finished the job with a pistol."

"Why would he do all that?" Carol said, almost to herself.

"I can tell you," growled a voice behind me. Guareschi was smoking a foul cigar and holding something in a large white handkerchief in both hands.

"Take a look at this, Aaron." It was the red sugar bowl, only half full now.

How many cubes were gone? A dozen at least. What was a normal dose of that stuff?

If anything about it could be called normal.

"Sugar?" asked Levy, eyebrows raised.

The sergeant grinned. "Sugar that can make you decide to peel your skin off with a knife. I'll tell you later. We don't want to give these kiddies more ideas then they've already got."

He looked at Carol and me. "You folks are late this time. We found the body without you."

"That's some sense of humor you've got," I told him. "You ought to be on the Ed Sullivan Show."

Guareschi started to speak but Levy jumped in. "Thought I'd show them the bathroom, Sarge. Maybe they can help us identify that stuff."

"Worth a shot."

The bathroom looked like hell and smelled worse. The walls hung with a gray film and towels lay half in and half out of the toilet.

Levy pointed to the bathtub. "What do you make of that? Whatever it was, he didn't want to take any chances on it being salvageable."

The thing in the tub was an empty plastic reel for audio tape. Ray had unwound the tape into the tub, breaking it every few yards by the look of it. Then he poured something on it—"Lighter fluid," Levy explained. "We took the can away for fingerprints."

Audiotape doesn't burn well. It melts. The whole thing had charred to hell and filled the room with a foul, acrid stink. After the lighter fluid had had its way with the tape Ray filled the tub with water. Ruined scraps of tape still floated like seaweed in a sickening brown broth. It was Ray's last chemistry experiment, unless you counted his own death.

Carol and I looked at each other. Of course this had to be the last copy of Dean's tape, the one Ray has assured us was safe in his office at the laboratory.

"The bastard," I muttered. "He killed him twice."

"What was that?" snapped Guareschi, standing in the doorway.

"Nothing," I said. "The smell in here is making me sick."

We moved back into the hallway. "Is that what we think it is?" Levy asked. "Coffey's demo tape?"

"It must be. Ruined, of course. And don't ask me how Ray got it. I have no idea."

"Any idea why he killed himself?"

Then Carol started to talk, telling them that Gus had been Ray's best friend—which was true enough—giving them a comfy motive so they could file it away as a closed case. I think she was mostly talking so I could catch my breath.

"We came by to visit him yesterday afternoon, just to cheer him up. He was upset, but we never thought he'd do a thing like this."

"Thanks for the help," said Guareschi. "Now beat it."

Outside, I sucked cold air into my lungs until I started coughing like Max.

"It's not your fault," Carol told me. "The tape was just Ray's little gesture of vengeance."

"Some gesture," I said. "Dean's music is lost forever. If I hadn't played judge and jury…Hell. You were right about that. As usual."

The coroner concluded that Ray's death was a suicide, under the influence of booze and LSD, so you might say he was the first of my friends to die from drug abuse.

God knows he was not the last.

CHAPTER 43

I don't know how much more to tell.

Dean Coffey said the song should stop when you reach the punch line. Katy Poe said the song ends when the story is finished.

But who decides what the punch line is? And who knows if the story is ever really over?

Maybe the story ends with Ray's death, or even with Dean's. But when I think back to that time I remember one more thing.

Two years later: March 1, 1965. The last day of the Riding Beggar.

After all those years of struggling with his lungs, it was his heart that finally forced Max to retire. He had a heart attack in 1964, a few minutes after the Republicans nominated Barry Goldwater for president. He moved to Israel and we agreed to close the joint and sell the proceeds.

The folk scene wasn't what it had been, of course. *Hootenanny* had lasted a year on ABC and then died from a combination of blacklist, boycott and the Beatles. The British Invasion of sixty-four had crushed the folk revival, swamping our little boat before Michael could row it to shore.

I had even started opening the joint for lunch, and put in a juke box. The box was stocked with every folk 45 I could find, but it was mostly the Beatles and their compatriots that people dropped their coins to hear.

The machine contained two singles by a minor U.S. rock-and-roll band with the deliberately British sounding name of the Lyonhearts, featuring a bass player named Matthew Oliver. The day after the Beatles made their first appearance on Ed Sullivan, Matty Mark had sold his stand-up bass and banjo and gone electric.

Believe it or not, the flip side of the Lyonhearts' second single was *Let Me Take Your Side*. Matty Mark never explained his change of heart on that song, but it is the only existing recording of a Dean Coffey song. I guess that makes the Lyonhearts pioneers of what became known as folk rock.

We moved that juke box up to the Bag of Nails on the day I turned the Beggar's space over to a couple of recent NYU grads. Late that summer they opened what today would be called a gay bar. Ahead of their time, I guess.

Bob Braubinger helped Les Newcomer and me drag the big machine up the stairs and Katy came along, mostly to shout encouragement. We dropped some coins in the box to make sure it was working, then sat down to kick a few memories around like a flea-bitten dog.

"I'll miss that dump," said Katy, as she looked around the bar. Technically, women still weren't allowed in there, but Les winked an eye for a member of the moving crew. "But I won't pretend I'll miss playing for those crowds. I don't know what they were looking for, but I don't think they ever found it."

"Star quality," said Braubinger, solemnly. "That's what they wanted, and that's why the Limey's are so popular. Funny haircuts. Long hair. Suits with no collars. They don't look like the jerk next door."

He pointed a pudgy finger at Katy and me. "You folksingers always wanted to represent the People, capital P. But there isn't any People. There's just, well...people.

And they don't give a damn. So you can't make it work with *just* the music. That ain't enough."

"Sometimes it is," I said. "If the audience is right, and the singer."

"Well, I'm glad I got a day job, again," said Katy. "Teaching music theory at NYU is a lot easier than entertaining drunks."

"There's good money in drunks," said Braubinger. He looked thoughtfully at Les, who was building martinis for a couple of art gallery types. "Booze and drugs: they make the world go round."

I made a face, trying to keep familiar memories from gathering.

"What's that starting on the juke box?" asked Braubinger.

"*Mr. Tambourine Man* by Bob Dylan," Katy told him.

"Not the one I know."

"You're thinking of the cover version by the Byrds," I told him. "That was the big hit. This is the original, sung by Dylan. He wrote the song way back in 1963, the year everything fell apart."

"I thought you didn't like his voice," said Katy.

"It's growing on me," I admitted.

"The cover version is better," Braubinger decided. "Fewer words, more rock-and-roll. Those Byrd boys are gonna move some vinyl with that one."

"What does it *mean*, though?" asked Katy.

"It doesn't have to mean anything," I told her, "anymore than we do. It's just...."

"Joe? Something wrong?"

Something was. Dylan was singing about weariness, but I heard another voice, Ray's voice saying: "I'm so tired, so damn tired...." I shuddered.

Dylan sang:

My weariness amazes me
I'm branded on my feet
I have no one to meet
And the ancient empty street's too dead for dreaming.

Well, Ray was dead. Dean and Gus, too. And the streets of New York were dead for me.

"Joe?" said Katy. "You look like you've seen a ghost."

"Not seen one," I said. "Heard one."

"What?" Braubinger's eyes went wide. "You believe in ghosts?"

I shook my head and quoted: "'If you had met as many as I have you wouldn't believe in them either.'"

"That's from *archy and mehitabel*," said Katy, smiling. "Who taught you about Don Marquis?"

"Carol Meisel."

"Carol, of course. How's she doing?"

"She's okay. Living in some hellhole called Thailand, up to her knees in mud and having the time of her life, according to her letters."

Carol had joined the Peace Corps a few months after Kennedy was killed. "I can only do this because of you," she had told me as she packed. "You gave me the faith to believe in myself, and I'll always love you for that."

Speaking of love, Sovay was still in England, our occasional letters little more than nostalgia now. She had recently been arrested at a nuclear disarmament rally in Birmingham, which didn't exactly improve her chances of getting an American visa.

Women who fall in love with me seem to get a strong urge to save the world, starting as far away from me as possible.

"Thailand," said Katy. She shook her head. "Seems like everyone we know is gone or going."

"Me too," I admitted. "I've got plane tickets to L.A. the day after tomorrow."

"Aw, Joe, you should have told us. We would have held a party."

I smiled at her. "That's why I didn't tell you."

"Why California?" asked Braubinger. "Gonna try the movies?"

"No. To get away from here, more than anything. I keep looking for people I'm not gonna see. People who have gone elsewhere, or who aren't anywhere at all."

Katy nodded sympathetically. "Time to move on. You have relatives out there, don't you?"

"My brother and his family, yeah."

"But leaving New York, my God." Braubinger raised a hand in a gesture of bewilderment. "You're in the big time right here. There isn't any place that's better than this."

I laughed and stood up. "Let's hope there is, Bob. Let's hope so, anyway." Then I paid my bill and got out of there.

Robert Lopresti is the author of more than thirty mystery stories, some of which have won the Derringer Award, and been nominated for the Anthony Award. He edited the book *Thurber on Crime*. He is also a singer-songwriter whose CD *Can I Blame You?* features *White Wolf*, which appears in this novel. Raised in New Jersey, he has lived for almost twenty years in Bellingham, Washington, where he is a librarian at a university. His website is www.roblopresti.com.